"*A Change of Plans* will keep readers up way too late in this fast-paced tale of love lost and found again."

~Melanie Jacobson, author of
The List, *Not My Type*,
Twitterpated, and *Smart Move*

"*A Change of Plans* is lots of romance sprinkled with pirates, shipwreck, and adventure. Donna Weaver spins a tale that you will fall in love with, think about for days afterward, and then go back and read again. I laughed, I cried, and I couldn't put it down."

~Betsy Love, author of
Identity and *Soulfire*

"A captivating tale of love, grief, and hope that will tug at your heartstrings until the very end."

~Laura Josephson, author of
the *Rising* series and *Confessions from the Realm of the Underworld*

"When someone says pirates and novel in the same sentence, I usually say, 'Thanks, but no'. Not in this case. Ms. Weaver brings a warm humor to her story of romance, travel, and overcoming skeletons in one's past with her vivid characters and delightful scenes."

~Shaunna Gonzales, author of
Dark Days of Promise

EMERALD ARCH PUBLISHING

A Change of Plans
Second American Paperback Edition

Edited by Katharina Brendel
Edited by Diane Dalton
Cover design by Melissa Williams | MW Cover Designs
Cover photograph waves by Solovyova Lyudmyla
Cover photograph couple by Hot Photo Pie
Author photo by Sidney Ulrich http://sidneyulrichphotos.blogspot.com

ISBN Paperback: 978-0-9899928-1-7

Donna K. Weaver's author website is
http://www.donnakweaver.com

For Edward

Forget zombies!.
Plan for pirates!!.

Donna K. Weaver

A CHANGE OF *Plans*

DONNA K. WEAVER

EMERALD ARCH PUBLISHING

Part 1

CHAPTER 1

*S*TARING AT the cruise ship, a shiver of anticipation ran through me. After almost a year spent saving on a high school teacher's salary, I could hardly believe we were here. Even the clank of luggage and supplies being loaded intensified my excitement, and I decided the rare blue Seattle sky had to be a good omen. Elle was right. This trip would be just the diversion I needed. But I would never admit that to her, or she would keep trying to run my life like she had since kindergarten.

I watched with amusement as she stretched up on her tiptoes, scanning the crowded dock. "Looking for handsome pirates?"

"Oh, please," she snorted. "Modern pirates don't look like Johnny Depp. Besides, there aren't supposed to be any in the Pacific Ocean."

"Johnny might be a little tall for you, anyway. Maybe we can find you a handsome Hobbit in New Zealand." I kept a straight face.

She fixated me with a mock glare and opened her mouth to retort, but something caught her eye and her reply died on her lips.

"What's wrong?" Alarmed, I started to turn around.

Elle grabbed my arm to stop me. "Don't look, but there's a guy over there watching you."

"Sure he's not watching *you*?" I tried not to peek in the direction she had indicated.

"I know when guys are watching me." She wasn't being arrogant, just honest, and after twenty years, I should have known better than to ask.

The man supposedly eyeing me had just finished checking in, and we ended up next to him and his group as we made our way to the ship.

He was tall. Really tall. At nearly six feet myself, I paid attention when guys were taller than me. I caught a whiff of pleasant cologne.

Elle gave him a sideways glance, and I casually turned my face in his general direction. He *was* looking at me. When our eyes met, he looked away and said something to a little girl whose hand he held.

"He's cute," Elle whispered.

That's what she said about every guy she tried to set me up with. "Looks like he has a daughter."

Elle shook her head, keeping her voice low. "I overheard them. The little girl called him uncle. She belongs to the couple he's with."

As we went up the gangway, I squinted at the ship's

balconies, wondering which one might be ours. I paused on the threshold and took a deep breath, hoping to capture this memory. The interior smelled like a hotel, lacking the engine stink I remembered from my single day-cruise experience. Several feet ahead, Elle signaled for me to catch up.

I hurried over, and we stepped inside an elevator. I turned to face the doors and found myself meeting the eyes of the tall man in the elevator opposite ours. He nodded and didn't break eye contact until the doors closed.

Flushing, I remained silent as the elevator moved, wondering about the guy. He looked a few years older than me … I stopped that train of thought. Elle was already sucking me into her nefarious plan to get me dating again. My plan was to read a lot of books.

And get past the first anniversary of Jace's death.

We rode to the lido deck, where we had been instructed to eat and entertain ourselves. Elle turned toward the taco makings spread out on the buffet and reached for the tongs.

"You're brave." I moved behind her. "We have five days at sea before Hawaii." I nodded toward the taco shell. "Won't be as tasty coming up as it was going down."

She glanced over her shoulder at me. "All the more reason to enjoy it in at least one direction," she said with a wink.

The smell of broiling meat drew me to the grill. While I doctored my burger, Elle headed straight to a nearly full table. She already had the ship's schedule spread out for everyone to see by the time I got there. Sighing, I slid into the chair beside her and turned my attention to the food on my plate.

I hoped this wasn't a sample of what was to come, the way she was already collecting 'friends,' acting like the last year hadn't happened. We had agreed—I thought—that I would have plenty of quiet time. I watched Elle as she immediately took control of the conversation, introducing herself and pulling the others into the discussion. Her knack for managing any social situation was one I had always envied, especially in high school. Eventually, I had learned to accept that I was just more reserved—and that was okay.

Social butterfly Elle would tell me what events I needed to attend. We had come to terms with our different social preferences once we had reached high school. Elle would have been out with friends every night, while I would have been happy with just the weekends.

Finishing, I pushed away my tray. "I wonder if I'll fit in my clothes after eating like this for four weeks."

Elle looked up from the schedule and grinned. "I'll worry about it then."

"Keep telling yourself that." She liked her trim figure too much to overindulge too often. I stood. "I'm going to look around."

She considered me, wary. "Don't go signing me up for any tours. I won't go with you to see the engine room."

Laughing softly at the memory of the nasty little engine room on our day cruise, I went in search of the gym. Situated at the bow of the ship, it had an entire wall of windows. I sighed, standing in the warmth of the sunlight and imagining running on the treadmill with nothing but the ocean before me.

"Nice, yes?" asked a deep voice behind me.

I spun around and couldn't help a soft gasp. Before me stood the most beautiful human being I had ever seen. A little taller than me and probably close to my age, he must have been a direct descendant of some Scandinavian god with his pale blond hair and light gray eyes.

He raised his hands. "I didn't mean to startle you." His voice had a hint of an accent I couldn't place. "My name is Jori. Jori Virtanen."

"Nice to meet you. I'm Lyn North." I shook the hand he extended. Like the other guy, Jori also wore nice cologne, subtle and masculine. "Where are you from?"

"Seattle."

I blinked. "Seattle? Your accent …."

"My parents and I emigrated from Finland about nine years ago." Jori's smile made him even more beautiful. He glanced at the wall of windows and said, almost to himself, "It will be interesting to do some sketching in here."

"Are you an artist?"

He hesitated, his shoulders shifting a bit as though uncomfortable. "I hope to be someday."

Curious. In my experience, beautiful people had a tendency to be self-absorbed. "Are you going to sketch the scenery in New Zealand?"

Jori nodded. "I do plan to do some drawing there."

"Wouldn't it be faster to fly?"

"I prefer to sketch people. What better place than a cruise ship for people?"

Remembering why I had come to the gym, I asked, "Have you seen any of the staff around?"

Jori's eyes did a quick scan from my head to my feet, and my jaw tightened. "Are you interested in some of the classes?" he said.

"I want to see if it's okay to use that open area by the door." I indicated the location, taking a step toward the exit.

He arched a brow. "Are you a dancer?"

"No, I want it for karate practice." At that moment, a staff member entered the gym. "Well, it was nice meeting you." I raised my hand in farewell. "I need to go talk with him and then meet my friend."

Jori glanced at my left hand. "Your boyfriend?"

"No." I edged away. "Just a friend."

"Are you going to the departure party?" he asked before I managed to leave.

"Uh, yes. For a little while."

His pale eyes glittered. "Then I will look for you." He did a little bow and left.

With a frown, I watched him leave. That incredible specimen of male perfection couldn't have just been coming on to me. No way was I telling Elle about the encounter.

After getting permission to use the exercise area, I was about to leave the gym when the loudspeaker squeaked, and a voice announced that the cabins were ready. By the time I found ours, Elle had already put her things away and left a note on the table saying she had gone out to explore but would be back in a little while.

After unpacking, I wasn't sure what to do. With nearly fifteen hundred passengers aboard, I didn't want to risk missing her. She would have to return to the cabin to get her lifejacket for the lifeboat drill, so I decided to explore our balcony.

The little terrace was only somewhat private. While it had a partial barrier next to the wall, I could see straight down the side of the ship to the other balconies. This was both good and bad. Good because I would get a broader view of the ocean. Bad because I had two swimsuits, and only one was fit for display.

I glanced at the balcony next to ours, straight into the face of the man from the dock. His eyes twinkled, lighting up with interest. He raised the glass he was holding, starting as his cell phone rang. As he moved to answer it, I heard Elle return and hurried back inside.

The drill turned out to be a bit anticlimactic, the cruisers taking a long time to gather. The need to wait as more people pressed into our assigned lifeboat area itched at my nerves. I tried to think about something besides the close press of bodies, taking shallow breaths to keep from smelling the mixture of perfume, sunscreen, and liquor, plus a dash of cigarette smoke for variety.

Elle nudged me and tilted her head to my right. Our tall neighbor stood beside me, observing the people around us.

"He's in the cabin next to ours," I whispered to Elle.

"Convenient." Her eyes took on a contemplative gleam.

I gave her a warning look. More people arrived, forcing us to squeeze in tighter, and my arm pressed against our tall neighbor's. He leaned toward me. "Look at them." He pointed ahead.

Startled at his uninvited comment, I shot him a quick glance and edged a little closer to Elle. I immediately felt silly when I saw he wasn't even looking at me but at an elderly couple a few feet away. The tiny white-haired woman wore dark glasses, a walking cane for the blind hanging from her hand, as an equally tiny white-haired man guided her to a spot not far from us. He played with her short, curly hair, his fingers twirling a strand around and around. The unconscious familiarity of the movement spoke of decades doing it.

Intrigued that this love story had captured my neighbor's attention, I peeked at him from the corner of my eye. He had a pleasant enough face, though his nose was a little too prominent for him to be considered handsome. His dark, almost black, hair had a stylish cut with nice body to it. I imagined it would be wavy when long. When he noticed my scrutiny, he smiled like we were sharing a secret before turning back to the couple.

The frail gentleman had shifted the old woman so we formed a tight circle. With a quick glance my way, he nodded to the man beside me. "You take good care of your lovely lady there, young man."

Elle choked back a laugh, and our cabin neighbor coughed. My face went hot.

"When times get tough, you should always talk about it." He gave us a conspiratorial wink. "The ladies need to talk it out, you know."

As the blind woman laughed and swatted his arm, the crewmembers launched into the briefing and a last-minute group crushed us tighter still. I clutched Elle's arm and closed my eyes. I didn't catch a thing the crewmembers said. When the people finally drifted apart, I took a deep breath of fresh air.

The tall man reached his hand out to me. "I'm Braedon Randolph."

"Lyn North." A tingle spread through my hand where his dry skin touched mine. I pulled Elle closer. "This is my friend and roommate, Elle Reinhardt. Elle, this is Braedon."

Before Elle and Braedon could do more than exchange greetings, his phone rang. "It was nice to meet you," he said as he stepped away to answer it.

I stared at my palm, wondering at my response to his touch. A sharp horn blast signaled the ship's departure, and my stomach noted the first sensation of movement. My heart raced, and I nearly whooped, forgetting the tingle in my hand. "Let's go to the bow." I tugged on Elle's sleeve.

She made a face. "I said I'd meet the others from lunch by the pool."

I hesitated, darting my eyes between her and the receding dock.

"You go." Elle gave me a gentle push. "Just be sure to meet us for dinner at seven, okay?"

I hugged her and made my way to the lower deck, which had a track going completely around the ship. I found a place along the railing, relieved to be alone. I let the ocean breeze blow my hair in a dizzying swirl around my face and shoulders, relishing in the sense of freedom that came with it.

My mind drifted to Elle. I wondered how seriously she would take her self-designated role of matchmaker.

I knew I waited in limbo, like someone who had been injured in a diving accident and sat on the edge of the high dive, trying to decide if she could face the water again. The idea of dating had teased the back of my mind for a while, but I was determined. Not yet. Not on a ship. Fairy godmother Elle couldn't truly believe a cruise would ever provide me with a happily ever after.

Just as I decided to search for her, I heard voices and turned to find Braedon and his family strolling around the corner. I sighed. Elle would love this.

CHAPTER 2

RAEDON RAISED his eyebrows in recognition. There was no avoiding them then. He had the little girl from earlier in his arms and was accompanied by a man and woman I assumed were her parents.

"Hello again," I said when they reached me.

Braedon smiled warmly in response and turned to the woman by his side. "Ash, this is my cabin neighbor Lyn North. Lyn, this is my sister, Aislinn Armstrong, and her husband, D'Arcy. This little princess is my niece, Kate."

D'Arcy locked eyes with me as he took my hand. "Don't say it." He ruined the effect by putting on a brooding expression.

I burst out laughing and Kate giggled. I reached to shake her hand, but she buried her face in Braedon's shoulder, suddenly shy.

After the introductions, they turned to admire the shrinking shoreline, and I wondered how to make a strategic retreat.

Kate raised her head from her uncle's shoulder and regarded me, her face solemn. "Those are seagulls." She pointed to two of the white, squawking birds as they glided alongside the ship.

"Yes," I agreed, equally serious.

"They poop a lot." Her face scrunched in disgust.

Braedon and I laughed. He tickled her tummy. "Yes, they do."

His phone rang, and I wondered if he was one of those people who had to be connected at all times.

Aislinn glared at him and whispered, "You promised."

"Just this one last time." He tried handing the little girl to his sister, but Kate stretched, wiggling her little fingers for me to take her. I looked to her mother for permission, and Aislinn nodded.

I settled Kate on my hip and pointed at a new seagull that had joined the others. "Look at it squawking at them. What do you think it's saying?"

"It wants to know if you're married."

"I'm not married."

Kate got a big grin on her face. "You can marry Uncle Bray and be my aunt. I want an aunt. I only have uncles."

I swallowed wrong and choked, grateful the others weren't watching us. I hoped so, anyway.

Braedon put his phone back in his pocket and returned to us.

With a pinched mouth, Aislinn held out her hand to him. "You promised, Bray. Hand it over." Awkward. Braedon relented, and Aislinn stuffed his phone in her purse. I avoided looking at him.

"Sorry about that." Aislinn scrutinized me. "Kate doesn't usually take to strangers so quickly. We do really need to get her to dinner now, though."

The little girl shifted, indicating she wanted to get down, but she took my hand once her feet were on the deck. "I can walk with you guys," I offered. "I need to find my cabinmate anyway."

Now that the ship had moved out of the harbor, the impact of its motion on my balance became more pronounced. Kate giggled at me stumbling as I climbed the stairs. Braedon took my elbow to steady me, clasping the handrail himself. I would be glad when I finally adjusted and got my sea legs. I said a silent prayer of gratitude that I at least didn't suffer from motion sickness.

"See you around," I said to Braedon and his family when we reached the lido deck. Kate let me go with a little kiss on the cheek, and I went to join Elle. Naturally, she stood among a circle of people. I could almost see the words 'date potential' in her eyes as she glanced between Braedon and me. I ignored her and we headed to the dining room.

Later, we returned to the lido deck for the sailing party. Elle clapped her hands in delight. This was her environment: people, food, and music. She pointed to the band in the middle of the deck. "I want to request a song."

"I'll get us some seats," I shouted over the din of people. She waved her approval.

After I secured a table and some chairs, I sat guarding them. I planned to stay only a few minutes and then make my escape to listen to a chamber group performing somewhere else. Somewhere more quiet and less crowded.

I smelled Jori's cologne before I heard his voice behind me. "I didn't see you at dinner."

So much for not telling Elle. I glanced up. "Hello again." I did a quick scan of the band area—no sign of Elle.

He sat beside me, pulling a sketchbook and pencil from under his arm. "Are you saving all these seats?"

I craned my neck again in the direction of the band. "Yes, Elle's just stepped away …."

"Your friend from earlier?"

"Yes." Elle was nowhere in sight. I surrendered to the inevitable. "If you aren't a full-time artist, what do you do for a living?"

He made a wry face. "Modeling. It pays well enough, but I don't like it." He observed the people around us as he toyed with his pencil. "I wish I'd thought to come on a cruise before."

I pointed at his sketchbook. "May I see?"

After a slight hesitation, Jori handed it to me. I flipped open the cover and was immediately captivated. Some would consider his sketches unfinished. They weren't quite complete pictures but rather parts of pictures—a child's face, a young woman's profile, an old man's hand. Jori used relatively few strokes, yet he still managed to capture the essence of his subjects.

"These are beautiful." I looked up from the last page. "Have you sold any of your pieces yet?"

"I haven't tried." He shrugged. "I guess I don't believe anyone would want them."

I was perplexed by his insecurity. "I'm no authority on art, but I know what I like. Your pictures touch me."

"Thank you." The tightness around his eyes relaxed. "That's the nicest thing anyone's said about my work."

I suddenly understood. "Your family doesn't get it, do they, your love of art?"

The sound of the pencil as he tapped it on his knee turned to sharp smacks. "No. Especially my father. He thinks I'm wasting my time."

I hated it when parents tried to crush their children's dreams.

I had only been teaching for three years, but I had already seen too much of it. "You're good, Jori." I reached over and touched his agitated hand. "I hope you don't give up on this."

"Give up on what?" Elle asked as she walked up behind Jori, followed by her growing entourage. Her eyes widened when he turned to look at her. "Who's this?"

He stood and took her hand. "You must be Elle."

Unlike me, Elle didn't flush very often, but she turned pink as he did his little bow over her hand. For a fleeting moment, I considered playing the matchmaker with them, but I quickly dismissed the thought. That just might give her further ideas regarding me.

"Elle ... and everyone." I waved the rest of Elle's group over. "This is Jori. He's an artist—come and check out some of his drawings." Before he could stop me, I handed Elle the sketchbook.

I checked my watch and whispered to Elle, "I've got to go." She nodded, occupied by Jori's sketches.

The Explorer's Lounge was a small area on the upper deck. Several people had gathered there, and the musicians— consisting of a pianist, a violinist, and a cellist—had already begun playing. The ambiance created by the low lighting, the gilded murals of old sailing ships, and a map of the world made me think of a drawing room. I found a small loveseat to sit in and closed my eyes, savoring the combination of the ship's sway and the lovely music.

At the end of the third piece, a man whispered, "Excuse me, Lyn. Do you mind if I share your couch?"

Recognizing Braedon's voice, I opened my eyes. His sister and her family had found places on a sofa to the side, but no other empty seats remained.

"Sure." I slid over, and he sat down next to me. I closed my eyes again as the next number began, trying to ignore how nice his cologne smelled. What was it today with men's cologne, anyway?

When the number finished, Kate turned to her mother. "Mommy, I want to sit with her."

Aislinn looked at me questioningly, and I nodded. Kate headed to me and turned her back so I could lift her onto my lap.

She smelled like baby shampoo, and as she snuggled against me, I had a fleeting thought that I might have been expecting a child of my own by now. Jace and I had talked about not wanting to wait to start our family. I shut down the painful thought, blinking against the sudden burning in my eyes.

After several more numbers, I checked my watch. "Kate, I have to leave to go meet my friends." She gave me a hug, slid from my lap, and returned to her mother.

As I rose, the ship suddenly swayed and, to my horror, I toppled onto Braedon's lap.

"Decide to stay for the rest of the music?" he said, trying not to laugh.

My faced burned. "Excuse me." I tried to figure out where to put my hands to lift myself again. I finally got to my feet, supporting my weight on the arm of the couch. I attempted to straighten, but another shift of the floor sent me askew again, and I landed back in Braedon's lap.

By then Braedon was laughing outright, and everyone stared at us. This was ridiculous. Braedon raised his hands but didn't seem to know how to help. The best thing he could have done was give my bum a push, but he had the good sense *not* to do that.

Luckily, D'Arcy came to help and pulled me to my feet.

"Thank you." I turned to Braedon, mortified. "I'm so sorry."

He shook his head, still chuckling.

I walked from the room, hoping I didn't look as ridiculous as I felt and praying I could make it down to the Show Lounge without another blunder.

Elle was waiting for me, sitting among some of her new friends. I waved hello to them and sat in the chair she indicated.

"Where did you find Jori?" she asked.

"I know, right?" I peered around her to see if he had come.

"He was feeling seasick, so he went back to his cabin." Elle looked at me. "He seemed interested in you."

I leaned my head back and shut my eyes for a moment before glancing at her from the corner of my eye. "How many guys do you plan on playing matchmaker with?"

She made a face. "Just flirt with them. You can date a guy without marrying him—" Elle snapped her mouth shut when she saw the pain in my expression. "I'm sorry. But you know what I mean."

I sighed and squeezed her hand. "I do. Have you given that job offer anymore thought?"

Elle made a face. I wasn't surprised. She had worked at half a dozen different things since high school. Recently, she had gotten her Colorado court reporter certification. I had told her that sitting invisible in a corner would never suit her. Evidently, now that the job offer had made that a reality, she was having second thoughts.

"Then don't take it," I said.

She leaned her head back. "I wish I could be my own boss, doing something I like."

"Play to your strength—people." We had been over this

before, but fear of failure kept her from starting an Etsy business with some online friends. It was the same problem she had with guys, but I wasn't going to go there.

At the end of the show, the members of Elle's group who hadn't gotten seasick wanted to go to the Crow's Nest, the ship's dance club.

"You're coming, aren't you?" Elle asked.

I shook my head, thinking of my mishap with Braedon. "I'd prefer to wait until the deck is steadier before going dancing."

Elle put on a martyred expression. "Well, based on the stormy weather forecast, you'll have to get used to it. I'll let you go today, but tomorrow you *will* come."

"Okay," I agreed. "Night, everyone."

CHAPTER 3

*T*HE SHIP'S rocking was so much gentler in the morning that I felt it was safe enough for a workout. Though I arrived at the gym early, two guys were already there on the treadmills. I went to the workout floor near the entrance and took off my hoodie and shoes.

I sipped some lime-flavored water and took a couple of minutes to admire the view of the ocean. I couldn't help but notice the nice physique of the shirtless man jogging on the treadmill. He must know what he was doing when he lifted weights; it took time and knowledge to get such a defined build without the grotesque bodybuilder look.

I suddenly realized it was Braedon and choked on my water. Embarrassed, I turned away, trying not to draw attention to myself with my coughing.

While I did my sensei-required thirty minutes of stretching, I focused my attention on the list of books I planned to read on the cruise, refusing to look at the treadmills again. Once finished, I took a long drink and allowed myself one peek in his direction. He had moved on to the weights. I tried not to remember my humiliation at falling all over him last night.

I began the kata, starting with yellow belt forms, and lost myself in the movements. When I completed the forms for the brown belt, I took a break. Braedon stood by a young guy and a pretty Hispanic girl I had seen at dinner last night, apparently giving them instructions on how to use the weight machines. I scrutinized Braedon, curious about what kind of teacher he might be. Our eyes met before I had a chance to look away. Busted! My face went hot.

I spun, stumbling a little over the first moves of the black belt kata, so I had to start over. I could almost feel Braedon's eyes on my back as I returned to the beginning position. I closed my eyes and slowly did the opening bow, forcing my thoughts into the next move. After a pause, I exploded to the right, performed a right strike and Haku kick, stepped into a left stack, and followed with a right augmented block. By the time I moved forward to do the next block, I had found my zone.

After completing the six required forms one after the other, I was drenched in sweat. I grabbed my towel, wiping my face. Water bottle in hand for a refill, I didn't see him until I turned around.

Braedon leaned against the wall, watching me with his arms crossed in front of his chest. A towel hung loosely over his shoulder, his skin glistening with a faint sheen of perspiration. He straightened. "Karate?"

"Yes." I moved toward the water cooler.

Braedon followed. "Are you a black belt?"

"First degree." I bent to fill my bottle. "I should be ready to test for my next level by fall."

The lanky guy Braedon had helped joined us, the girl following closely behind. "You're Elle's friend Lyn, right?" He thrust a tanned hand forward. "I'm Jimmy Hewitt and this is Maria Sandoval." His eyes lit up. "Was that Kung Fu stuff you were doing?"

With that accent, he had to be from the south. Texas, maybe. There was something so likeable about him that I couldn't help smiling. "It's karate."

"I'd love to learn some moves sometime." Jimmy glanced from me to Braedon.

Maria moved closer, taking Jimmy's arm. "Elle and a bunch of us are meeting for breakfast. You two coming?"

"I'm heading to the first class in that series about Hawaii, so I won't have time." I threw my canvass bag over my shoulder and headed toward the elevator, followed by the others.

"I'll have to pass too." Braedon reached his arm past me and pushed the elevator button. "I'm meeting my family for that same class."

"Oh, okay." Jimmy nodded. "Hey, I was wondering—"

The elevator opened, and we stepped aside to let out the people, Braedon's hand on the frame to keep the door open. I looked at Jimmy. "Yes?"

"Well, see, I play the guitar, and I'm looking for other people who play instruments."

I glanced at Maria, who was watching him in obvious adoration. "Why?" I asked him.

Jimmy's face glowed. "I'm trying to talk the cruise director into letting us have a passenger talent show."

I hoped Elle hadn't told him that I played the piano and the guitar. I was on vacation and had no intention of performing. "I'll let you know if I find any."

Jimmy gave me a big grin. "Wicked. Thanks!" He headed toward the stairs.

"Hang on a sec," Braedon said to me. He let the elevator door go and dashed toward the buffet by the pool area. He grabbed a few things and hurried back, handing me a muffin. "After that workout, you can't skip breakfast."

"What?" I laughed and pushed the elevator button again. "Are you a doctor or something?"

He nodded. "Surgeon."

That explained the cell phone obsession, but he looked too young to be a doctor. "General surgery or did you specialize?"

"I'm a thoracic surgeon."

"Wow. How old are you?" I blurted and immediately covered my mouth in dismay. "Sorry. It's just I know that involves an extra four years after medical school, so it's what? Fifteen years of training *after* high school?"

Braedon blinked. "I *am* younger than most in the field." The elevator door opened again, and we entered. "I graduated early from high school with an associate degree, so I had a head start."

"How old were you when you graduated?"

He paused. "Fifteen."

"You graduated from high school at fifteen *with* an associate degree? I'm … speechless."

Braedon chuckled, but there was a hint of bitterness to it. "You wouldn't be if you'd known my mother."

The doors opened to our floor, and we stepped into the narrow hallway.

"Did your mother push you to graduate early?"

He shrugged. "No more than I pushed myself."

Cocking my head, I lifted one eyebrow.

"What?"

"I'm a high school teacher. Even graduating at eighteen with an associate degree is a big deal. Did you do *anything* but study?"

"My mother was a very determined woman, and she knew how to get what she wanted … and, to be honest, what I wanted. I had a rigid schedule, but I did have a social life."

The smile left his face. "She wanted to keep me from growing up to be like my father. He's a rancher in Montana, and she knew how much I loved to be out on the range with him. So when I expressed an interest in medicine, she jumped on it with a vengeance and made sure I never had time to change my mind."

He winced. "I'm sorry. You don't need to know all this."

Yet at that moment, I wanted to know the whole story. "Did you ever? Change your mind, I mean."

He shook his head.

"How did your dad feel about you becoming a doctor?"

Braedon snorted, but his expression softened. "He can be really hard on people, but he supported me in whatever I wanted—as long as it was my choice. Dad's not one to trust people who aren't family. After the divorce, my mother was no longer family."

Being caught between them must have been tough. My heart swelled at the thought of my own parents. "Your mother and father sound like they're from two very different worlds."

"It's amazing they ever got together—the cowboy and the debutante. Their story was the stuff of a chick flick … if there'd been a happy ending." He lifted his chin toward me. "What about you? How did you get into martial arts?"

"There'd been a rash of rapes around campus, so I registered for karate. I loved it and kept going even after the police caught the guy."

"I studied Taekwondo in school—traditional, not sport. I only got up to my red belt, though. Other things became more important to me at that time in my life." He gave a soft chuckle. "Like cars and girls."

"Cars and girls. Makes me think of my brother." I grinned and paused when we reached his door. "So you didn't go beyond red. What level is that? I'm not familiar with Taekwondo's belt colors."

"In my dojo, it was just before black."

Elle stuck her head out of our door a few feet away. "There you are!" Her eyes widened when she noticed Braedon.

"See you," I said to him and nudged Elle into our cabin.

I had to give her credit for trying to hide her smug expression. "You coming to breakfast?" she asked.

Stepping out of my gi pants, I nodded toward the day's itinerary on the desk next to her. "Don't you remember I said I wanted to go to the briefings?" I took a big bite out of the muffin.

She scanned the paper and frowned. "But there are five days of them. All first thing in the morning."

"You want to come with me?" I tried not to push too hard. Elle hated sitting through lectures, and I figured she would decline this time too. We had learned to respect our differences and accept the give and take.

She surprised me by considering my offer, and my hopes rose, but she finally made a face. "No, but you'll still come to the hula class after lunch, won't you?"

"Of course. I love making a fool of myself in front of others." Grabbing my clothes, I headed to the bathroom.

"We'll have company. Jimmy's coming," Elle called as I shut the door.

*I*T WAS probably safer for me to go to the briefing without Braedon since I was finding him a little too interesting for my comfort. I had survived the last eleven months by removing all evidence that Jace had ever been a part of my life. Mentally, I had known it would take me time to get over him, but the betrayal confused everything. I had set progress markers to prove to myself I was moving on, like finally eating at our favorite restaurant or accepting a Facebook friend request from someone in high school we had both known. My pride had demanded it. Like a racehorse wearing blinders to avoid distraction, I had refused to see anything but getting past the anniversary of Jace's death … and all that had followed. I hadn't been able to bring myself to consider my raw and wounded heart. That would come. Eventually.

Braedon's cabin door opened just when I was about to pass it. He grinned. "Good timing. Do you mind if I walk with you?"

"No," I lied. Kind of. He smelled fresh from his shower and had put on that yummy cologne again.

"What's involved in your belt test?" he asked as we walked down the corridor.

"I have to do all my degree kata. Sensei will have me choose one of my favorites from any color belt, and he'll choose one or two for me to do too."

Braedon frowned. "So you have to remember all the forms?"

I nodded. "And there's unpadded sparring—three against one—plus a bunch of self-defense techniques."

We had reached the auditorium, where a crowd of people gathered at the entrance, slowly making their way inside. In front of us was the elderly gentleman from the drill. Braedon's eyes flicked to me, and the corner of his mouth twitched. If I had known him better, I would have smacked him. Instead, I laughed.

The old man looked back over his shoulder, his eyes sparkling in recognition. He nodded to us and turned back to another elderly man. "What was it you said?"

"That stuff doesn't happen out here, does it?" the other man asked him.

"Not that I ever heard of. I wouldn't go on any of the excursions if I had. Who'd ever think pirates …."

Their voices faded as they entered the auditorium.

Aislinn and D'Arcy were seated at the front. She waved for Braedon to come over, and he looked at me. "It didn't sound like you were meeting anyone here. You're welcome to sit with us."

The invitation was hardly unexpected, but my heart still sped up. I had never been able to come up with excuses quickly enough in order to get out of things gracefully. I could be rude, and had to admit I had overreacted at first after Jace—just ask all those guys who had asked me out over the last year—but this was different. Braedon was just being nice. "Sure."

"No Kate?" I asked when we sat down next to the Armstrongs.

Aislinn bent forward. "They have a lot of activities for the kids. I could hardly get her to eat her breakfast first."

The sound of drums blasted through the speakers, and the lights slowly dimmed. A large Polynesian man in a flowered shirt came on stage and opened the day's lecture on the history of the Hawaiian Islands.

"How do you practice self-defense on your own?" Braedon whispered.

"I don't. I'll have to wait until after the trip."

After a few minutes, Braedon leaned toward me. "Is it hard?"

I turned to him. "Is what hard?"

"Being a self-defense dummy." He tilted his head closer, his hair tickling my ear and making goose bumps break out along my arms. "I could be your guinea pig."

Jace had hated my love for karate. He had said he worried someone would hurt me. Yeah, right. He hadn't liked me being punched but hadn't minded breaking my heart.

When I didn't answer right away, Braedon said, "But only if you want." He sounded unsure.

I didn't want to be distracted from my goals, and Braedon was definitely distracting, but I told myself it was just a kind offer. "That'd be great. I do need to practice." The last part at least was true.

The brightness from the low lights made his eyes glimmer. "Just don't hurt me."

I choked back a laugh, and the woman behind me shushed us. We faced the speaker, our shoulders shaking.

$\mathcal{I}$ LEFT BRAEDON with his family at the end of the lecture and went back to the cabin in search of Elle. She hadn't returned from breakfast, and I had no idea where to look for her before lunch. Time to take advantage of the sunshine. I changed into my barely-there bikini that I only wore to tan when no guys were around, put on a robe, and went out onto the balcony.

Leaning against the balcony rail, I tasted the salty air. Seagulls glided the drafts of wind that swirled my hair. I had come on the cruise for this—quiet solitude and the majesty of the ocean.

From what I could see, none of the nearby balconies were occupied, so I slipped off my robe and lay down on the lounge chair. I read until my eyes grew tired from the glare. I set the book aside, the toasty warmth of the sun trying to lull me into a doze. It was time to go inside.

The sound of Braedon's balcony door opening sent a shock through my body. I choked back a cry, scrambling for my robe.

"Nice bikini," he commented, his tone appreciative.

My stomach churned as, cheeks burning, I flipped the robe the rest of the way around me and rose to face him. First I fall all over him and now this. Was I forever destined to be embarrassed in front of this man?

He stood with his back to me, his shoulders shaking with silent laughter.

I didn't know if I should be glad he had turned around or mad he was laughing at me. I chose to go with the first option. "And they say chivalry is dead."

Braedon turned, trying to look penitent and only succeeding a little, the humor still in his voice. "Sorry, but you should have seen your face."

I laughed softly. I was surprised at the number of times he had made me do that. "So where do gentlemen like you come from?"

"New York. I grew up on my mother's estate in Long Island. The estate itself has around a hundred acres of formal gardens." Braedon chuckled. "There's a walled garden where Aislinn used to like to pretend she was Mary Lennox. She'd bribe me to be Colin."

After biting back a smile at the picture, I considered the implications of growing up in a home like that. It was something far beyond anything I had ever experienced. "Does your mother still live there?" I shifted. My robe was getting hot.

"No ...." He grimaced. "She died about six months ago."

I straightened. "I'm sorry."

Braedon gave me a tight smile, his expression making it clear he didn't want to talk about it.

When I tried to think of another subject, an image of my parents' tiny house in a middle-class neighborhood flashed through my mind. "It sounds like you had a privileged childhood."

I didn't mean to sound accusatory, but Braedon became defensive. "We did have a privileged childhood, but it wasn't from living at Winterwood or going to yacht races; it was from spending our summers and holidays on a Montana ranch working our butts off. I spent only about a quarter of my time with my dad, but it's his house that feels like home to me."

We stared at each other for a moment, and I had the strong impression he had not spoken of this with many others. I felt honored he would share something so personal with me.

My balcony door opened, and I jumped. Elle slipped outside but stopped when she saw Braedon.

"Sorry I talked your ear off, Lyn." He turned toward his door. "I'll see you around."

"I liked getting my ear talked off." I kept my voice low. He must have still been able to hear, because he glanced over his shoulder, and the corner of his mouth turned up before he went back inside his cabin.

I turned toward Elle. "Been having fun?"

She considered Braedon's closing balcony door but didn't say anything for a moment before finally asking, "You ready for lunch? I'm starving."

CHAPTER 4

I SPENT PART of the afternoon reading in the ship's library. When I returned to our cabin, I found Elle had almost finished dressing for dinner.

"Did you get lost in your book?" She dangled her wristwatch. "You're cutting it pretty close."

"I won't be long." I slipped out of my shoes.

When I had undressed, I chose one of the four formal dresses I had purchased for the cruise. Since Elle wanted to go up to the Crow's Nest, I chose the simplest one. It was a black, knee-length chiffon piece.

I twisted my hair into a loose, curly updo, leaving a few strands hanging around my face and down my neck.

After slipping on my heels, I stood beside Elle in front of the mirror to check the overall effect. She was more striking than beautiful. While her eyes were a little too wide for her small nose, their bright blue color offset her dark blonde hair. It had amused us when we were growing up that people often mistook my fair-haired brother as hers. I was dark where Elle was light, tall where she was not. Elle's soft, feminine shape contrasted with my more angular, athletic form.

"You'll do," we said together and giggled.

The Crow's Nest sat on the top floor of the ship with a panoramic vista of the ocean. Elle's little social group had grown, and Jimmy helped me push a few of the small tables together.

"That should give us a good view of the dance floor." Jimmy patted the table before turning to me. "Guess what."

"You found someone who plays an instrument."

He snorted. "I've already found three—a drummer and two guitarists. One's good at bass too. Now I just need a keyboardist." His eyes glowed. "The news is I'm wearing the cruise director down and ... Hang on." He scooted around a couple and dashed to the door where Maria stood searching the crowd.

Jimmy brought her over to the table. "I'll be right back," he said and headed toward some guys who were waving him over.

Maria didn't seem to know what to do with herself, so I patted the chair beside me. "He's not excited about his little band at all, is he?"

Her face shone with pride. "He's so talented."

"Did you two just meet?"

Maria shook her head, glancing over her shoulder like she was afraid someone might overhear. "We're kind of engaged," she whispered. "But it's a secret. He's not sure his mother will approve of me."

Grimacing, I wondered if it was because she was Hispanic. Not that I could ask. "With him in the family ranch business, it'll be hard to keep secret."

"I know, right? His mom's determined to set him up with a

family friend. Jimmy's going to break it to her when—excuse me." Maria jumped from her chair and hurried over to where Jimmy was signaling her.

I watched them talking with the group of guys. Jimmy and Maria made a cute couple. I hoped things worked out for them.

Elle slid into the chair beside me as a feedback squeal came from the sound equipment. The DJ made a quick adjustment to the microphone. "Welcome, cruisers!"

The crowd roared their approval.

The DJ introduced himself and then officially opened the floor. D'Arcy led Aislinn out to dance. She winked at Braedon as her husband took her into his arms. As Santana's "Smooth" began to play, they flowed into the cha-cha like their bodies were being guided by one brain.

The crowd got into the rhythm, and I found myself grinning. I loved to dance, and I hadn't had a good partner since college. I wondered if Braedon could dance that well too.

My curiosity was soon satisfied. The song had barely played halfway through when Braedon suddenly jumped up and cut in on D'Arcy, Aislinn laughing as he swept her away.

No, Braedon couldn't dance like Aislinn. Or wouldn't. His sister tried to do the cha-cha with him, *tried* being the key word. His steps reminded me of the out-of-sync movements from guys at my high school graduation—then I realized he was pretending to be a robot. Braedon was trying to suppress a smirk, and Aislinn finally laughed, hitting his arm and letting him lead her in a bizarre two-step that didn't match the music at all.

When the song ended, Braedon approached my table, extending a hand. "May I have this dance?"

I hesitated a moment, thinking it might be better if I didn't, but Elle gave me her you-had-better-say-yes-or-you're-so-dead look. I took his hand, prepared for the tingle this time. He smelled good. Great.

The second song, "In the Mood," had begun by the time we reached the floor. Braedon placed his right hand high on my back and, taking my other hand, went into the two-step again. At least this time he moved with the music.

"So, where are you from?"

I didn't realize I had been holding my breath. After talking about his medical training earlier, I had been expecting questions about college. Maybe someday I could look back on my own memories of that time without thinking of liars and cheaters. "Colorado Springs. I've lived there all my life."

"Excuse me." Jimmy tapped my shoulder. "I'm cutting in."

He stole me away, pulling me into an awkward embrace and swinging me into what could only be a Texas two-step. Almost immediately, I missed Braedon. Stupid me.

Jimmy was followed by a host of guys in what became a session of speed-date-dancing. Exhausted, I returned to our tables, where I found Elle had just finished dancing with D'Arcy and invited the Armstrongs to join us.

I slid into the seat next to Aislinn. "You *had* to have been on a ballroom dance team."

"I was." She winked at her brother. "I used to try to make Braedon practice with me."

He grimaced.

"Which was worse, dancing with Aislinn or playing Colin to her Mary?" I teased.

Aislinn darted her eyes from me to Braedon. "You told her that?"

"I may have mentioned it." He rose from the table, took my hand, and pulled me to my feet. "Let's finish our dance."

A slow, modern song played, and Braedon pulled me near, swaying back and forth to the music. Except for karate, I hadn't been held so close in almost a year. My senses awakened to him; his subtle but pleasant cologne, the weight of his hand on my waist.

I needed to think of something else. "I'm sorry if I said something I shouldn't have back there."

He lowered his eyes to mine. "About me playing *Secret Garden* with my sister?"

I laughed. "I have a younger brother I used to torment, and I love the thought of Aislinn doing the same to you."

Braedon smiled, but it didn't quite reach his eyes—like the smile he had given me on his balcony when he hadn't wanted to talk about his mother.

"I think you would probably do anything for Aislinn," I said, hoping my instincts were right.

His smile then did more than light up his face. I almost forgot we were surrounded by a crush of people. He was a *very* good dancer.

"You said you were a teacher."

I was on edge, kind of like when I was blowing up a bunch of balloons for a school event and just waiting for one to pop. Braedon continued to make easy conversation, and I wondered what I had been worried about.

When we returned to the tables, the Armstrongs were rising to leave.

"We need to get Kate to bed, or she'll be a bear in the morning." Aislinn twisted so her husband could help her with her wrap.

When D'Arcy looked at Braedon, he nodded. "I'll come with you." Braedon finished the last of his drink. Turning to the rest of us, he said, "I have to get up early. Good night." The three of them left together.

I looked at my watch. "I should probably go too."

Elle tapped the seat beside her. "I don't think so."

"But I have to get up early too."

She tilted her head and pinned me with her eyes. It always struck me how so much strength of will could be housed in such a little person.

Laughing, I sat down. "Fine. I'll stay a little longer."

CHAPTER 5

RAEDON HAD already begun his workout on the treadmill when I arrived the next morning. Before I had fallen asleep the night before, I had reminded myself of my reasons to stay aloof. As soon as I saw him, I had to go through them again.

I went through my stretches, and by the time I took my break, Braedon had moved to the weights, giving Jimmy and Maria tips. They joined me when I had completed my forms. I took a few minutes to teach Jimmy and Maria some kicks and punches, sending them off to practice before the gym got too full.

I was pleased to be collected and businesslike as I turned to Braedon. "You ready for this?"

"Of course."

I pulled a pair of mats from the corner. "We need to use these because in my escapes I'm required to take you down."

"Okay," he said slowly. "What kind of escapes?"

"Holds, mostly. Let's start out with you behind me." I turned my back to him. "Pin my arms to my sides."

He grasped my arms, his skin warm and surprisingly soft, and held them in place, though without much strength.

I shook my head. "You need to bring your arms around me and *pin* my arms to my sides."

He did as instructed, but I could tell he still wasn't using his full strength. I would have to get his attention. Before he could react, I pulled one of his fingers free and bent it into a joint lock, careful to not apply too much pressure, just enough so he released my arms. Still in control of his finger, I twisted around so he was forced to drop to his knees. He tapped out to let me know he'd had enough, and I let him go.

As he rose, I said, "Braedon, you need to hold me like you mean it."

A funny expression crossed his face.

Curse my traitorous hot cheeks. Okay, maybe not so under control. I sighed. "I mean hold me tight like you're a bad guy trying to keep me from getting away."

He pinched his lips. Stepping behind me, he wrapped his arms around me and pinned my arms to my sides. His skin didn't feel so soft now.

I simulated a stomp on his right instep and swiveled my hips out of the way for a right ridge hand strike—sometimes called a karate chop—toward his crotch. In a flash, he released me, leaping out of the way.

Having arrived in time to see Braedon's leap, Jori grinned.

"*You* grab her from behind and let her take a shot at you," Braedon growled.

I held up my hands in surrender. "I won't *really* hit you. It's an escape move." I leaned down to pick up the mat. "It's okay. I'll just work on my self-defense stuff when I get back home."

"No, I'm good." He stepped onto the mat so I couldn't lift

it. "Just tell me if there's anything else I should know about first."

I let go of the mat. "Are you sure?"

He lowered his voice, a mock-grim expression on his face. "I have to save face now. We've got an audience."

I did a quick scan of the gym. He was right. We had become the center of attention. All right. I would play along. "Save face, huh?" I gave him a 'come on' gesture.

This time when he moved, he moved *fast* and held my arms tight, my back pressed against his chest, his right hand clasping his left wrist in front of me.

I quickly considered my options. Since he would be expecting a foot stomp and the groin strike, I went for his fingers again. As soon as I tried to pull on one, he tightened his grip, turning his fingers in. I made a fist and ground my knuckles into the bones on the top of his hand.

Braedon hissed but kept his arms rigid around me, bringing them down to keep me from bending my elbows. I threw my head back fast and connected with his lower face. I cringed, hoping I hadn't made him cut his lip, but I still followed up with a foot stomp and the hip twist.

Distracted by an anticipated groin strike, he moved up his grip on my arms when he shifted his hips out of the way. Just what I needed to grab a finger again. The little one is the weakest and therefore the easiest to get loose. I bent it back, locked the joint, and gave it a slight twist.

He released me, and I spun, swinging my right leg behind his and sweeping his legs out from under him. I caught him as he went down, breaking his fall. Twisting around, I put my right knee on his chest and threw a throat strike, stopping just before it connected.

"Dead." Grinning, I straightened.

Everyone broke into applause, and I jumped to my feet, reaching down to give Braedon a hand up. He took it and stood, brushing his lip with his tongue, his eyes narrowed. I reached to touch his lip to see if it was bleeding. To his credit, he didn't flinch.

"Sorry about that. I didn't think you'd keep your head in such a vulnerable place. Your lip's not bleeding."

He touched his lip and then brushed his chin again.

Jimmy rushed over, dragging Maria with him. "You have to show me how to do that!"

"We'll see." I glanced at Braedon.

His face remained expressionless. "Do you want to practice some more?"

I looked at the group of people watching us. "Not with this crowd."

He bowed to me, keeping his eyes to the ground as he would to his sensei, turned, and left. I stared after him.

Maria shot me a sympathetic glance before Jimmy took her hand and they left. So it wasn't just me thinking Braedon was unhappy about something.

Jori came over and helped me put away the mats. "I'm impressed." He sized me up as though he had never seen me before. "Remind me never to make you angry."

Already disappointed at Braedon's attitude, I glared at Jori.

"Wait. I can sympathize with Braedon. I wouldn't be happy to be shown up by a girl."

I tossed my water bottle in my bag. "Shown up by a girl. Really?"

"No offense … Hey, Lyn, don't get angry. It's a guy thing."

Jori moved closer. "We all suffer from it, some more than others."

Then he struck—so fast I never had time to think of throwing up a defense. He swept me like I had swept Braedon, and Jori had me in a full mount with my hands pinned over my head. It was a sweet move.

"Nice." I tried not to smile. "Sneaky, but nice. Now let me back up."

His face broke out in a wicked grin. "I don't think so." He leaned forward, his face only inches from mine. I gave him a crusty look, but he continued. "I find this an interesting predicament."

When I realized his intent, my body went still. How had I not seen this coming? He must have taken my shock as permission because he moved his lips toward mine.

Angry heat flooded my body. I jerked my face away while bending my knees, twisting my foot around one of his. Locking it in place, I pushed all my weight up and to the side, throwing him off balance. He didn't resist and had to release my hands to catch himself, but I reached up and yanked his hair as he flew over me, forcing his head to the side.

Where the hair goes, the head follows. Using my feet to finish the movement, I was now on top of Jori, pinning his hands. He had the advantage of size and strength, so I didn't stay there long enough for him to reverse us again. I leapt up and out of his reach.

He lay on the floor smirking, not the least bit repentant.

I grabbed my bag. "Don't *ever* try to kiss me again."

Jori sat up. "Don't be fussed about it."

I stared daggers at him and snarled through my teeth, "*Never* again."

Realizing I wasn't feigning my anger, he jumped to his feet. I stepped out of his reach. "I'm sorry about the kiss. I promise I won't try it again." He held out both hands in supplication. "Friends still?"

I glowered at him for a moment but decided he was sincere. I wasn't going to let him off that easy, though. I turned my back on him and left the gym without a word. He didn't follow.

$\mathcal{I}$ MUTTERED UNDER my breath as I waited for the elevator. It wasn't like Jori hadn't given me any clues. He had even mentioned looking for me at dinner that first night. I should have made it clearer I wasn't interested in him like that, but I had been too busy thinking about Braedon.

Braedon. His attitude had surprised me. Even as I assured myself it would be better if he were mad at me, I wondered if he would be willing to practice with me again. Stupid.

Elle had gone to breakfast without me but left a note reminding me of our hula class and telling me where to meet for lunch. After showering, I called room service and had some breakfast brought to my room.

When my food arrived, I took it out onto the balcony to eat. The gloomy sky matched my mood. I stood glumly at the rail for a while, staring at the dark gray water.

At the noise of Braedon's balcony door opening, I considered making a quick retreat back inside but found I wanted—no, needed—to make things right with him. I turned slowly toward the sound.

Braedon stood in the doorway and watched me. He had showered, and his hair glistened with moisture. After a moment's hesitation, he strode to the rail separating our balconies. "I hoped you might be out here."

I joined him at the railing. "I owe you an apology. I assumed you knew what you were getting yourself into when you offered to be my self-defense dummy. I promise I would never really hurt you."

"It's been a long time since I studied Taekwondo, and I've forgotten more than I realized." Braedon touched his lip with his tongue and chuckled. "It's me who owes you an apology. I was pretty abrupt when I left."

I opened my mouth to reply, but he caught my eye, and I stopped. "However, I've swallowed my pride about how fast you put me on the floor, and I'm willing to risk being put there again."

"Really?" I hated how relieved that made me feel.

"I wouldn't miss it now, but you'll need to give me a training session before we have another go. I'm not much into public humiliation."

I squeezed my hands together, surprised at the moisture on my palms. "Then please understand the whole point of this practice is for me to refine my defense skills … you *have* to go down."

"I can do that." He checked his watch. "I'm supposed to meet Aislinn and D'Arcy again for the Hawaiian geography class. Do you want to walk together?"

"Sure. I'll meet you outside."

$\mathcal{I}$ DIDN'T EVEN remember the incident with Jori until after I entered the dining room, when he slipped in a few minutes late. I was glad the closest chair was at the other end of the table.

While I might not have been clear enough before, I would be now. During the meal, he kept trying to get my attention; I ignored him.

"Wait, Lyn," Jori called later as I hurried Elle out of the restaurant.

He had to know I was serious. "I'm not talking to you, Jori." I continued to walk away.

Elle glanced back at him. "What's this about?"

"I swept her this morning, and now she's mad at me." Jori caught up, but I kept Elle between us.

She frowned, knowing that shouldn't have bothered me. "You're mad at him because of *that*?"

I continued to walk, staring straight ahead. "I'm not talking about this."

"No," Jori corrected. "She's mad because I tried to kiss her."

Elle's teasing expression disappeared. Her eyes widened. She looked uncomfortable in her position between us.

Jori took Elle's arm and traded places with her, so I stopped and faced him, folding my arms across my chest. "Lyn," he brushed back a wisp of his pale blond hair, all contriteness. "I said I was sorry for offending you, and I meant it." He did his little bow.

"With Elle as your witness, you'll never do that again?"

"Never again." He blinked as though something occurred to him. "Unless you ask me to."

I spun away, but he grabbed my arm. When I moved to pin his hand to my elbow in the beginnings of a joint lock, he jerked it out of my reach. "Okay. Never."

At Elle's encouraging glance, I gave in. "Apology accepted."

With a grin, he bowed and left us.

Elle nudged my shoulder with hers. "See, that wasn't so hard." She slid her arm through mine. "Let's go see if we can convince the dance teacher to let us merge hip-hop and hula for Jimmy's talent show."

A NEED FOR solitude drew me to a window nook in the ship's library. Hidden from most of the other occupants, I squished a soft cushion behind my back and tried to settle into reading.

For nearly a year, I had looked forward to this uncomplicated cruise, excited to have time to be at sea, read, and visit places I had always wanted to see. Elle thought the temporary nature of the cruise would make for a perfect dating environment. No risk of involvement. But I had vowed I would not consider it until I got past the first anniversary.

I don't know how long I had been staring at the water when I heard someone sit at the piano just around the corner from my nook. I pinched my lips. I would have to move if the player was too distracting.

Because of the way the nook was situated, I couldn't see the person who began to play finger drills. Great. Not exactly music to read by. I picked up my book and tried to find where I had left off, hoping to ignore the sound.

After going through several drills, the player went into the insane fingering of the beginning of Chopin's *Fantaisie-Impromptu*. This was no kid practicing scales.

When I was eight, I had sat beside my father in the Boettcher Concert Hall in Denver. The special guest was a world-renowned performer, and she had played this song. Her fingers had flown across the keys, and I had determined then and there I would be able to play it someday.

I sighed and closed my eyes, leaning against the window, the glass cool against my cheek. My hands automatically picked out the notes as I accompanied the unknown player on my imaginary piano.

When the number ended, I considered clapping, but the pianist went right into one of my favorite New Age pieces. I thought of how Braedon's long, graceful fingers had clasped around my waist. He would have great hands for playing the piano. A little shiver sent goose bumps along my arms and up my neck. It couldn't be ….

I peeked around the corner.

CHAPTER 6

I WONDERED HOW he had learned to play like that with everything else he'd had to do as a kid. And it had to be the piano, one of my great loves. I leaned my chin against my raised knees. I could just see him around the nook wall.

Braedon focused on playing and didn't appear to notice me. I played several instruments, though only the piano and guitar well. I found pleasure in the piano, and when I'd had a bad day, I would play to relieve my stress. As I watched him, I thought perhaps Braedon did too. His face in this private moment made me feel like I had captured a glimpse of his soul. I was fascinated.

When he finished, I leaned forward enough to be seen. "That was lovely."

He started at the sound of my voice and snapped his head in my direction.

I smiled. "You need a small orchestra to bring out the full depth of that piece. Nice interpretation, though."

He twisted on the bench. "Do you play?"

"I work at a small school, so I teach both music and

science. I teach band, orchestra, music theory, and I'm the choir director."

Braedon grinned. "Do you know any duets?"

I snorted. "Not from memory. Well, 'Chopsticks' and 'Heart and Soul' are two pieces I do know how to play."

"Wait a minute." He rose from the piano bench and approached the librarian.

The crewmember went to a locked cabinet and handed him a stack of sheet music after taking his ship card in exchange. He riffled through the sheets as he ambled back, and I moved to the piano.

He scanned a piece of music. "How familiar are you with Mozart?"

"For four hands?" I tried to read the title upside down.

Our eyes met over the music, and he quirked an eyebrow. "That is the nature of a duet."

I scowled, almost sticking my tongue out at him. "I'm familiar with the piece, but it's fast to sight read."

"Want to give it a try?" His eyes dared me to say no.

He had been a good sport earlier, so I moved over to the piano bench. "I get the easy part."

Braedon pulled out a second piece. "Here's Brahms's Hungarian Dance no. 1 in G Minor for Piano, Four Hands, if you prefer."

I looked over his arm at the page as he read through the music. "I haven't tried this one in a long time." I ran my fingers over the keys. "If we do this one, I claim the secundo part."

After a couple of false starts, I relaxed. Braedon didn't play it flawlessly either, which gave me more confidence. When we were done, we tried the Mozart piece, but I gave up. "I need to practice this one by myself. I'm not up to it."

He took the stack of music and went through it again.

"Look." He turned the piece so I could see it—a ragtime duet of "Cantina Band" from *Star Wars*. "We have to give this one a try." He set it on the holder.

I was more than familiar with this piece because two of my students had performed it this year, and I had learned it while helping them. Most of it was really only three hands, but it was quirky and fun. We were both laughing by the end.

As we rose, I blinked, surprised to find Elle and her group standing behind us. Braedon slipped away to return the music.

Jimmy rushed forward. "Why didn't you tell me you could play the piano? I need a keyboardist."

"You should ask Braedon. He's much better than I am."

Braedon heard this as he rejoined the group. He and Jimmy argued about it as we made our way to the cafeteria-style restaurant. We collected our food before heading to the sky deck.

After eating, I took a few minutes to review with Braedon some of the self-defense techniques for the next morning. His graceful hands were a combination of strength and gentleness. I had seen how strong he was that morning, and I now could also imagine those hands doing delicate surgery.

Two of the guys from dinner—Wes and Ryan—observed us and came over, followed by Jimmy and Maria.

"You know karate?" Wes flipped his dreadlocks over his shoulder. "We're brown belts."

"What style?" I asked.

"Gosoku."

I raised my eyebrows. "Hard and fast, huh?"

"Hard?" Maria looked first at me and then at the two guys. "Like, they hit hard?"

We laughed. "Not like you mean it. A hard style means it has linear motions. A soft style is more circular." I said to the two guys, "Mine's a hard style too. Braedon and I have been practicing self-defense techniques in the gym in the morning. You guys ought to come."

Maria shook her head, rubbing Jimmy's arm a little anxiously. "Not me. I don't mind kickboxing for cardio, but I don't want anyone hitting me."

"You don't have to come," Jimmy interrupted, kissing her cheek. "But I would like Lyn to teach me more than kicks and punches."

With his request came sudden inspiration. I scanned the area for Jori, who was chatting with a couple of girls in a corner. I wondered which one would be his partner that night. "You should talk to Jori about teaching you some self-defense techniques."

Jori turned toward me at the sound of his name and strode over.

I smiled at Jimmy. "I think Jori knows Hapkido."

Jori nodded as he reached us.

"I just volunteered you to teach Jimmy. Wouldn't you say you owe that to me?"

Jori sent me a shrewd look over the head of his soon-to-be student.

Jimmy looked confused. "What's … what did you call it? Hop-kee-something?"

Jori slugged Jimmy's shoulder. "It's a Korean martial art."

"That also uses joint locks for self-defense," I added. "Jori can bring you up to date."

"Hapkido is much better than anything from Japan." Turning, Jori sent me a sideways glance, the twinkle in his eyes

taking the barb out of his words. He led Jimmy and Maria—
who wore a martyred expression—toward an open area.

I giggled, thinking Maria must really be in love to go along.
It was kind of sweet. Leaving the others, I made my way to
one of only two remaining lounge chairs and lay down. The
two guys would make interesting additions to my self-defense
sessions.

"Mind if I join you?" Braedon sat in the empty chair beside
mine.

Just friends. "Sure."

He leaned back, his eyes gazing at the star-studded sky.
"Do you teach your students about astronomy? Can you tell me
about the constellations?"

This I could handle. I ran my hand up and down the arm
of my chair, the smooth plastic cool under my touch. Clearing
my throat, I began in my lecture voice, "I'm sure you've heard
of the North Star." I pointed to one of the bright stars. "As
we haven't traveled too far south yet, we can still see it. It's
been used for navigation for centuries. Because it's the 'North'
Star, we can only see it while we're in the northern hemisphere.
Once we cross the equator, we won't be able to see it anymore."

Braedon looked at me. "I didn't know that."

I lifted my head. "You didn't take astronomy as an
undergrad?"

"No." He faced the sky again. "Premed requires plenty of
other science courses."

"I take my students up Pikes Peak every spring to stargaze.
Most people don't realize there isn't a bright star in the southern
hemisphere—a South Star, so to speak. Makes navigating
harder. If we're going to get shipwrecked, we better do it before
we cross the equator."

Braedon chuckled. "We should be sure to mention it to the captain."

*L*ATER, WHEN I came out of the bathroom in my pajamas, Elle sat on her bed waiting for me. "So." She played with the bedspread. "Two guys are showing interest in you, and you've only told one of them off. That's good."

I raised my hand to stop her. "It's not like that. Braedon's just a friend."

"Still, this is progress for you." She concentrated on plucking at the bedspread before continuing. "It's time to trust again."

I grunted. "Oh, right. In this fake place?" I grabbed my pillow and fluffed it up. I didn't want to have this conversation.

She watched me with sad eyes as I crawled into bed and turned away from her. It was easy for her to believe; she had never been deceived.

Memory brought the scent of blooming lilacs blowing in my window on a warm summer breeze. I doubted I would ever like the smell again. It took me back to that night almost a year ago when Jace's father had called.

Dan's voice cracked as he said my name. In spite of the warm night, my blood turned to ice. "What is it, Dan?" Through the phone, I heard his sobs. My stomach knotted. I sat and tried again, clenching the phone to stop the shaking of my hands. "Dan. What happened? Is Jace all right?"

"He's ... gone," the older man croaked.

"Gone?"

"Dead."

My whole world spun, and I grasped the table edge for

support as a wave of dizziness smashed into me. My body reacted while my brain played dumb, tears flooding my eyes.

"His car went into the canyon and rolled," Dan whispered, the weight of his loss heavy in his voice.

The blood pounded in my head. "Why?"

"They don't know yet."

Jace was supposed to have gone out with some guy friends. "Was anyone else hurt?"

Dan paused. "The ... girl's still unconscious, but they think she should recover."

My fingers holding the phone shook. Girl? What girl? Someone must have made a mistake. Hope rushed through me. Maybe it wasn't Jace after all. "There could have been a mistake."

"No, Lyn." The tone in his voice was final.

I slumped against the back of my chair, rubbing at the pain in my temple. Jace gone. At the sound of Dan's sobbing, I pulled myself together. "What can I do to help?"

"I have to call family. Can you ... call his friends?"

"Yes. I'll do that," I whispered. I felt like my insides were exposed, jagged nerves aching and burning with every breath.

The horrible evening had continued as I phoned my family and Elle. She rushed to my apartment and helped with the calls, staying with me through the night. The girl who had been with Jace haunted my dreams, and I roused after a few hours of troubled sleep. I had to see her to understand why she had been with him. Elle went with me to the hospital.

That was when the real nightmare began.

The young woman had regained consciousness during the night. I would always remember the hospital smells: cleaning chemicals, cotton bedding, iodine, even the fragrance of the front desk nurse's too sweet perfume.

The girl, her head bandaged and one arm in a cast, looked up when Elle and I entered her room.

Elle got right to the point. "We're so sorry about Jace. How did you know him?"

The girl's eyes glistened, her bottom lip quivering. "Are you some of his friends? Didn't he tell you about me?"

Elle shook her head.

"He was my boyfriend."

As I stood there, playing with the engagement ring on my left hand, the memory of the time Jace had put it there after a day on the ski slopes flashed before me.

"I think he was going to propose last night." The girl burst into tears, turning her head away from us.

I was suddenly numb, the lack of sensation hitting me so fast it was as if someone had severed my heart from my body. Like I was dead. Elle, her face pale and bleak, took me by the elbow to guide me from the room. I resisted, watching the girl's grief a moment longer.

As I had watched the sobbing form, Elle pulling on my sleeve, I had debated correcting the girl. But somewhere, as though from behind a thick wall, I had felt compassion for her. I hadn't been able to do to her what had just been done to me. I had slipped the ring from my finger, allowing it to drop to the floor as I had finally let Elle guide me from the room.

Trust. Elle wanted me to trust. Here. On a ship's tiny, phony world with its fake relationships. In a couple of days, it would be a year since I had discovered everything I had believed in was a lie.

I lay awake long after Elle fell asleep. I had been devastated last year, but I had survived. I didn't think I was bitter. I was simply a realist with a more practical view of people now. Best to keep it that way.

$\mathcal{T}$HAT SECOND day at sea established a pattern for the rest of the trip before the ship's four Hawaiian Island stops. Wes and Ryan joined us for the morning workouts while Jori shared some of his Hapkido techniques and took Jimmy under his wing for special instruction. Maria came for support but just watched. I hoped he realized how caring she was being.

On the fourth day, I passed up a hula class to take advantage of the tour of the engine and control rooms.

Running a little late, I dashed out of the elevator on the deck where the tour group was scheduled to meet and bumped right into Jori.

"Careful there." He grabbed my arm to keep me from falling as I bounced off him.

"Sorry." Everyone in the group stared at us.

The ship's officer began his explanation, and the others gave him their attention.

Jori leaned toward me and whispered, "I didn't know you were into cutting classes."

"I didn't know you were into engines—" I snapped my mouth shut as the officer opened a door and led us down some narrow stairs into a noisy room.

Jori signaled for me to go ahead down the tight, narrow stairs and then joined me at the railing that overlooked the ship's huge engines. The warm air held a sharp tang of oil and paint, and crewmembers went about their business ignoring their audience.

I glanced at Jori. He held a small notepad in his hands, his pencil making swift strokes on the paper. I leaned over to see what he was drawing—an older man in the tour group—and cast a shadow on his notepad in the process. He flashed me a cross look. I shifted a little and got so caught up watching him sketch that I forgot to listen to the officer's explanation.

When we moved to the quieter bridge, I whispered, "Are you a natural or have you taken art classes?"

"My electives were all art classes." He flipped his pad shut and indicated the officer, who had begun speaking again.

The command center for the ship had a sophisticated array of computers to monitor the various aspects of the floating hotel.

Jori seemed entranced by the view, and I asked, "Do you ever draw landscapes?"

"Sometimes." He flipped open his pad and showed me a couple of sketches of western ranch scenes with cattle and horses. One included a large log and stone ranch house with a huge bank of windows facing a distant mountain.

"Where's this?"

He chuckled, his tone rueful. "I *hope* it's Braedon's family ranch as he's described it to me." Jori closed the booklet and shifted his gaze to a group of passengers cavorting by the pool below. "I'll always prefer to draw people, though."

In a quiet voice, he asked, "Do you ever wonder what their stories are? Why they came to be where they are, at this time, with these people? What drives them?" He glanced at me. "Is it love? Adventure? Greed?" He faced the windows again and, so softly I almost couldn't hear, added, "Is it pain?"

The raw agony in Jori's eyes made me stare at him, and I felt a sudden kinship. What had caused that pain? I regretted how testy I had been with him after the incident in the gym. He had been true to his word and never made another flirty comment.

"That's odd," Jori muttered, the hurt suddenly gone.

I bent forward to see where he pointed his finger, kept down so the others didn't notice. There was an officer on lookout at the bank of windows. He had raised his binoculars to peer off to the side, looking tense. In the distance, a small craft headed right toward the cruise ship.

The officer snapped a few terse sounding words in another language—I guessed Norwegian since the ship originated from there—and the bridge crew jumped into action. Our tour guide hustled us out of the room. Jori and I tried to hang back. A crew woman stationed at the radio seemed to be trying to make contact with the other vessel as our guide finally pushed us out and shut the door.

CHAPTER 7

"WHAT THE ...." Jori scowled and looked at me.

Almost as though we had choreographed the movement, Jori and I pushed past the other tour members waiting for the elevator and dashed up the stairs.

We burst through the door onto the running deck. A few passengers had noticed the small vessel but most seemed oblivious. My heart pounded as we leaned over the railing. The boat had come quite close.

As we watched, the smaller vessel stopped. Jori and I stood silently with a handful of other passengers waiting for something to happen.

"Do you think they need help?" asked an elderly woman.

"I'm glad they don't have trouble with Somali pirates out here," said her male companion.

"Did they get those hostages back yet?"

The man shook his head.

I shivered at that thought. The rusty vessel seemed dwarfed by the large cruise ship. It was difficult to tell much about the crew on it. They were partially hidden by bags of some kind stacked around the deck. Could there be men with weapons hidden behind them?

"Do you know what modern pirate ships look like?" I whispered.

Jori snorted. "Do modern pirate ships have a 'look'?" He leaned farther out and peered more closely. "I wish I had some binoculars."

A dark-haired, dark-complexioned man on the other ship waved his arms. From above us came the sound of a lowering tender, one of the little lifeboats that doubled as transportation when the ship couldn't dock. We backed up a little as it dropped by us, and I realized our section of the deck was getting crowded with other curious passengers.

Jori put his mouth to my ear. "He's got a gun."

Beside the white-uniformed ship's officer sat a man with a sidearm at his waist. I was glad to know the cruise line had armed people on the ship—and that they kept it low key. I nudged Jori's arm. "And that guy has a rifle. Is it just a precaution?"

Once the tender was in the water, I could tell the men on it were tense. Was it because they didn't know what they were heading into? The man with the rifle took up a defensive position in the tender as the officer and two crewmen climbed aboard the other ship and disappeared from sight.

As the minutes passed, more people crowded into our section. Jori, standing directly behind me, finally took up a rigid stance to keep from being pushed into me. "Sorry. I'm not getting fresh."

I was about to suggest we find somewhere less crowded when the passengers started murmuring. Our crewmen appeared on the other ship's deck again and climbed back into the tender.

Once the cruise boat was clear, the ratty old ship sailed away, its crew waving at us.

A woman's voice from farther down said, "I know who that is. That's the ship's doctor." She pointed toward one of the men on the tender.

The other passengers broke up rather quickly, and Jori moved to my side to watch the tender rise to its dock. The man with the rifle had pushed it out of sight, and they all nodded to us as they went up.

"I don't get it. Why all the drama if they just needed the doctor?"

An old man with tattoos on his arms was passing and paused. "They were using arm signals because their radio was down."

"Makes sense." Jori turned to me. "Where are you headed now?"

"Library."

"Mind if I come with you?"

"Of course not." I shook my finger at him. "As long as I'm not one of your subjects."

Jori exhaled. "Why do you make my life so difficult?"

I nudged him with my shoulder. "Someone has to."

He opened the door into the ship's interior and its filtered air, and we walked in silence to the library entrance. Jori paused. I followed his gaze to the piano where Braedon sat playing.

"I just remembered I promised to help Jimmy with … something." Jori bowed to me. "I'll see you later."

What was he playing at? I stared at Braedon's back. I had an easy out. All I had to do was walk away.

I almost did. Just as I made the decision to leave, Braedon looked over his shoulder and our eyes met. His slow smile grew, and he beckoned me to join him. I could have left. I even told myself to turn around and follow Jori, but that's not the direction my feet took me.

I SAT WITH Elle on the sky deck after dinner, and we watched where the guys in her little social group had gathered. It amazed me how quickly they had bonded, and I wondered if some of the friendships would last beyond the cruise.

Braedon said something, and Jori laughed. Odd that two such different men had hit it off so well. Then I thought about Elle and me and decided it wasn't so strange after all.

Elle sighed and leaned her head back on her lounge chair. "Do you think there's something wrong with me?"

I peered at her in the too-bright ship lights. "Because you get bored with every guy you date after a couple of months?"

"Yes," Elle groaned. "Look at Jimmy over there with Maria." She pointed to the couple who sat on the edge of the group, completely absorbed in each other. "I want someone to be crazy about me like that."

I would have teased her, but she sounded genuinely sad. "You just haven't met the right guy yet."

"Wouldn't you think that after all the people I have met I'd have connected with *someone*?"

"We both know you don't want just anyone." This was a side of Elle I hadn't seen in a long time, not since I had gotten engaged to Jace. Why was she feeling insecure now? In the distance, Braedon laughed, and I glanced in his direction.

"You going to be okay tomorrow?" Elle asked.

"Sure. Why?"

She hesitated, and with a jolt, I understood. How could

I have forgotten even for a moment? Tomorrow was the anniversary.

My attention shifted back to the guys just as Braedon looked in my direction. He held my gaze, and warmth spread from my stomach to my chest and then my face. I broke eye contact, squeezing my tingling fingers into fists.

Elle put her hand on my arm. "I've got some ideas on things to do to help distract you."

Oh, I had something ... someone to distract me. But I couldn't go there. Not yet. Not here.

 That night, I dreamed of Jace for the first time in months, and it set my mood for the next day, making me edgy. Elle did her best to keep me occupied with activities and conversation. How ironic that her efforts kept me from thinking about Braedon too.

She must have been exhausted as everyone gathered around the piano by my nook after Jimmy's jam session. The group had spread around the area, a few on the sofas, some at the game tables, and others on the carpet. It was the second formal night, and we needed to leave earlier than usual to get dressed, but no one seemed inclined to move. The Armstrongs had joined us, and Kate sat at the piano picking out "Heart and Soul."

Finally, Aislinn rose with a sigh. "I suppose I should take Kate and get her fed."

Kate turned toward me with a huge grin. "We're having a pajama party with lots of goodies."

Elle rose and waved to me as she left with some others from her group. With their departure, more people drifted away.

"Come on. We should go too." Braedon stood and reached to pull me up.

Even expecting the tingle, I jumped a little, and his eyes danced. He kept my hand in his as we made our way around the people still sitting on the floor. My stomach twisted. He knew we were just friends. Didn't he?

Once back in my cabin, I spent extra time in the shower. I considered faking a headache and skipping dinner and the night's festivities. But Elle wouldn't want to leave me alone, thinking I was stewing over Jace.

I chose a floor-length sheath dress in a luscious dark gray for dinner. Elle entered while I was working on my hair, which I had decided to wear down tonight. She nodded in approval and did a little straightening for me. "He's outside waiting for you."

I spun, my breath catching. "Braedon? What's he wearing?"

"A tux." She grinned and slipped off her sandals.

For nearly a year, I had turned down every guy who had asked me out, and I hadn't always been very civil. Braedon had made the assumption I would spend the evening with him. Kind of like a date. How had this happened?

He waited outside my door, just as Elle had said, leaning against the wall and fiddling with one of his cuff links. The tux made him swoon-worthy, and my knees shook a little. This was ridiculous. I was too old to act like this.

Braedon straightened when I stepped out of the cabin door and offered me his arm. "You look beautiful."

"Thank you." With my trembling hand on his arm, I had a hard time denying we were on a date. He had on that cologne I liked, the one that made me want to snuggle up against his neck and breathe him in. Maybe Elle was right, but I wasn't ready for more than friendship with Braedon.

As we made our way to the restaurant, Braedon spotted a roaming photographer. "Come on. Let's get our picture taken."

I stood with him to be photographed. Like a couple.

The Armstrongs were waiting for us when we finished, and the four of us continued to the restaurant.

We were seated at a table across the room from where Elle and the others sat. She smiled, her expression full of encouragement. Jori leaned back in his chair to get a good look at me and mouthed, 'Wow.'

I couldn't help but smile and settled down to what ended up being a pleasant dinner. Braedon and the Armstrongs always set me at ease with their comfortable camaraderie. The dinner discussion flowed easily from the restaurant to the Explorer's Lounge where the chamber group played.

As we listened, Braedon's arm rested lightly on the couch behind my shoulders. I had no idea what music the chamber group played because 1 couldn't think of anything but the proximity of his arm, worrying that he might bring it around my shoulders. Or that he might not. My obsession with it made me feel like I was in high school.

I couldn't lie to myself anymore. For the first time in a year, a part of me wanted a man's attention—*this* man's attention—but acknowledging it didn't stop the fear that I wasn't ready, that I couldn't trust my feelings in this temporary world. My head pounded.

The four of us found seats on the Lounge's balcony for the floorshow. Instead of resting his arm on the back of my chair, Braedon slid his fingers between mine, his thumb brushing the top of my hand. It sent a little jolt of electricity up my arm and gave me goose bumps. My palm was wet against his soft, dry skin. He had to be sensing my agitation.

After the floorshow, Braedon and I followed Aislinn and D'Arcy, ending up on the sky deck rather than the Crow's Nest where we usually went.

D'Arcy surveyed the area. "We should play a game of miniature golf."

I stared at him. "In this?" I gestured at our formal clothing.

"Sure." Braedon removed his jacket. "It'll give me an excuse for playing terribly."

D'Arcy took off his coat, and Aislinn went to select a club, so I followed her. The game would be a good distraction. No more nerve-wracking arms close to my shoulders or handholding that sucked my wits from me.

I gave all my attention to the game—not that it improved my playing. Both Braedon and I scored badly, which gave us something to commiserate about.

Aislinn stepped into place to take her last shot of the game. It went in, and she squealed, "I win!" D'Arcy hugged her, and they kissed. Aislinn sighed before turning to me. "We need to get Kate."

D'Arcy put his arm around Aislinn's shoulders. "Good night, you two."

Braedon stepped beside me, and we stood in silence as they disappeared down the stairs.

The music from one of the ship's bands drifted to us on the soft breeze, the moonlight and gentle rocking of the ship enchanting.

The last of the paralytic numbness that had fallen upon me a year ago in the hospital room melted away, leaving me alive again. Exhilaration washed over me, and I thought for a moment I might float away, free from the chains that had bound me. I wanted to throw my arms up in the air and let loose a cry of joy.

I even raised my hands from my side, but I caught Braedon watching me with the hint of a smile. Braedon. A little chain reached up and gripped me, pulling me back to reality. I dropped my hands. I couldn't forget where I was.

Braedon, his expression now unsure, held up his club. "Should we play another game?"

"Okay." I stepped toward the first hole and tripped on my skirt. "Oh no!" I bent down to examine the fabric. "It tore."

Braedon bent to look at the hem. "Then we should postpone our game to another day."

He smelled so good. I clenched my suddenly shaking hand to stop it from reaching over and brushing aside a strand of hair that had fallen over his eye.

While he returned the clubs and balls, I debated if I should make a move toward the stairs, to get us around other people. The ambiance was dangerous to my resolve. Elle's earlier comments came to mind. Maybe I should just see what happened. I might be making more of this than was really there.

I stepped to the rail overlooking the ocean. Braedon came to stand beside me, and we faced the water in silence. The soft wind blew a strand of my hair in front of him, and he caught it in his hand and began rolling it between his fingers.

My already pounding heart sped up.

Braedon released the strand and laid his hand softly on my shoulder.

My breath caught. I stepped out from under his hand as I turned toward him and asked in a rush, "So where did you go to medical school?"

Braedon dropped his hand and watched me, a slight crease between his brows. "Harvard."

I clutched my fists at my sides, forcing them to stay there. "Where did you go for your thoracic training?"

"The Mayo Clinic." He moved closer.

Blood pounded in my ears. I wanted to run away. I wanted to step closer. "Where do you work?"

"Cornell University Medical Center." He lifted his hand toward my face. "What's wrong, Lyn?"

I could hardly breathe. Never in my life—not even with Jace—had I been such a ditz over a man. I met Braedon's dark eyes. He lowered them to my mouth.

Memory rushed back of the first time Jace had kissed me. My newly alive but raw emotions pulled back. As much as I wanted to be, I wasn't ready. "I can't." I opened my mouth to say more, to explain, but those words wouldn't come. "I have to go." Like Cinderella faced with reality, I fled.

CHAPTER 8

*M*Y NIGHT was full of both pleasant dreams and dreadful nightmares. I knew leaving Braedon alone on the sky deck had been the smart choice, even though I had left him with no explanation. Regardless, I hadn't wanted to hurt his feelings by leaving so abruptly.

I woke bleary-eyed and sat by Elle, talking about the sights while we rode the tour bus to the Maui Ocean Center. Walking around the aquarium, I occupied myself with taking notes for the next school year. I knew I wasn't acting quite right, and I didn't fool Elle. The collection of gardens around the Iao Needle, the mountain overlooking the site where the Maui king had stood in his final battle against King Kamehameha, didn't have me gushing as they should have.

When we returned to the ship, Elle got dressed for the sailing party. I sat in the chair with my feet curled under me and stared at the balcony. This was all my fault, and I needed to explain to Braedon, but I didn't want to do it with a crowd.

"You're not going to wear that, are you?" Elle fastened her necklace.

I laid my head on the arm of the chair. "I'm going to eat in tonight, but I may come up for the sailing party later."

Elle raised an eyebrow. "Did you and Braedon have a fight?"

"No," I answered a little too sharply.

She scrutinized me for a moment, doubtful. "Well, get some rest. We've got lots to see tomorrow."

I ordered a light supper and watched from the window as the ship left the dock. I wanted to kick myself for not sticking to my plans. After I had discovered the truth about Jace, I had forced myself to get up every day and move on. I had refused to let his betrayal destroy me or waste my time grieving a lie. Anger had gotten me through the last year.

I went up to the party on the lido. The place was so crowded it was hard to locate the group off in a corner. Everyone was laughing and eating. Except Braedon. He sat with a drink that he played with, smiling every once in a while at a comment.

How could I get his attention without alerting the others? He glanced my way and straightened in his chair when our eyes met, sending a thrill through me. I took a step toward him but stopped. Last night had shown me I was healing, but fresh scar tissue must be treated with great care. I couldn't do it yet. Turning, I went back to my cabin.

The weather on Kauai the next day was clear and warm, and Elle and I spent most of the day riding in a sightseeing bus. The long ride to Waimea—the Grand Canyon of the Pacific—gave me something else to ponder, and I jotted down more notes.

No insight on how to broach the topic with Braedon had come to me by the time we returned to the ship. Perhaps it was shame that I had treated Braedon so horribly. What had he done, anyway? He must hate me, thinking I had led him on. That thought alone tied my stomach in knots.

Elle didn't question me again, but I could tell she wasn't happy when I came up with more excuses for not going with her to dinner. With two-thirds of the cruise left, I knew I would have to face him. Whoever thought being locked up with the same people for four weeks was a good idea, anyway? I didn't care how good the food was.

The milder weather made for a comfortable trip to Pearl Harbor. By the time we finished a tour of the Arizona Memorial and the *Battleship Missouri*, it had begun to sprinkle. I was glad to get back to the ship, curl up in bed, and fall asleep.

I woke to find Elle gone and the hour late. Her note stuck on the television said I could join her in the Crow's Nest. Bless her. She knew me well enough to give me space to work things out myself. I couldn't stand being stuck in the cabin another night, though. To ensure I wouldn't see anyone from the group, I slipped into the ship's movie theater. The film had already started, and I let the mindless action play in the background of my mind.

The last island stop before we headed for American Samoa was Kona. The day had seemed promising when we had signed up to go on a catamaran snorkeling excursion. A powerful squall that lasted perhaps an hour made a mess of everything. The only excursion I had been able to muster up any real enthusiasm for and they canceled it.

The storm fit my mood as Elle and I ate breakfast in our soggy clothing at an open-air restaurant near the beach. From our vantage point, we could see that even the ship's tenders were stuck until the ocean calmed. We spent the rest of the morning at a local flea market.

On that last Hawaii night, I went to the movies again. Jori surprised me by slipping into the seat beside me just as the lights dimmed. Neither of us spoke. When the room brightened at the end, we sat mutely in our seats until the room emptied of passengers and the crewmembers came in to clean up.

Jori stood. "Take a walk with me. Please."

"I …."

He put his hand on my shoulder. "I'll keep an eye out for him and make sure you don't have to see him. Okay?"

My eyes misted at his kindness. I nodded, and Jori led the way. The wind whipped my hair, a sign of another storm kicking up. He found us a sheltered niche, and we sat down on a bench, side by side.

He twisted to face me. "Elle told me you had a bad experience last year. I'm sorry about teasing you."

I gritted my teeth. I hated people talking about me behind my back.

"You know," Jori continued when I didn't respond, "in spite of my reputation, I do believe that love—a lifelong love—is possible."

I stared at him in disbelief. I had overheard several conversations and, if they were true, he had rarely slept alone since the cruise had begun—and always with a different girl. When I couldn't think of anything polite to say, I faced forward and stared at the clouds.

"I've seen it. My grandparents had it." He straightened, resting his head against the bulkhead behind us. "You know, you light up whenever you see him."

I tilted my head toward him. "What are you talking about?"

He watched me from the corner of his eye. "Braedon. You practically glow when you're around him."

No way was I going to talk about Braedon. I stood, but Jori pulled me back down beside him.

"I would love to have a woman look at me like that." He stared at his hands, clasped loosely before him.

"Oh, please. I've seen how women look at you."

He shook his head. "It's not the same thing." He glanced at me before returning his gaze to his hands. "It's shallow. They only care about the attractive package and have no interest in the man inside."

I stared at him. "And you care so much about them? I got the impression you liked the emotional distance."

He winced. "Ouch. The hypocrite gets it right in the heart." He mimed being stabbed in the chest and then looked at me, his face serious. "I liked the attention when I was younger. It fed my ego, and I thought it validated me."

"What happened to you, Jori?' I asked.

He leaned his head back against the wall and exhaled a deep breath. "Your first time ought to be with someone you love."

"How old were you?"

"Fifteen." His voice was soft, his eyes closed. "And she was my brother's wife. She liked to be a boy's first experience. When I confessed, it tore the family apart."

My heart tightened for him, and I squeezed his hand. "You were a kid, and she was a sick woman. You can't let that experience define you."

He looked at me. "You must see the irony of two emotional cripples giving each other advice on romance." Jori poked my arm. "But this isn't about me. It's about you running away from someone you should be running to."

I straightened. "Jori, I don't—"

"Listen to me." He grabbed my hand. "I wasn't kidding

about you and Braedon. Something good is happening to you. Don't throw it away. It's special, and it's rare. I've taken the time to get to know Braedon. He won't disappoint you if you give him a chance."

Jori stood and offered me his hand. I took it, and he slid my fingers around his arm, silent as he walked me to my cabin door.

"Think about it," he said before he left.

Once in the empty cabin, I meditated on what Jori had said. Was I an emotional cripple? Would Jace win by making me forever afraid to trust anyone? But even if I could trust again, was this the place?

I hadn't seen Braedon for four days. I wanted to cry.

$\mathcal{I}$ WOKE EARLY on the eleventh day of the cruise, our first full day back at sea. The ocean was rough again, which seemed a fitting setting. It also meant the group wouldn't gather for our self-defense session. So much for pulling Braedon aside and talking to him there.

The light by Elle's bed flicked on. "No practice this morning?"

I shielded my eyes against the sudden glare. "It's too rough."

She sat up in bed, rubbing her eyes. "Braedon's been as mopey as you. Are you going to tell me what's going on?"

"You were right. He wants more than friendship."

"What's wrong with that? What scares you about dating on a ship?"

I heaved a sigh and waved my hands. "All of this."

"I don't understand."

"It's all a fairy tale." I sat up, throwing my blanket from me. My eyes burned. "We live in this luxury, spoiled by fine food and pampering servants. All around us are fun activities and attractive people while we visit exotic places."

Elle shook her head. "You're not making any sense, Lyn. If you're so afraid of connecting with people here, why do you go out of your way to make them feel comfortable and confide in you?"

"I don't."

She crossed her arms. "Oh, please. All you have to do is talk with people and they're spilling their innermost secrets to you. You've always been able to do that." She sighed. "Until a year ago. I think it's healthy that it's coming back."

Standing, I rubbed my pounding temples, remembering how I had felt in the hospital room. "Not in this environment. I trusted a fairy tale once. I won't do it again."

I retreated to the bathroom, undressed, and cried in the shower. So much for the diminishing of my emotions.

CHAPTER 9

$\mathcal{E}$LLE REMAINED quiet when I came out, slipping into the bathroom for her own shower. I dressed and tried to put on some makeup. It seemed pointless to work on my red nose and puffy eyes, so I blew my hair dry first.

I didn't say anything when Elle came back into the room. I didn't want to talk about it. I felt exposed and tender. She put on her clothes, and I stepped beside her at the mirror to finish applying my makeup.

"I'm sorry," she said softly. "I didn't mean to push you."

Elle had been such a stalwart friend and supporter. She must be tired of me. "I didn't know my feelings were still so raw."

She paused and raised her eyebrows. "I'm not sure it's—" she stopped herself before saying Jace's name aloud, "um, your past that's the problem. I think you're afraid because you care a lot for Braedon."

My chest ached. She was right about him, but it didn't change anything. It's not like we would see each other after the cruise. I had been right not to let things go any further. It was pointless to take a chance on something that couldn't go anywhere anyway.

We finished in silence, and Elle faced me. "We have a social problem we need to decide how to handle."

I knew what she meant. The only way for me to ignore Braedon completely was to keep to myself. Elle would never stand for that. Yet I couldn't subject everyone in the group to the awkwardness between Braedon and me. I sighed.

"Lyn, you need to tell him."

"What, you didn't tell him like you told Jori?"

Elle averted her eyes. "Braedon needs to hear this from you. Don't you think he has the right to know why you've been avoiding him? Everyone's been asking him if you guys had a fight."

My stomach churned. I should have done this days ago, forged my way through the embarrassment. Only Elle understood the hell I had been through the last year. And Braedon, he didn't deserve any of it.

A year ago, I had refused to admit I was wounded, not saying Jace's name or allowing anyone else to do so in my presence. Yeah, that had gone well.

I dropped into the chair. "I'll talk to him. I would have done it this morning if I could have been sure of a little more privacy."

Her expression lightened. "You will?" Elle, the eternal romantic.

I scowled, my stomach tightening again. "What did you think was going to happen, anyway? That the nice doctor would sweep me off my feet, and we would ride off into the sunset and live happily ever after? This isn't *The Love Boat*."

"It sounds stupid when you put it like *that*. But I don't think I deserve your sarcasm."

I stared at her, remembering all she had done for me. "You're right. I'm sorry. But admit it. You thought that could happen, didn't you?"

"It still could." Her eyes pleaded with me to make it so.

"As if he'd even talk to me after …." I squeezed my lips shut. She was sucking me into it. "Stop it, Elle. Please."

She studied me before nodding. "We're late for breakfast."

By the time we got there, only two empty chairs remained at the large table where the group sat. One by Jori and one by Braedon. I lengthened my stride and passed Elle to take the seat by Jori, across the table from Braedon.

"Good morning, everyone." With hands like ice, I placed a napkin in my lap.

Maria picked up her juice glass. "Nice to see you're feeling better. That must have been quite the bug you caught. I'm glad no one else got it."

"Me too," I mumbled, sneaking a quick look at Braedon before lifting my menu. He watched me, his expression dark, his brows knit. I felt an almost overwhelming urge to reach across the table and wipe the frown from his face. Instead, I asked Jori. "What are you having?"

He leaned inside my menu and whispered, "Have you talked to him?"

"Stay out of it," I hissed.

"You're an idiot." Jori sat up, his mouth tight. His volume increased. "You should eat something easy on your stomach. You wouldn't want to get any *heart*burn—ow!" He leaned down to rub his shin and glared at Elle.

Jimmy nudged my arm. "Hey, I don't know if Elle

mentioned it, but the cruise director's letting us have the talent show, and our first rehearsal is this afternoon. I really need you to play the keyboard with Braedon."

My heart sank. Why did this need to be any harder? "I'm not interested in performing."

"But Braedon wrote you a special part."

Curious, I looked at Braedon.

He shrugged. "You volunteered me to play the piano for him, remember?" He glanced at Jimmy, who stared at me, his hands together as if in prayer, his eyes beseeching.

I asked Braedon, "When did you write music for me?"

He didn't even blink. "I've had a lot of free evenings lately."

My face burned. I had hurt him ... or embarrassed him. Yet he had composed music for me? I took a deep breath and turned to Elle. "What are you doing to help Jimmy?"

"Costumes, of course." She gave me a 'you can't be that selfish' look.

"You'll help Jimmy, won't you?" Maria asked.

All eyes rested on me.

"Please," Jimmy begged.

He had told me this trip was to be his last hurrah before he bowed to his parents' plans. The talent show was his one chance to perform power metal before an audience. I considered first Jimmy and then Elle, who watched me expectantly. I owed Elle for worrying her during the Hawaii days.

Sighing, I rubbed my temple. I was an adult. I knew how to be pleasant to people I didn't like. Or liked too much. "I'll take a look at the music."

Jimmy whooped and jumped from his seat to hug me, and Elle beamed. I didn't look at Braedon, who left to get the sheets from his cabin.

When he came back, he slid some handwritten music across the table. I picked it up and read through the piece, surprised at what he had written. It was perfect for me. The music was a descant to one of Jimmy's favorite songs, "Shining Star" by Kinslayer. As I played the notes in my mind, I felt a chill at its beauty. My hands itched to play it on the keyboard.

At the end of the meal, I held back while the others rose. Braedon also remained in his chair.

I clutched my cold hands on the table before me, my heart pounding as I waited for us to be alone. "I ... I'm sorry."

Braedon leaned forward, stretching his hands across the table toward me. I pulled mine into my lap and sat back. He stopped but left his hands there, his eyes concerned. "Did I do something wrong?"

"No. I just—" I still couldn't say Jace's name. "I got burned really bad last year."

His expression softened, compassion in his eyes.

I didn't want his pity. "I'll help play the keyboard, but ...." My face grew warm. "I'm not interested in a shipboard romance."

He met my eyes. "Neither am I."

My heart fluttered, and I swallowed, unsure how to respond. That so didn't clear anything up, but it didn't matter. I clenched my hands so tight they went numb. "I just want to be acquaintances."

"Acquaintances." Braedon pulled his hands to his lap and leaned back in his chair, mirroring my posture. "Not even friends?"

Jace's charming face flashed through my mind, followed by a memory of the hospital room. "I'm just not ready." I stood and hurried from the restaurant, leaving him alone. Again.

I passed Jori where he stood watching us by the entrance. I pushed the elevator button and glanced back to where Braedon sat. He hadn't moved.

Jori stared at Braedon and shrugged, waiting until the last minute before sliding into the elevator beside me. As the doors closed, he put his arm around me. "It'll be okay," he said.

Just like my brother had done a year ago.

*J*ORI BECAME my shadow. He was always nearby to help if things became awkward. When I went to the library, he came along to sketch, never bothering me, but always there in the background. In the morning self-defense sessions, Jori served as my new partner.

Braedon maintained a pleasant manner and continued to come to all the group activities. He only spoke to me if the situation required it, though I caught him watching me several times. His expression reminded me of someone trying to solve a puzzle without all the pieces.

Rehearsals were the most awkward. Braedon and I had to stand side by side at the electronic keyboard, playing the notes he had written for me. I couldn't get the lovely music out of my mind. I caught myself humming it several times, the lingering descant haunting my dreams.

*T*HE DAY before we reached American Samoa, everyone gathered backstage after lunch for the performance. Elle gave us our costumes, comprised of an eclectic assortment of black formal attire and leather boots. All the costumes included decorative chains and spikey jewelry that looked suspiciously like they might have been purchased at a pet store. She had worked on them in the evenings while I had been so self-absorbed.

Jimmy had arranged to have us perform last, after a parade of passenger acts that included everything from a little girl singing "Over the Rainbow" to an old man whistling the *William Tell Overture* through his dentures while doing percussion on his chest and thighs.

When our turn came, we took our places on stage behind the closed curtain. Jimmy got himself set up and glanced back at us to make sure we were ready.

With his right hand raised, he bowed his head for a few seconds before dropping his arm. As it fell, the curtain opened, and he lifted his head while shifting into the perfect metal rock star pose.

Springing forward, Jimmy cried, "Are. You. Ready?"

The crowd screamed their agreement. Drawn by the audience's enthusiasm, more people came into the lounge.

Jimmy paced the stage like a caged animal before throwing his arms above his head, clapping his hands, and yelling, "What will you do?"

The lead guitarist began a complicated riff, and the audience got up and clapped with the beat.

At a signal from Jimmy, the drummer and the bass followed the guitarist. After a few measures, Braedon and I joined the song on the keyboard, and Jimmy began to sing. He dazzled them. It was like someone else inhabited his body, energy emanating from him.

Jimmy connected with the audience, and they loved him. He could feel it, and he seemed to draw even more energy from it. He hadn't been quite like this in the practices. I understood it to a degree. Performing with an audience always made me feel like I had become part of something bigger than myself. I forgot to be self-conscious.

By the end of the song, everyone in the audience who could stand was on their feet, cheering and screaming for an encore. Savvy Jimmy had prepared us for this possibility, and we had a second song ready.

At the end, I stared at my shaking hands. "Wow."

Braedon watched as Jimmy bent down to talk with audience members who had rushed to the stage to meet him. "I think he'll be famous someday."

"I think you may be right."

After congratulating Jimmy, Jori jumped up the stairs, hugged me, and then clapped Braedon on the back. "None of the practices prepared me for that. It was nothing short of amazing." Jori eyed Jimmy. "I've got a friend who's a promoter. I'm going to do everything I can to get Jimmy in to meet him."

Applause greeted us as we entered the restaurant for our celebratory dinner. Jimmy accepted their acknowledgement with Maria on his arm, waving to the crowd.

The party continued on the sky deck where we finalized plans for our Pago Pago snorkeling trip the next morning. The entire group had signed up for it.

CHAPTER 10

*J*ORI STRAIGHTENED my face mask as he treaded water beside me. "You good?"

We played around in the water for a while before I felt ready to try snorkeling. "Yeah, I think so." I pointed to one of the girls waving her arms at him. "You'd better hurry. I think she needs your help more than I do."

After he left, I floated, swirling my hands and flippered feet in the water. I wanted to remember all the details: the comforting warmth of the crystalline water on my skin and the soft caress of the breeze as it ruffled a few strands of my hair. The small island with its pristine beach lay a short distance to one side, and the catamaran floated in the little bay on my other side.

The catamaran was a sweet little vessel, much smaller than the ones I had seen around Hawaii. It sat low on the water with two sections of trampoline made from white rope in the front. Unlike larger vessels, this one had only a simple canopy with no walls.

After a review of Jori's instructions, I closed my lips over the snorkeling mouthpiece. When I slipped my face into the water, I almost gasped. The view under the surface made it seem as though I had put on magical glasses that revealed a secret, chaotic world of multicolored fish glowing in the reflected light of the sun. As I kicked my fins, the fish flitted around but didn't move too far away, a few tickling my legs when they came too close.

My right eye burned, and I lifted my head from the water and removed the mask. A small amount of seawater dripped from the interior, and I shook it out before putting the mask on again, adjusting it. As soon as I put my face back in the water, my right eye burned again. Groaning, I lifted my head and tried tightening the straps.

"Something wrong?" Braedon appeared at my side and took the mask from me.

It took all my control to maintain a level voice. "I keep getting water in my right eye. I can't tell where it's leaking."

Braedon put the mask back on me and adjusted the straps, taking my jaw in his hand and gently twisting my chin back and forth, scrutinizing the fit.

At his touch, my cheeks flamed. I tried to keep my expression neutral as he examined my face. "Ah, I see the problem." He tugged a small strand of hair from under the mask on the right side. "Your hair was letting the water get through. Give it a try now."

I slid my face under the water again, kicking my feet to propel me forward. No stinging right eye. I looked up, treading water, and faced him. "That fixed it."

"Did you see the shark?"

I jerked at the word, drawing my feet up and whipping my head from side to side.

Braedon chuckled. "It's just a whitetip reef shark. They're not dangerous and leave people alone. I'll get a picture of it for you." With a twist, he dove under the surface.

"Wait!" I tried to grab his arm to stop him, but he was already out of reach. With shaking hands, I slipped the mouthpiece in place. Through the mask, I could make out his form sliding through a kaleidoscope of fish that darted away from him, opening my field of vision to large rocks at the bottom. I blinked back dizziness at the sight of the fin that identified the small shark.

My mind envisioned the monster turning on him, and I went deeper. Too deep. Ocean water poured through the snorkel tube, and I inhaled the salty liquid. I launched back to the surface and ripped off the gear, choking and gasping for air.

Jori was beside me in a few strokes and helped keep me afloat while I hacked. By the time Braedon resurfaced, my coughing had lessened, but my throat was raw.

He tore off his headpiece and hurried over. "What happened?"

Chuckling, Jori shook his head. "She tried to go after you and nearly drowned herself."

I tried to argue, but all I did was trigger a fit of coughing.

Jori patted me on the back like he would a baby. I elbowed him and wheezed, "You should have more ... respect ... for poor drowning women."

Rubbing his ribs, he snickered. "Well, you're back to normal."

I gave him a crusty look, which only made him laugh harder. I was about to elbow him again when the catamaran crew called us back to the boat.

Jori rolled on his back, acting all dramatic with his hand

on his rib. "I owe you." He twisted to his stomach and swam toward the catamaran.

Braedon scowled as I coughed again. "You're okay to go back?"

Nodding, I stretched my hands toward the catamaran, still holding the face mask, and kicked my flippers. By the time I pulled myself up on the ladder, Jori had already turned in his equipment and stood next to Elle.

"What do you mean you owe me?" I tossed my gear in the box. "What did I do?"

Jori touched his rib, faking a grimace. "I owe you some payback." He grinned and followed Elle to the main group under the canopy. She looked back at me with a quizzical face.

I sighed.

Braedon came up beside me. "You two act like siblings sometimes."

"Yeah, well, sometimes he does remind me of my younger brother."

As the captain started the engine, I moved toward the trampoline, sorry to see the crew had lashed the sail. No more wind sailing. I joined Jimmy and Maria—on the opposite end of the boat from Jori.

Braedon followed. "I got a decent picture of the shark."

"We heard about that thing. Can we see?" Jimmy asked. He and Maria made room on the trampoline.

Braedon sat next to them, pulled his camera from its underwater case, and turned it on for the others to see.

After drying off, I slipped a cover-up over my tankini before lying on the netting. It had been a long morning, and my eyelids were heavy. We had one more island to visit, where we would have lunch and then head back to Pago Pago.

I barely noticed when Braedon reclined a couple of feet from me. I opened my eyes at the movement, catching him watching me. It must have been his peaceful gaze combined with my fatigue that kept me from searching for an excuse to move.

"Would you like to see the picture?"

I shivered and closed my eyes again. "I hate sharks."

Jimmy exhaled. "I wish every day was like this."

I peeked over where he and Maria lay cuddled on Braedon's other side. "We might get tired of it if we did this every day." I yawned.

"Nah. I wouldn't." His eyes closed, a contented grin growing up his cheeks.

I had just drifted to sleep when a loud crack jerked me awake. Braedon jumped up, lunging forward. Someone screamed.

CHAPTER 11

*I*STRUGGLED ACROSS the netting to the main deck, trying to make sense of the screaming and shouting around me. I jolted at another sharp crack—gunfire—and then there was only sobbing.

Jimmy and Braedon were the first off the trampoline, but they stopped, both raising their hands. Like in a movie. What was going on? I tried to look around Braedon. He threw out one of his hands, keeping me behind him.

A voice shouted for him to stop. Braedon's hand froze. The voice barked for him to move. His shoulders rigid, Braedon hesitated before stepping aside. One of the crewmen stood before us with an AK-47 pointed at Braedon, his eyes on me. My stomach lurched, and the scene before me took on a surreal, nightmarish quality.

The Asian crewman glared at us, but his hands shook as they gripped the rifle. What if he squeezed the trigger by mistake? Fear tightened my chest, making it hard to breathe.

"Move down," the other crewman bellowed, his rifle indicating the settee where everyone else huddled.

Maria gasped. The captain lay on the deck, dark blood pooling around his sprawled body. My stomach twisted with a wave of nausea, and I looked away, my hands shaking. This couldn't be happening.

As we moved closer to the others, I caught Jori's gaze across the settee. His eyes blazed. Elle cried into his chest while the others huddled away from the body. I shuddered.

"I'm a doctor." Braedon pointed to the body. "May I examine him?"

The crewman-turned-pirate nearest us sneered, "You can toss him in the water."

Braedon's jaw muscles tensed, his eyes narrowing. "I'll need help."

"I'll do it," Jimmy offered, his fists clenched at his sides.

The gunman grunted his approval. Jimmy followed Braedon over to the body, his Adam's apple convulsing. I took Maria's cold hand. She clutched mine, moaning as she watched.

Braedon checked for a pulse first and shook his head. They carried the body to the back of the boat, where they dropped the captain into the water. A bloodstain ran the full length of the white netting.

When they returned, Braedon's tight expression and Jimmy's pale face did nothing to calm my stomach. I released Maria's hand, and Jimmy put his arm around her. I huddled close to Braedon as I stared at the pool of blood on the deck. It had been inside a living, breathing man just a few minutes ago. I shivered, wanting to be gone, be home.

I jumped when one pirate started the boat's engine. In the chaos, I hadn't noticed anyone shut it off. A girl by Elle let out a sob. The Asian pointed the rifle at her, his hands twitching. "Quiet!" Everyone became still, but not for long.

"Where are you taking us?" Wes called.

The man at the wheel looked like a different person than the one who had passed out drinks to everyone a few hours ago. "You'll find out soon enough."

Wes swore, leaping at the pirate nearest him. The man swung the rifle, striking Wes in the face and dropping him to the deck. The pirate at the wheel trained his gun on us. His companion kicked Wes in the stomach before backing up with a sneer.

Braedon made a move toward Wes, but the pirate at the wheel growled and Braedon froze. Ryan and Jori helped Wes back on his seat and pressed someone's shirt against the cut on his jaw.

My mind was awhirl. For years, I had trained in the martial arts and self-defense. None of it did me any good against semiautomatic weapons.

The pirate near us leered at me in a way that sent a chill up my spine. What were they planning? I scanned the row of passengers, half of them young women.

The man at the wheel had been watching me. He must have liked the look on my face. He smirked, steering the pirated catamaran away from American Samoa.

$\mathcal{T}$HE FEAR was palpable as we sat crammed in two rows along the edge of the settee area during the long journey. The catamaran's engine sped us toward the increasingly ugly clouds.

I couldn't get that look the pirate had given me out of my mind. It made me feel dirty. We might not know what they meant to do with us as a group, but I had no doubt what this guy had in mind for me. I felt queasy.

When I looked at Elle, she stared at me glumly, but Jori's face beside her reflected the darkness of the gathering storm in the distance. Small waves from the churning water splattered my back, making me shiver.

Jimmy, who had been fidgeting beside me for a while, muttered, "We have to do something."

"Against guns?" I breathed.

The pirate on guard gave us a withering look. We went silent, but Jimmy kept exchanging glances with Wes between glares at our captors. A sudden slow-motion scene played in my mind of Jimmy and Wes making mad rushes at the pirates, who simply squeezed their triggers and sprayed the group.

I clutched my stomach, the muscles knotting at the thought of either of them trying to do something by themselves, of their bodies lying on the deck, *their* blood spilling onto the wood. The pirates had already shown what they were capable of with the captain. I doubted they would limit themselves to simply hurting the guys next time.

What did they want with us, anyway? I tried not to think about the leer. Surely, they couldn't want us just for that. Please let it be for ransom, though my family didn't have money and neither did Elle's. Were they hoping to get money from the cruise line?

I couldn't imagine them getting anything from the US government, which I didn't think would bargain. But our government might send in people to negotiate our release. And America had snipers. If we were patient and did what they said, there might be a chance for rescue.

But could we take the chance that help would be coming? If we did fight, it would have to be a coordinated effort. But how could we do that with everyone lined up? My head hurt, and I rubbed my temple as a strand of my hair whipped across my face. The wind had picked up.

Jimmy pointed to the horizon. "Look."

Against a backdrop of black clouds, trimmed with a fading reddish-orange glow from the setting sun, I saw what looked like the shadow of another boat. Adrenaline shot through me; it might be an American military vessel.

But the pirates jabbered to each other, excited. If they were happy, it couldn't be good news for us.

"We should have tried to jump them earlier," Jimmy grumbled, his eyes tight. He looked from Maria to the pirates on the catamaran to those on the new ship and back to Maria.

I stretched forward, peering across the settee, my mind racing. Did we have the right to decide for everyone if the risk was worth it to try to take the boat back ourselves?

The pirate nearest us gave Maria another one of those looks, turning back with the hint of a smile. Jimmy tensed beside me. We had to have a plan, in case we had an opportunity to do something. I straightened.

Braedon put his arm around my shoulders and turned his face into my hair near my ear. "What are you thinking?"

"Jimmy's going to do something," I whispered into Braedon's neck. "Right now we're twenty against two. That boat is sure to have more men—and more weapons."

He pretended to nuzzle my hair. "We won't have a lot of fuel left after the distance we've traveled. We won't get very far."

The lead pirate noticed us and growled at Braedon, who sat up and tightened his arm around me. Jimmy fidgeted, and I reached over and squeezed his hand. His eyes met mine. 'We'll figure something out,' I mouthed.

The roughness of the waves and wind continued to increase. I had to splay my legs to stay on the bench. Braedon's arm around me helped me stay put, but it was the warmth of his body next to mine that strengthened me the most.

As the larger boat pulled beside the catamaran, possibilities flooded my mind. The lead pirate caught a rope thrown from the ship while the nervous one commanded a couple of our men to tie the rope to the catamaran.

I groaned inwardly. At least three more pirates were visible on the new boat, and they all had weapons. My heart sank. If we tried anything now the men on the boat could just shoot us from above ... but ....

My pulse raced. Wes and Ryan sat near Jori and Elle. Based on how close they were to the rope ladder being lowered from the craft, there should be a point when there would be three people with at least some martial arts training on the larger vessel and three of us on the catamaran.

I nudged Jimmy, his skin hot on my arm. When I indicated our friends up front, he surveyed them for a moment. He nodded and tapped Maria, who in turn touched the person next to her and so on down the line. I think the only reason we got away with it was because the pirates were distracted by the increasingly rough seas, struggling to take the rope ladder.

The guys looked at Jimmy, who mouthed our intent to fight once they were above. They glanced at me, and I nodded. Their eyes got the same shrewd look as Jimmy's. I could only hope we were all thinking the same thing.

One of the young women stood first in line to board the larger vessel. She glanced back at the group, her eyes glassy, breathing ragged.

When she reached for the rope ladder, the pirate pointed his rifle at her. "Wait."

The pirate checked her out like a stockman examining a cow for sale. He picked up a strand of her long brown hair. She twisted away from him. Dropping her hair, he pulled the tie string of her bikini. I had never thought you could smell fear, but I could have sworn that's what came off her.

Shrieking, she grabbed the front of the swimsuit to keep her chest covered. We all surged forward, but suddenly all the rifles from both boats were trained on us. A single round fired into the catamaran's deck, inches from the girl's foot, silenced everyone.

I clutched Braedon's arm. No way was I getting on that boat. He pressed his mouth against my ear and whispered, "Be patient. We can't help anyone if we're dead."

Yeah. That made me feel better.

Once we were back in line, the lead pirate turned back to the girl. He tugged at her top, still held in place by her shaking hands. When she resisted, he put his face to hers, growled something, and placed the barrel of the rifle against her bare abdomen. She closed her eyes and dropped her hands.

With his legs spaced wide to keep his balance in the pitching catamaran, the pirate turned the girl so the men on the boat could see her. He spoke in an Asian sounding language. Two men on the larger vessel laughed and nodded, while the third regarded the rest of us with concern, keeping his rifle pointed at us. The lead pirate on the catamaran told the girl to climb the ladder. He did not give her back her top.

The occasional flash of lightning in the now almost black sky flickered across the fearful and angry faces of the passengers. As another girl approached the ladder and had to remove her top, the tension in the group intensified. The energy coming from Jimmy reminded me of a boiler about to blow.

"Wait for my move," I breathed.

Then it was Elle's turn.

When the pirate commanded her to step forward, all my ideas of a coordinated effort flew from my mind. Before I could move, though, Braedon tightened his grip on my shoulder, and Jimmy stepped back, grabbing my other shoulder. Even though I knew they were right, I moaned in frustration.

Elle marched forward, her back stiff with pride, untied her bikini top, and handed it over as if she was handing her jacket to a coat-check. I could tell by her red face how much it cost her, but I had never been prouder of her.

After she climbed onto the large boat, Jori sped up the swaying ladder behind her. He ripped off his T-shirt for her as soon as his feet hit the deck. A shouting match ensued with two of the pirates up there. Jimmy caught the attention of Wes and Ryan where they stood by the rail. Ryan looked at me. I nodded. With a grim smile, he dipped his head in return.

Braedon and I now stood almost abreast of the pirates on the catamaran. While the shouting match continued above us, I began to make loud sobbing noises. The lead pirate growled at Maria to step forward. Bending, I turned away from the other pirate, who stood to my left. I cocked my arm into my side.

The wind whipping my hair into my body, I fake-sobbed louder, pulling the energy of my wrath inside. My knees bent to accommodate the heaving deck. Sucking in my breath for a loud kiai, I spun around, fast and hard. I didn't feel the pain as the heel of my palm connected with the pirate's chin, and he flew up in the air.

I hoped he bit his tongue off.

Braedon lunged forward in sync with me, jerking the rifle from the flying pirate and twisting to aim at the loathsome beast by the rope ladder. Jimmy, however, had already jumped him and struggled to take his rifle.

A series of lightning flashes across the black clouds turned the fight above into a macabre dance under a strobe light. The sharp cracks of thunder almost covered the sounds of shouts and screams.

I wanted to cheer. Our people were fighting back. Jimmy ripped the rifle from the pirate's hands, spinning in a deft move and taking aim. Both pirates leapt from the catamaran into the churning water.

A spray of gunfire ripped into the exposed deck of the catamaran, and we jumped for cover under the canopy.

"We're free!" Maria screamed, hurling aside the rope that had tied us to the other boat.

Braedon tossed me his rifle and started the engine. "We've got to get out of their range of fire!" He gunned it and, with a sharp turn, sped us away from the boat.

Ping. Ping ... ping. The sound of bullets striking the catamaran decreased the farther we got. I fervently prayed no one had been hurt. And that the catamaran hadn't taken too much damage.

Then the full force of the storm hit us.

CHAPTER 12

*C*LINGING TO the settee rail, I tried to stay on my feet as a wave crested over the side. The pelting rain stung like little pebbles. I squinted against the burning salt water. Braedon clutched the wheel, fighting to maintain stability, his muscles taut with the strain. The catamaran was a fair-weather craft, never meant to be at sea in conditions like these.

And what about Elle and the others? If they weren't successful, how angry would those men be? I heaved myself next to Braedon. "Can you see the other boat?" I yelled. "We've got to go back!"

"Not—look out!" He jerked the wheel to meet the onslaught of water as a new wave crashed into us.

I slipped and lost my footing, sliding to the deck with the water. My shin bashed the corner of the seating. I cried out and grabbed a pole.

Braedon, his fists clenched on the wheel, called over his shoulder, "Are you all right?"

I got to my feet and tested my leg. It hurt but held my

weight. "Yes." Pulling myself again to Braedon, I picked up the radio mike. It came away in my hand.

"They shot it," Braedon said and then swore as he steered into another wave.

Once it passed, I located life vests in a seat box and helped Braedon put one on. Once I had mine fastened, I grabbed two more and staggered in search of Jimmy and Maria.

I found them on the other side of the settee. Jimmy lay on his back. Maria knelt beside him, pressing on his chest. Her shoulders shook with sobs. In the dim light, I didn't comprehend at first that his white T-shirt was pink and red.

"No, no," I cried, dropping beside her, heedless of my shin.

A swell peaked and crashed over us, and Maria bent to shield him. Jimmy, his face pale, coughed as he choked on the water.

"I called and you wouldn't come," she cried.

I pressed my hand against his forehead, my eyes burning. I swallowed the bile that rose to the back of my throat. Not Jimmy.

His lips moved, but I couldn't make out his words. I put my ear by his mouth.

"Sorry"—he coughed, his face contorting, body tensing—"I didn't move … fast enough."

"Oh, Jimmy." I touched his cheek, wishing I could tease him back, but his pale skin and shallow breathing filled me with dread. I had to get help. I jumped to my feet. "I'll get Braedon." Jimmy nodded weakly.

"Hurry!" Maria shrieked, almost baring her teeth. "Oh, God! Don't let him die."

I stared back at her. She shouldn't talk about dying when Jimmy could hear. I darted a glance at him, but his eyes were closed. I stumbled to Braedon and shouted, "Jimmy's been shot in the chest. He's bleeding a lot!"

His jaw tightened, and he took my hands, wrapping my fingers around the wheel. "Keep it turned into the waves." He ripped open a cupboard with a red cross on it. Snatching the kit inside, he clung to a main mast as another wave hit us before lurching to Jimmy.

I clenched the wheel, straining to keep it in place. Hands trembling, my mind filled with the memory of the captain's blood on the deck overlaid with the image of Jimmy.

Had it been less than twenty-four hours since he had been in his glory? As I spun the wheel to meet another wave, I screamed out my frustration, the sound lost in the gusting wind.

While I fought my personal battle with the sea, all my angst of the past week drained away, trivial and petty in the face of Jimmy's fight for life.

The need to fight the waves and the wind forced me to focus on the moment. I lost count of the time or how many waves battered us before Braedon was back, freeing my cramped fingers and taking the wheel from me. I rubbed my hands to get the circulation flowing again. "Is Jimmy …?"

Braedon, his face grim, shook his head and shouted, "He didn't make it. We're taking on too much water. You and Maria need to bail it out."

I stumbled to the side, only part of it from a swell. Choking back a lump in my throat, I turned. Maria sat, a dark shape huddled on the bench, shaking with sobs. Resisting a sudden sense of weakness that threatened to overwhelm me, I focused my thoughts on the moment. I located two buckets in a closed cupboard nearby and staggered to her. Still weeping, Maria came with me when I showed her the pail. We went to work, tossing out bucket loads of water.

For an eternity, we fought the ocean, bailing water that was replaced with another wave. Thoughts of Jimmy and Elle—and all the horrible things I kept imagining those men doing to her—continued to nag at me, but I forced the burning pain in my back and arms to be my only reality. I came to think each bucketful of water would be the last; I simply could not continue. But there was always more water at my feet. I kept telling myself I could do one more, just one more.

I was a robot, not noticing when the rain had slackened or that the amount of water coming over the side had diminished. When I sensed the cool water depth on my legs had dropped to my ankles, I came back to a physical presence and straightened to relieve my muscles, rubbing at the painful cramps. Maria did the same.

Braedon's hunched form at the wheel was a silhouette against the nearly full moon, the stars in the dark sky patchworked with drifting clouds. We had survived.

What was happening to Elle? I shook my head. I had to deal with what I could control. "Maria, I need to check on Braedon."

"Of course." Her tone had a sharp, accusatory edge to it.

Braedon sat with his fingers still clenched around the wheel, his forehead resting on his hands. When I touched his shoulder, he sat up. He looked beyond exhausted. I peeled his fingers free, massaging the cramps from them.

He stared at me as I worked on his fingers. I wanted to say something about Jimmy, but when I tried to speak, my throat closed up. I blinked burning eyes and finally squeaked, "Rest."

The engine sputtered and died. With a cry, I reached for the ignition key. Braedon put his shaking hand on mine. "It's out of gas. We're lucky the captain did so much sailing during the excursion, or we'd have run out during the storm."

I turned to find Maria behind us, her knees curled under her bedraggled form, her muscles tense. When I reached out to her, she pushed my hand away.

"Maria, you should lie down." Braedon staggered a little as he tried to take her hand.

She jerked it from him, her eyes blazing, and let loose a stream of words in Spanish. I couldn't make them out, but her rigid posture and the venom in her tone said plenty. When she was done, she returned to Jimmy's body.

I looked at Braedon. He shrugged and sat in the captain's seat, his eyes bloodshot and red-rimmed. He looked like I felt. I dropped to the bench and buried my face in my hands, rubbing my aching temples, and fighting the lump in my throat. At the sound of a clang, I looked up. Braedon had pulled a bucket from a bin.

I went over to him. "What's that?"

"Hopefully an emergency kit." He got the lid up on one corner, and I reached to hold it in place as he eased the rest of it off. Lifting two plastic containers from inside, he handed one to me.

I peered at a package of green tubes.

Braedon tapped one. "Glow sticks." He unzipped the bright orange bag on his lap and removed a first-aid kit, also handing it to me. "Well, that's something." He held a mirror and a white plastic package with the words 'SOS flag' printed on it.

Balancing the two packages, I craned my neck to see inside the pack, the bright light of the moon casting eerie shadows inside. "Are there any flares?"

Using his foot, he slid the larger plastic container toward

me, making a little ripple in the water. I set my items aside, reached inside the bucket, and pulled out a long yellow tube. "There are three more of these."

His expression lightened, and he stuffed everything back in the orange bag and handed it to me while he took the tube. "Anything else?"

I removed a package with four yellow and silver tubes and held them for him to see.

Still sniffing, Maria came over to look at them. "What's the difference between them?"

Braedon acted as though her little explosion hadn't happened and held up the sickly yellow—distorted in the bright moonlight—and silver tube. "This is a regular flare. Sometimes they have locators built in that are activated when lit. None of these do. This larger one is a rocket parachute flare."

As I unscrewed the red cap of the regular flare, I asked, "How long do they last?"

"Only a few minutes, so we won't use it unless we spot a ship or a plane." He touched a little string that came out of the now exposed end. "Pull on this when we're ready to use it."

While Maria picked up the mirror, I screwed the cap back on the flare and handed it to Braedon. "How do you know all this?"

"My mother was into sailing and insisted Aislinn and I knew the basics." He returned them to the plastic bin. "We'll need to take turns standing watch. The first twenty-four hours are critical. Our chances of being found go way down after that."

Maria handed me the mirror, and we watched in silence as she opened a bin and dug around, finally pulling out a tarp. She took it and covered Jimmy's body with it, then sat down. I wished I knew what to say to her to offer comfort. I did, after all, know exactly how she was feeling, but I wasn't Elle who always knew what to say.

My stomach growled. How absurd—with us adrift at sea, Jimmy dead, Elle and Jori who knew where—for my stomach to need something as mundane as food. I bit back a laugh at the ludicrousness of the situation but then had to choke back a sob.

I had to think of something else. My stomach gurgled again, and I remembered we hadn't eaten since breakfast. I scouted out our uneaten box lunches and found them in a galley fridge stocked with cold water bottles.

"Braedon, can you come here?"

"What is it?"

I handed him one of the bottles.

His eyebrows shot up. "That's the first bit of good news we've had." He frowned at the refrigerator. "Where's it drawing its power from? A battery?" He knelt and tried to examine the wiring but straightened when a cloud covered the moon, hiding most of the light. "Too dark. At least the food will last longer."

I took Maria a bottle and a box, but she barely looked at me before resting her head against her knees. The light breeze shifted the tarp around Jimmy's foot, exposing the water shoe that covered it, the partial light from the moon making it a sickly green color. We were all so fragile. Life could be taken from us in a moment. I set the box and bottle beside her.

Returning to the food, I gathered boxes for Braedon and me. He had returned most of the emergency items to the bin and took my offering with a soft "Thanks." He riffled through the lunch, settling on the large chocolate chip cookie, his expression contemplative.

"Lyn, what was it you were telling me before Hawaii?"

"What?" I blinked, confused.

"About the stars and navigating on this side of the equator."

My eyes darted to the controls. "Isn't there a GPS?"

He finished his cookie and moved on to the sandwich. "They shot it along with the radio."

"No compass?"

"Not that I can find."

I sighed. "We can't see the North Star here and there isn't a South Star." My tired brain still understood what he was really asking. "We have no way to guess where we are, do we?"

He shook his head and took a bite of his sandwich, mumbling, "Doesn't appear so."

I held my unopened box. "How long before they come looking for us?"

Braedon eyed me over his food. "Which ones?"

A chill ran up my spine. I hadn't thought about the pirates finding us before the authorities did. My stomach twisted, hunger gone.

"Eat." Braedon stood, squeezing my shoulder, the warmth of his fingers comforting. He remained there until I finally opened the box and took out the cookie. "We'll need our energy." He went over to Maria and knelt beside her.

I sniffed the tuna in the sandwich. It didn't smell spoiled, so I took a bite, watching the two. Braedon kept his voice low, so I couldn't make out what he said, but it wasn't working considering how tense Maria looked while she waved her arms. I wondered if I had been like that a year ago. I didn't think so. Not quite the same, anyway.

Poor Braedon. I didn't know how he did it. Did they teach classes like Calm Demeanor 101 in medical school?

I was closing up my box when he returned and dug out a tarp from a cupboard. "I'll take the first watch."

Maria, who had followed him, held out her hand for the tarp. "I'll do it. I won't be able to sleep anyway."

When she started to walk away, he grabbed her arm. "Don't forget these." He handed her large, heavy looking binoculars and two kinds of flares. With a nod, the tarp over her shoulder, she stepped on a chest and climbed on top of the canopy.

"Hey, there's a solar panel up here," she called from above.

Braedon jumped on the chest and looked over the top of the canopy. "That explains the fridge." His finger appeared through a hole. "We're lucky they missed it." He touched Maria's shoe. "Wake us if you see anything—ship or plane."

She jerked her foot back. "I get it, Braedon."

He held up his hands and stepped off the chest, turning toward me. The odd shadows gave his face an almost skeletal look, accented by the fatigue that radiated from him.

I took out the only remaining tarp and held it up. "We'll have to share."

He hesitated. "Only if you're okay with that."

We stretched out as best we could on the netting. The captain's blood had washed away in the rain, for which I was grateful. I doubt I could have lain there otherwise. With nothing but rope underneath us, I hoped the ocean stayed calm or we would get splashed from below.

Staring at Maria's shadow, outlined by the night sky, I worried about Elle and Jori. What had the cruise people thought when our excursion hadn't come back? How long before they notified my family back in the States? What would Aislinn, who had just lost her mother, do when she was told her brother was missing?

I rolled away from Braedon, trying to cover my mouth so my crying wouldn't wake him. Then he was next to me, his body molding around mine, and his arm around my waist. I felt his body behind me shudder with a sob he tried to swallow. I moved to turn over, but his arm held me in place. "No," he whispered, his voice ragged. "Just let me hold you."

We clung to hope and each other. I covered his arm with my own and offered what comfort I could.

$\mathcal{T}$HE SUN had just begun to lighten the horizon when I woke, bleary-eyed after my middle-of-the-night watch. Maria still slept, so I slid off the netting, trying not to wake her. When my feet touched the remaining water on the deck, I shivered and hurried through it.

Braedon sat in the captain's chair, documents spread on the instrument panel, the binoculars hanging around his neck.

Feeling a little awkward after the previous night, I glanced over his shoulder. "Found anything that might help us?"

"Nothing yet." He let a map drop onto his lap. "We may be okay if we're rescued soon."

I scanned the vast expanse of empty ocean again and took a deep breath, overcome with a feeling of insignificance. "What if that doesn't happen?"

He gathered the papers into a stack. "We have more food than water."

As soon as he mentioned the water, my throat went dry.

Braedon glanced over to where Jimmy's body lay covered. It would be exposed to the full sun soon. "We won't be able to keep his body aboard if we're out here very long."

Tears swelled in my eyes. I hadn't wanted to consider that.

He reached a hand out for me. I stepped back. If we managed to survive this, I could never tell Jimmy's parents that not only was he dead but we had dumped his body in the Pacific.

Braedon stood and took me by the shoulders, forcing me to look at him. "We have to be practical." He tilted his head toward Maria's resting form.

I regarded her for a moment. He was right, but I hated it. She needed to know what would happen. I sniffed. "She's going to have a hard time with this."

Braedon gave me a quick hug and released me. "I think we all are."

I needed to think about something else and glanced up to where the sails were tied to the mast. "Do you know anything about actual sailing?"

His eyes followed mine. "Some." He looked at me. "You?"

"Nothing."

Braedon let out a deep breath. He considered the rigging again. "We need to find out if those bullets did any damage."

He set the stack of paperwork neatly aside and put a flare on top. I woke Maria to take the watch while Braedon unlashed the sail. We painstakingly searched it, finding only one bullet hole. The mast had been hit a handful of times but seemed intact.

He wiped the sweat from his brow and sat in the captain's chair. "Until last night, I'd never sailed a multihull before. The rudders worked fine through the storm. All we need now is to harness the wind."

The hot sun had given me a headache, and my stomach rumbled. "And figure out which way to go."

Braedon gave a soft grunt as he poured over the map again. "We need to go west."

Something nagged at my memory but slipped away. I touched his sleeve. "Can we really make it back?"

A cloud blew across the sun as his eyes met mine, the shadows making his expression inscrutable. I could imagine him wearing this face when he spoke with the family of one of his patients ... and didn't want to tell them the truth. My shoulders drooped under the weight of everything we had been through.

We were going to die.

CHAPTER 13

$\mathcal{U}$NTIL THAT moment, I hadn't realized how much confidence I had put in the man before me, and now he was signaling that he couldn't save us. My entire body turned cold.

He put one hand over mine and cupped my cheek with the other. "There's always hope. We *can* beat the odds."

I leaned my head into his palm, wanting to believe him—needing to believe him.

Maria jumped onto the deck, and I pulled away.

Braedon regarded her with a frown. "You okay?"

She looked awful, but she nodded.

He moved to the cooler and pulled out three lunch boxes. After handing me one, he sat by Maria.

In a flash, I knew what he was planning, and I jumped to my feet. A sick feeling stabbed my stomach, and I set my box down. I couldn't be here when he told her. The knot in my throat told me I would be no help.

"I'm going to wash up before I eat." I grabbed the bottle

of liquid soap by the portable toilet and looked at him over my shoulder.

His eyes were reproachful as he mouthed 'Thanks.'

When I returned, Maria was crying over her sandwich, her eyes red and swollen. Braedon's didn't look much better.

"I need a wash," he said, rising from his seat as I approached.

"I'm sorry," I whispered.

"I can tell." He practically grabbed the bottle of soap I held out to him from my hand.

"I just thought—"

"What? That since I'm a doctor, I was trained to handle all the crappy bad news jobs?"

"No, I ...." Yes. I had assumed that very thing, but I was also honestly sure I would have made it worse.

"Thanks for nothing." He pushed past me.

When he returned, I pointed at the portable toilet. "Speaking of crap ...." I paused, waiting for some sign of humor. He gave none. Fine. "We need to empty it. Soon." I couldn't help a slight gag.

After we dumped it, we decided not to put it back, simply tying up a couple of large towels to have some semblance of privacy. I took the next watch while Braedon and Maria napped. I hated the sense of being alone while they slept. It made me feel small and helpless. The fact that it was Elle's towel flapping in the increasing breeze around the toilet didn't help.

Staring at the cloudy horizon and trying to listen for the sound of an airplane gave me a headache. It did beat the night watch, when I had strained my eyes hoping to see a distant light. Both were better than thinking of Jimmy's lifeless body or worrying about Elle and Jori.

When they woke, Maria took the watch while Braedon and I checked the lines for the sails.

He shielded his eyes as he examined the sun's position midway between its peak and the horizon. "That's the way we need to go."

Maria put down the binoculars. "I heard if you're lost at sea, you're supposed to just drift and let the current take you where people can find you."

Braedon squinted at her. "That's fine if the current will take you where you want to go."

She jumped to her feet. "How do you know it won't? Why do you just assume I'm wrong?"

Braedon's eyes narrowed, the veins in his throat pulsing. He stabbed his finger toward the sun, his words barely understandable through his tight jaw. "Does it *look* like we're drifting that way?"

Maria moved closer, her fists clenched, her jaw working. She was going to lose it. Alarmed, I jumped between the pair, raising my hands to keep them apart. I pulled out my teacher voice. "Let's look at this calmly. See the way the water—oh!" The memory that had been playing hide and seek in my mind finally showed itself. I grabbed the map and turned it so both of them could see it. "Look here. The ocean in this area has a circular current, kind of like an oblong hurricane. Braedon's right. This current will take us away from American Samoa."

Maria gave me a crusty look. "How do you know we're not in the part that would take us west?"

I ground my teeth. Had I been this horrible after Jace died? "The current that flows west is above the equator. If we'd gone that far north, I'd have been able to see the North Star last night."

"Whatever." Maria curled her lip. "No surprise you're

going to agree with *him*." Without another word, she stomped over to Jimmy's body. She jerked to a stop, her hands going to her mouth and nose. Turning, she hurried back, not taking another breath until she reached us.

Braedon and I exchanged quick glances, and my stomach dropped. "Is it time already?" I asked.

"No, it's not time!" Maria glared at us. "Why are you in such a hurry to dump him?"

Her unfair accusation irritated me but must have really pricked at Braedon's raw nerves because he spun on her. "Why are you in such a hurry to pick a fight?"

Maria made an obscene gesture and ran to the trampoline, muttering in Spanish. I didn't want a translation.

I rubbed his arm, hoping to calm him. "Anger's the third phase in the grief cycle."

He jerked away. "I don't need a clinical analysis."

With a sigh, I glanced toward the girl. "Why is she mad at you?"

Braedon blinked, his throat working. When he spoke, his voice was rough. "Because I couldn't save him." He turned and went over to Jimmy's shrouded body.

My eyes burned at his unexpected show of emotion. I hurried after him. "But that's not your fault."

The smell of rotting meat brought me to an abrupt halt. Choking, I covered my nose and mouth and stepped behind him, peeking around at Jimmy's covered body.

Braedon looked to the back of the boat. I turned to see Maria watching us, tears running down her cheeks, her lips trembling. Braedon extended an arm out to her, but she shook her head. "Maria," he called, "how bad do you want us to let him get, lying there in the sun?"

"All right!" She jumped to her feet, arms straight and rigid by her sides, hands clenched.

He continued to hold out his hand to her. I thought he would have to go ahead without her, but then her shoulders drooped, and she slowly reached out to take his hand. Once she clung to it, he took mine with his other.

"Maria, do you want to say anything?"

Crossing herself, Maria said something in Spanish. Braedon bowed his head, and I said my own silent prayer, taking shallow breaths and trying to ignore the stench.

I needed a different memory of Jimmy—not like this and not him lying pale and bleeding. Him on the stage at the end of the song, the audience screaming its approval. I hummed the descant Braedon had written. His eyes darted to me, and he took up the melody.

Still humming softly, he released our hands and took one end of the shroud. Maria and I grabbed the other, stumbling as we carried Jimmy to the edge of the boat and dropped his body into the water. Maria spun and dashed to the rear of the catamaran.

I turned into Braedon's chest, keeping my eyes on the water. With his arms around me, we stared as the body drifted away.

"I wish …." I coughed, rubbing at the cramp in my throat. "I wish we had coordinates to give Jimmy's parents. I'd want to know where my son was buried."

Finally, Braedon dropped his arms and nodded toward the sail. "You ready to get to work?"

I blinked and shook my head, feeling that to just move on would be disrespectful.

Braedon's voice was soft. "It will help to distract us."

With a sigh, I followed him to the corner of the deck. He

took hold of the rope while I grabbed the corner of the sail. "Was that stuff about the currents true?" he asked.

I frowned. "Of course. I spent a lot of my spare time last winter studying the locations on our itinerary. I thought it would help me decide which places to visit."

Braedon checked the direction of the little SOS flag at the top of the mast, looked at the sun again, and adjusted the sail before doing the final knot. The catamaran jerked a little in the light breeze, and the sense of purposeful movement made my heart jump. Maybe Braedon was right. Maybe we would beat the odds.

I followed him back to the captain's seat, where he steered the catamaran toward the setting sun and tinkered with a small gray box on the console. Letting go of the wheel, he paused as though waiting for something. When the catamaran didn't shift, he gave a hint of a smile.

"This thing has cruise control?"

Now he did grin. "Looks like the captain jury-rigged an autopilot. Powered from the solar panel, I think."

Later, after using our makeshift restroom, I reached over the trampoline toward the water to rinse my hands. A large and distinctive shadow flashed by.

I lurched back and scurried away from the edge. Three forms zigzagged underneath my feet.

"Lyn?" Braedon asked from behind me.

I pushed against the netting and flew off the trampoline, crashing into him. He caught my shoulders, and we fell back, landing in the settee with a thud.

"What is it?"

"Sharks," I gasped.

With a low curse, he gave me a gentle push, freeing his legs from underneath me and rising. He peered at the trampoline as he helped me to my feet.

A wave of nausea squeezed my stomach. "Do you think they *ate* Jimmy?"

"It's possible," Braedon whispered, his face pinched. "They may have been drawn here when we threw the toilet overboard."

We had dumped Jimmy's body in shark-infested water. The pain in my gut magnified and my stomach convulsed. I flung myself toward one of the buckets, dropping to my knees and retching. Braedon knelt beside me and stroked my hair until it stopped. Weakly, I leaned against him. "Do you think they'll go away when no more food shows up?"

"We can hope. I'm hardly an authority on shark behavior." He reached over and grabbed my half-full water bottle, handing it to me.

I took a swallow, wishing I could rinse away the image of sharks eating Jimmy along with the bitter taste in my mouth. From the corner of my eye, I noticed Maria sitting in the shade, using the binoculars to check the horizon. She mustn't know.

"THE WIND's picking up. Wake me if it gets too strong," Braedon told Maria when she came to take the watch from him. "I don't want to risk stripping the autopilot's gears or capsizing."

"That's an encouraging thought," I muttered.

He pointed off in the distance at what must have been northeast. "Pay special attention to that direction. I thought I might have seen a shadow that way. Let me know if you see any lights."

Maria put a hand on her hip. "I say we check it out."

I wanted to placate her, so I stood beside her in a show of solidarity.

Braedon shot me a look of betrayal. "Just know we can't chase every shadow out there." He turned to the jury-rigged autopilot box, adjusted it, and did something to the sails before returning to us. "I'll take the second watch and drop the sails then, unless it gets stormy sooner."

Maria grabbed the watch gear and climbed on the canopy.

I faced the trampoline and shuddered.

"What?" Braedon asked from behind me.

"Is there enough tarp to lie on and cover up too?"

He glanced at the tarp in his hand and back at me. "If you don't mind sleeping close. Why?"

Like we hadn't slept close last night. "Sharks, of course."

He was silent for a moment, and then he laughed.

"Yeah, he's a real keeper, Lyn." Maria snarked from her perch.

Braedon frowned and heaved a tired sigh. "Shut up, Maria." He caught my arm as I turned away. "I'm sorry I laughed." He pulled me around to face him. "Let's be logical, though. If there was a shark of movie-sized proportions that could come through that netting, the tarp isn't going to offer more protection."

I closed my eyes. "I'm not stupid, but this is like the monsters that used to live in my closet when I was a little girl." I opened my eyes, pleading with him to understand. "My dad told me it didn't make sense that my blanket would protect me, but knowing it was there let me sleep."

He regarded me for a moment and shrugged. "Okay. Whatever works."

The decent-sized tarp still did require us to lay right next to each other. Instead of thinking about Jimmy or the sharks or how much our odds of being found had dropped since passing the twenty-four-hour mark, I considered how much windier it was tonight.

As tired as I was, sleep wouldn't come. Back home, I would have gone running. Lying so close to Braedon, I couldn't even roll over. He had taken the open end of the tarp and would be uncovered if I shifted too much.

He heaved out a heavy breath. "You can't sleep."

"I'm sorry. I'll get up."

"No. You need a distraction."

My mind flashed to that night before Hawaii when Braedon had been too much of a distraction. My face went hot, and I was glad for the shadows, especially when he rolled over to face me.

He supported his head with one hand and tugged at the tarp to cover his back. "So, tell me something about you I don't know."

Okay, so not what had been on my mind. I thought for a moment. "Lyn is the short version of my first name. I don't particularly like my name."

When I didn't continue, he asked, "And …?"

I sighed. "Gwendolyn."

"That's a pretty name." He pondered it for a moment. "It's old. I can't remember—"

"In some legends, Merlin had a wife named Gwendolyn," I interrupted. "And there was a mythical queen of the Britons who defeated her cheating husband in battle." I paused, not having thought of that little bit of trivia since I was young. Ironic about the cheating. "It was our names that first drew Elle and me together."

"Elle is short for something?"

"Adelaide. Her parents tried to call her Addy, but once she

started school she insisted they call her Elle." I giggled. "She refused to answer if they called her anything else."

I thought of her rigid bare back as she had faced the pirates. "Do you think she's okay?" I whispered.

His voice was rough. "I hope so." He rolled over onto his back, the tarp pulling me a little closer.

*K*ICKING MY *feet, I swam from the monster, arms flailing. The blood pounded in my ears. Jimmy's pale face loomed beside me, his eyes sad as he pointed at the growing shape below, light gleaming from the crystalline triangles that filled the shark's mouth.*

I jerked, starting awake with a sharp intake of breath ... and relaxed as I felt the warmth of Braedon's body against my back. It was just a nightmare. I sighed, sagging against him, until the tug came again.

Disoriented from sleep and the unexpected darkness, I lifted my head to find Maria lurching as a small wave capped the side of the catamaran behind her. A surge pushed up under the trampoline, soaking Braedon and me.

I cried out and Braedon cursed. We scrambled to untangle ourselves from the tarp and each other. The sky lit up, lightning scattering spider-like legs through the ominous black clouds.

Finally free, he tossed the tarp aside and leapt to the deck. I landed behind him, clutching his taut arm as a swell lifted the catamaran and then dropped it. My stomach stayed up in my throat.

Braedon staggered to catch his balance. "Why didn't you wake me sooner?" he shouted at Maria.

Maria screamed back, "I fell asleep, all right?" A new wave crested the side of the catamaran and flooded the settee area.

In spite of already being wet, I sensed a cold sweat break out over my body. I wouldn't think about the sharks. I wouldn't. I reached my shaking hands toward a bucket.

"No." Braedon grabbed my hand, turning me toward the trampoline again. "You have to help me get the sails down. Maria, take the wheel and keep it pointed into the waves."

Even with Braedon supporting me from behind, I staggered on the uneven rope. Without the moon's glow, there was nothing to help me find the way. Lightning pierced the sky, followed by a boom of thunder. Like a sick amusement park ride in the dark, the catamaran shot up into the air, freezing at the top of the wave for a precarious moment.

The boat dropped at an angle and my stomach flipped. I careened to the side, a powerful gust of wind throwing me off my feet.

"No!" Braedon roared, his hands digging into my arms.

My fingers clawed into the trampoline ropes, legs kicking wildly. A wave caught us head-on. The force of the water pushed me farther over the side.

Braedon planted his feet against the catamaran's edge. Grunting, he straightened his knees and dragged me back onto the trampoline.

My entire body shook as I clung to him. "We have to get the lifejackets."

"You—" A wave dashed against us, water flooding his mouth. He gasped and choked.

I rolled off his chest, pulling him over onto his stomach. With a painful rasp, he forced in a breath, ending in a spasm of coughs. The ocean surged, lifting our end of the catamaran.

"To the edge," he wheezed, dragging me with him.

A sudden flash of lightning nearly blinded me, but I saw the danger even as our weight on the edge brought us level with the heaving ocean again. We couldn't let the wind capsize us. The sharks might still be out there.

Braedon moved toward the canvass again. "We have to get the sail down."

"Here!" screamed Maria, her shadow barely discernible. As she tossed something, the catamaran heaved to the side. She cried out and fell with a curse.

Two objects flew toward us, the wind catching one and almost blowing it past Braedon. He darted his hand out, stretching like a volleyball player in a save, and caught the lifejacket. Before I knew what he was doing, he was shoving my arms into it. I handed him the one I had caught, and he buckled it on while I snapped shut my belt.

"The sail." He scurried to the edge of the trampoline.

The sail's swollen rope wouldn't give. A powerful gust of wind pushed against us. Lightning flashed in the sky. In a slow-motion kaleidoscope of grays and whites, the large sail veered down as though a giant hand had flicked it. My stomach contorted as the catamaran rose again. I slid, clutching the trampoline.

Braedon and I clung to the netting. Our eyes met for an instant before a huge wave crashed against us, his body taking the brunt. I blinked and he was gone. Pain stabbed my chest and I screamed. In the light of a flash, the ocean seemed miles below. I couldn't see him.

Another gust of wind pushed against me. My cramping hand muscles slipped, and I fell.

Part 2

CHAPTER 14

A SHARP PAIN in my foot jolted me awake. I jerked my leg toward my chest and peeled my eyes open, squinting at the sharp light. Another stab of pain pierced my foot, and I gathered the strength to sit up … and found myself facing a seagull—a huge seagull. With a surge of adrenaline, I lunged forward at the bird with a pathetic kiai and fell onto my stomach. The bird flapped away.

I crawled to my knees and stood up slowly, staggering to find my balance. I could only bear to open my eyelids a crack.

My temples throbbed. I tried to rub my head against the pain, but it hurt to touch … and my hand came away wet. I squinted at my fingers.

Blood.

Okay. I needed to focus. Where were the others? Had only I survived? My body shook. I hurt everywhere.

Closing my eyes, I took some careful breaths, and calmed myself. Lifting my hand to shade my eyes from the sun, I glanced around.

I was on a beach. The light blue water close to the shore

transitioned to the dark blue cast of deep water not far out. Some nasty looking rocks and reefs painted the ocean closer in. Away from the shore, a small mountain rose in the distance, overgrown with vegetation. Could there be people here?

"Braedon!" I called, my voice raw and raspy. I pressed my temples and grimaced as the pain sharpened. "Braedon! Maria!" It came out louder, but a slow burn in my throat triggered a coughing fit. A wave of nausea washed over me, and I swallowed rapidly, managing not to heave.

I wanted to lie down. I wanted it to all go away. My knees went weak, and I almost gave in. But Braedon and Maria might be hurt, lying unconscious on the shore. If the tide came in, they could drown.

Taking it slowly, I trudged along the curving shore. The longer I was up and moving, the better I felt. After a few minutes, I scanned the horizon again. And found Braedon halfway in a tidal pool. He wasn't moving.

Stumbling toward him on the uneven beach, I forgot about the pain in my head. I dropped to my knees and felt for a pulse. When I felt the steady *thump, thump* of his heartbeat, I slumped over, laid my head on his life vest, and cried.

I lay on him until my muscles finally complained. Taking a deep breath, I straightened. "Braedon." I shook his shoulder.

No response.

"Braedon." He was alive now, but what if he died like Jimmy? "Please, Braedon. Please don't leave me here alone."

I reached toward his eyelids, my fingers shaking, but pulled back. I jammed my clenched fist to my mouth. Blinking, I tried again, lifting his eyelids one at a time, moving my head in and out of the sun shining on his face. When his irises reacted evenly to the light, I released the breath I hadn't realized I had been holding.

With gentle fingers, I felt around his head, finding an egg-sized lump toward the back. Because of his damp hair, I checked my hand for blood and stared at the red smeared on my fingers and palm. A moan escaped me, but then I remembered it could be my own blood.

Resting on one hand, I leaned toward the water and rinsed the other. Braedon grabbed my wrist.

I screamed in surprise. My arm slipped, and I collapsed beside him. "Braedon," I breathed, scrambling to my knees, blinking against a new onslaught of tears. "You're awake." I brushed some hair from his forehead. "You've got a nice lump on your head."

"Yeah, I'm lying on it," he rasped, his eyes still closed. He shifted his head slightly and groaned.

"Hang on," I sniffed. "I can't tell if your head's bleeding. I need to rinse my own blood off first …."

He sat up too fast and groaned, holding his head. I took advantage of his distraction to rinse off the remaining blood and then touched his lump. He jerked away.

"Sorry." I dropped my hand. "I think your pupils are dilating okay, and there's no blood on your lump."

He lifted his head, slower this time, keeping his eyes narrowed. He grunted at the bright light and reached for my face. "Let me see." He turned the bloody side of my head toward him. "We'll need to rinse this off."

We shrugged off our life vests, and I sat there with a stupid grin as Braedon cleaned off the sand and blood, not even wincing at the sting of the salt water. Until he probed the cut.

I tried to pull away, but his strong hands held my head firmly in place.

"It's stopped bleeding and is a pretty clean cut, if a little deep. Anything else hurt?" He scrutinized me through half-closed eyes.

"My lungs when I take deep breaths. My foot where a bird pecked me."

Braedon examined my leg and found the two bruises on my foot. "It didn't break the skin, but something else did here." He examined a series of scratches along the back of my left knee. "You probably got that from a rock coming in." He looked at me. "Do you know how lucky we are to be alive?"

My throat choked up, and all I could do was nod.

"Where's Maria?" he asked.

With that, my momentary relief shattered. "I haven't found her yet," I whispered.

Braedon swore under his breath. "Which direction did you come from?"

I pointed, and we helped each other up. My balance was more stable than his was at first, probably because I had been conscious longer. Braedon used me for support, and we made our wobbly way down the beach in search of Maria.

I cried out as a sharp pain went through my foot.

"You okay?" Braedon held my elbow to steady me as I lifted my foot to remove my water shoe.

"It's just a pebble." I shook the shoe.

"I'll be right back." Braedon moved ahead to examine a small pool.

As I put my shoe back on, I noticed one of our water bottles on the beach. I went to pick it up and saw a few more bottles floating nearby among some seaweed debris. I stepped into the surf to collect them. When I touched one of the bottles, my fingers tangled in some long, thin, black strands … of hair. Maria floated face down in the water, camouflaged by seaweed.

"Braedon!" I dropped the bottles and tried to turn her over. "She wasn't wearing a life vest. No. No."

He splashed through the knee-deep water and felt for a pulse. Twisting away from her, he slammed his fist into the water and let out a roar.

Stunned, I stood in place, my tears frozen on my eyelids.

Braedon went still. With obvious effort, his breathing slowed and his tense shoulders relaxed. He turned to me, his face red, his eyes glistening. He put a dripping hand to his forehead and rubbed it.

The memory of his grief over Jimmy flashed through my mind. My throat tightened and tears ran down my cheeks. I stepped to his side and took his hand. He pulled me into his arms, and we held each other and cried. Finally, he stepped back and squeezed my hand. Together we gently grasped Maria's cold, lifeless limbs and towed her body to the shore.

Seaweed stink didn't help my fear of dead bodies, and I had to resist the urge to rush to the water and scrub my hands. I collected a fallen palm leaf and covered her swollen, distorted face.

I sank to the sand. First Jimmy and now Maria. Was Elle also dead? What about Jori?

Braedon sat beside me, placing his arm tentatively across my shoulders. He cleared his throat.

Glancing up at him, I asked. "Are they all dead?"

"We can't think like that."

I wiped the tears from my face. "What about us? Are we going to die here too?"

He exhaled and straightened, peering around, squinting against the glaring sun. "If we can find fresh water we should be okay." He leaned forward and picked up one of the bottles I had dropped and handed it to me.

I took it and twisted off the lid, savoring the moisture as it ran down my parched throat. Braedon stood and took a drink, assessing the jungle behind us. He glanced back at Maria's still form. "Let's look for something to dig a grave with."

A search turned up what was left of the catamaran in an indentation too small to be called a cove, but large enough to hide the hulk of the boat from our initial view. I wrote out a large SOS in dark volcanic rocks while Braedon scavenged the sail, a bucket, a damp first aid kit, one metal fork, a hammer, a sewing kit, a couple of knives, a small ax, a machete, and a lighter.

Braedon's face was serious when he showed me the last item. "I haven't had to make a fire from scratch in years, and I'm glad we don't have to eat raw fish while I figure it out again."

*I*T was hot, miserable work digging Maria's grave. Sweat made the cut on my temple burn; I concentrated on the stinging rather than the purpose of our work. After we lowered her body into the hole and covered it with sand, I gathered some flowers and placed them on the mound.

"It's not fair," I sniffed.

"No, it's not." Braedon squeezed my shoulder. "I'll carve something to mark her grave."

Exhausted after the burial, we collapsed in the shade of

some trees bordering the beach and fell asleep. It was dark when the cool breeze off the ocean woke us.

"Mother Nature calls." Braedon jogged toward the gloomy foliage.

Suddenly alone, I almost called him back. I peered at the jungle, its sinister shadows elongated by the moon shining through the lattice of leaves. The scent of nearby flowers nearly overpowered the smell of rich earth and rotting leaves.

Shivering, I decided to go to the water to freshen up. When I rose, shaking the water from my hands, I glanced up the dim shore. A white shape reflected the moon's light near where we had napped. With trepidation, I approached it and discovered the white sail from the catamaran spread out on the sand.

I jumped when Braedon stepped out of the jungle, his hands full.

"Sorry. Didn't mean to scare you." He set some water bottles by the sail. "Have a banana." He handed me one along with a bottle of water and sat down to eat his own.

I joined him. "Not much variety in the food." I unpeeled the banana.

He watched the waves glittering in the soft glow of the moon. "At least there is food."

"Right again, Mr. Positive." I tossed the peel into the jungle behind us and bit into the fruit.

His attention shifted to me. "Don't."

"Don't *what*?"

Turning to stare back at the shore, his voice took on a deep sadness. "Dig at me like Maria."

I thought of the mound of her grave around the curve of the beach. No longer hungry, I tossed the rest of the banana to the side. "Do you think anyone is still searching for us?"

"Probably, but we could be a long way from where they're searching. At some point we need to be prepared to rescue ourselves."

I swallowed. "Build our own boat?"

He turned his head, scrutinizing my face. "Does the idea bother you?"

I rubbed my forehead, avoiding my tender temple. "If nobody finds us, we'll have to, but ... I keep having dreams of Jimmy being eaten."

"I know," Braedon replied softy.

I frowned, rubbing my arms against the cool breeze. "You know? How?"

"You talk in your sleep." He lay down. "Our first priority is to survive here. We might luck out and get noticed by a plane or passing ship. In the meantime, we can make escape plans. Just in case." He lifted a section of the sail in his hand and pulled it over himself. "I'm sorry there's just the one sail. We'll have to share again."

I lay down, and he flipped the narrowed end of the triangular sail over me. My feet were still uncovered, and I had to scoot closer to him to fit them under as well.

What would it have been like if Braedon had died too? I allowed myself to savor his body being so close to mine, the warmth of his shoulder, the comfort it gave me. I moved my hand closer to him, my fingers brushing his.

I listened to the surf for a few minutes. Finally, I whispered, "I never realized before how noisy waves are. I don't know if I'll be able to fall asleep again."

Braedon responded with a soft snore.

CHAPTER 15

SOMETHING BRUSHED my leg, and I jerked away. Terror cut through me like a shark's tooth. I knew I lay on the beach, yet I felt as if I was underwater. I couldn't breathe.

Suddenly warmth and security enveloped me, and my body unfroze. My lungs gasped in a breath of air, and my muscles relaxed. Safe. I was safe. I drifted back to sleep.

A bird cry startled me awake to bright sunshine. Braedon's arm around my shoulders tightened. I raised my head from his shoulder, my face growing hot as I realized he was awake.

"You okay?" he asked, his eyes twinkling. He didn't move.

I decided not to acknowledge his mirth, or my red face, and shifted to sit up. "How's your head? Mine stings like the blazes." I touched my tender temple.

He stood up. "It hurts." His stomach growled. "We need something to eat besides bananas."

I glanced at him through the corners of my eyes. "Hm. I wonder where I've heard that before."

Braedon eyed me, his eyebrows raised, but finally gave in and laughed. "All right, I deserved that." He turned to study the long stretch of beach. "If this island doesn't have a source of fresh water, we'll need to capture rainwater." It had rained on us during the night. Twice.

"What do you want to do first?"

He squinted over his shoulder in the direction of the wreck. "I need to get a couple of things from the catamaran. And we should check how far the other side of the island goes in case we're not alone here."

"Do you need help with the stuff on the boat? If not, I can see what's around the cove there." I pointed toward a curve on the beach opposite from where we had found Maria's body.

I took one step before he grabbed my hand. "Don't go too far, okay?"

Even now, my hand tingled where he touched me, and I pulled it away quickly. How stupid was I? This wasn't the time to reconsider something I had already walked away from.

The beach curved around the point of an overgrown hill of sorts and continued on a ways, stopping abruptly. I didn't have to walk very far to see there wasn't more to the island on that side. A long, skinny valley bit into the backside of the mountain, making the edge between it and the beach resemble an arm.

I returned to the catamaran. "The beach ends back there, and there's nothing but ocean beyond it," I called. "I didn't see any signs of people. I'll check the other direction."

He looked over the edge of the boat. "I'll join you when I'm done here."

The pristine beach curved along a wider, lower overgrown hill on the other side. A tall mountain rose into the air from the island, the front half sheared off. Maybe from an earthquake? That thought didn't give me any comfort. I kicked at the white sand. The island was old, probably remnants of a dead volcano. Under different circumstances, it would have made for a lovely vacation spot.

The island's oblong shape had a leg at the far end where the beach split to allow water into the jungle. The sand began again a few feet beyond. Curious, I examined the deep water and then peered at the jungle vines hanging just above the inlet, wondering what they hid.

I peeked through the thin curtain of foliage and stared at a circular lagoon. Vegetation of varying shades of green sheltered the encircling beach, but the sun shone on a good portion of the water. A thrill rushed through me, and I danced back and forth. A waterfall. I needed to tell Braedon.

As I turned, he shouted my name from the beach, and I dashed through the curtain of vines. He spun to face me as I came through the foliage.

"Lyn," he breathed. "Don't disappear like that."

He had been worried about me? Of course he would be. I would be worried about him. Who would want to be stuck here alone? "I'm sorry I scared you." I grasped his hand and pulled him toward the vines. "Wait until you see what I found."

Braedon paused at the entrance, his eyes zeroing in on the waterfall. "Well, my Gwendolyn, this almost makes up for the fright you just gave me."

I narrowed my eyes. "What did you call me?"

The hint of a grin tugged at the corner of his mouth, but he didn't look at me. "Gwendolyn."

"I did mention I don't like that name, didn't I?"

"So? I like it."

I wanted to argue further, but something in his manner

reminded me of that half dream's comfort. Plus, from the set of his jaw, I wasn't sure he would have done what I asked anyway.

I shook my finger at him. "If you ever—and I mean ever—call me 'Gwen,' I will hurt you."

He did grin then and stepped closer to the lagoon, pointing at the fish. "This is perfect. I can build a simple fish trap here. Much easier than trying to catch them out in the surf."

I moved beside him. "How do you build a fish trap?"

"I can show you later if you want. It's an old Native American trick my father taught me."

"We'll have more options than just fish. See how dark the blue is on that end? It's deep there. With the fresh and salt water combining, it should be a good spot for mussels and oysters." I scrambled up the rocks next to the waterfall, bent to the water, and scooped some into my mouth. I sighed. "Pure Adam's Ale."

Braedon sat beside me, our legs almost touching, and we stuck our hands in the stream of water and drank until we were full.

"How does a girl from Colorado know so much about mussels and oysters?"

I pointed at myself. "Science teacher." I rubbed the area around my temple. "Now, if I dared take one of those pain killers in the first aid kit for this headache."

"You can, if it's that bad, but it would be better to save them." Braedon moved his hand as though to touch the back of his head but stopped, pointing at the lagoon instead. "Look at the high water marks. I don't think this'll work as a permanent camp." He gazed around with a critical eye. "And it's too well hidden to get the attention of passing ships."

"Maybe we could get the mast off the catamaran and make some kind of flag."

"We need the sail for ourselves." As he rose, his stomach growled, and he grimaced. "I'll gather what I need for a fish trap and set it up in the lagoon."

"I'll check for coconuts up on that plateau and get some bananas."

I watched him until he was out of sight. The pleasant little lagoon area didn't seem quite so pleasant with him gone. A rustling in the jungle followed by the shriek of a bird made me jump. The beautiful lagoon turned sinister all of a sudden. I was sick and tired of being so jumpy at every little noise. Refusing to succumb to my fear, I forced myself to be slow as I got a quick drink from the waterfall before making my way up the hill—all the time trying to ignore how the hair on my arms stood on end.

The hill opened to a much larger plateau above the falls. The sheared cliff face I had noticed earlier rose what must have been several hundred feet above, making it the highest part of the island. The tree is what caught my eye, though.

"Lyn, you up there?"

"Yeah!" I ran to the edge of the plateau. "I've found something else I think you'll be interested in."

Braedon bounded up the hill. "Impressive." He examined the tree's aerial prop roots.

"It's a Banyan tree."

He nodded, running his hand along one of the roots. "We saw some in Hawaii. This thing's huge. It must span a good thirty feet across."

"Looks like it might have started out as two trees." I pointed to the middle. "See that opening at the base? The top has real potential. We'd have a great view from up there, and it'll be easier to keep watch for ships and planes."

"Is it just the way the branches have come together, or does it look like some of the middle has already been cleared out?" Braedon pointed to a low section between the top ends of the tree.

Unsure about what he meant, I backed farther away. From there it was obvious. The two ends were definitely taller than the section in the middle. "I think you're right."

His stomach rumbled. "I'm starving." He turned to go down the hill and then glanced back at me. "I'll go check the trap. That lagoon is full of fish." His eyes got a wicked gleam. "The rule in Montana is that the catcher of the fish is not the cleaner of the fish."

Gross. "I've never cleaned or gutted a fish. You'll have to show me—but you'll also need to teach me how to work your trap, because I have no intention of being the only fish gutter on this island."

Braedon laughed and jogged down to the lagoon. It was nice to hear him laugh again. I went in search of the fruit.

$\mathcal{L}$ATE AFTERNOON had come before we had gathered everything in our new camp. I squeezed out the water from my cover-up. A burst of rain had provided an impromptu shower of sorts, but it hadn't lasted long enough to do more than rinse off my arms and legs.

I rubbed the parts of my cover-up together, unsure if the red volcanic dust would ever come out. Monsoon showers would do it. I froze. "Please tell me we won't still be here during the monsoons."

Braedon paused at testing the strength of one of the Banyan

tree's lower roots and looked at me. "How much rain will the monsoons bring?"

"If this is like American Samoa, a lot. Some places on Samoa get close to 200 inches a year. But that's not an answer."

He frowned and stepped onto the lowest branch of the tree. "I don't have an answer."

Not what I wanted to hear. I followed him up the branches, stopping near the top. "So make one up."

Braedon considered me before giving me a hand over the last branch. "And have you mad at me because my prediction doesn't come true? No thanks." He turned to stare at the middle section.

"Why do you assume I'd be mad at you—" I stopped when I saw what held his attention. This part of the tree had indeed been cut … and a floor built on it. It was old and parts of it were rotting, but it was definitely manmade.

My heart thudded hard as I came to stand beside him. "This is good news, right?"

"Could be." He walked around the floor, testing sections with his weight. Most of them were solid, but a few crumbled. "If someone built this, then someone knows about the island. But how long ago were they last here?" Braedon asked as he finished checking the flooring. "You game to sleep up here tonight?"

$\mathcal{I}$ SET THE dinner fruit on a flattish rock, spread a large banana leaf I had cleaned earlier over the surface, and grabbed the machete. The jungle's lengthening shadows were turning into twisted fingers closing in on the cooking area. If Braedon didn't hurry, he would be stumbling around in the dark. He had better not get hurt. I was no doctor.

Just before the last of the light disappeared, Braedon burst over the hill from the lagoon and jogged to the fire with a big grin. "I didn't think I'd make it before dark." He set a mesh bag full of fish beside the fire.

I stood and reached over, picking up a large, yellowish-green ball. I held it out to him. "I've expanded our diet."

He took it from me, his brows creased. "What is it?"

"Breadfruit."

Braedon turned it toward the fire and scrutinized it. "Can you make bread out of it?"

My stomach gurgled. "I wish. It just smells like baking bread when it's roasted."

He handed the fruit back to me and picked up the bag of fish. "You're sure it's breadfruit? It would be the worst irony to survive everything and die of poisoning."

I moved to the fire and set the breadfruit onto the edge where the wood glowed. "I told you I studied up for the cruise."

"That's impressive. I did a little studying too, but not about stuff like this."

We worked in a companionable silence, and I considered the waning moon, wondering if we should dare to climb the uneven tree branches in the dark. It was risky, but I didn't want to sleep on the ground. The nightmares were bad enough without having to fear animals attacking us while we slept. I wasn't sure, but I felt the jungle hid more than we had seen so far.

Braedon picked up one of the coconuts and brought it closer to the firelight. "This doesn't resemble store-bought coconuts."

"Ever seen walnuts on a tree?"

"So we have to get the husk off?" He reached for the ax.

"A screwdriver or a sharp stick works just as well." I picked up a branch and sat on a large rock, holding the stick in place between my knees. With the coconut on the point, I pushed down. The stick pierced the husk but didn't go all the way through.

Braedon put his coconut down and came over to help. He held the coconut still while I shoved the stick down hard. The husk split.

"Once we have the husk off, I'll show you how to crack the inside." I thought of when Elle and I had done this on my apartment patio, and my eyes began to burn.

"You okay?"

The knot in my throat grew, and I waved my hand, croaking, "Don't get me going."

He shoved the stick through the coconut husk again, tearing a piece off. "You should talk about it, you know."

I shook my head. I hated crying in front of people, and I had already done it too many times the last few days.

Braedon leaned toward me, his eyes glistening in the firelight. "Can't you see …." His voice was rough. "Can't you see you're not the only one trapped here worrying about friends and family?" He swore softly and took a deep breath. "I'm sorry you're stuck here with me. I'm sure you'd have preferred Jori."

I burst out laughing, my sorrow forgotten. "Are you jealous of Jori?"

Braedon shifted uncomfortably.

I stopped laughing. He was. "I love Jori like a brother, but he'd be worthless here. He told me once he's never been camping. Ever. His idea of roughing it is a four-star hotel." I gave Braedon a soft push before handing him back the coconut. "Can you imagine me being the knowledgeable one here?"

Braedon's shoulders relaxed. "You're not doing so bad." He pointed at the stick I held. "Our knowledge is pretty complimentary."

Once we had the husks off the two coconuts, I showed him the three coconut 'eyes' on the shells. Following my instructions, he rapped the coconut hard four times on those spots, turning it in his hand after each blow.

The juice ran between his fingers and spilled into the bucket. He licked his fingers. "I thought coconut milk would be sweeter."

"That's coconut water. You get coconut milk from the meat, and it's a much more complicated process." I peered at the tall trees surrounding our cooking area. "The water is sweeter in young coconuts, and it's very nutritious, which we'll need. But the younger ones are still in the trees."

While Braedon went to work on the second coconut, I used the screwdriver to pry the meat from the cracked one. It was harder than I had thought. I ended up with only a single, intact half-shell. "We could use this as a cup or bowl."

Braedon considered the shell. "Our first step toward some kind of civilization."

CHAPTER 16

$\mathcal{W}$E SPENT the next two weeks doing little more than keeping watch, either on the beach or in the tree. No signs at all. Not even a glimpse of a plane or a teasing shadow on the horizon to give us some hope, even if false.

Silent, we sat side by side on the tree's floor, watching the sun set on yet another day. I wanted to cry. I was dirty. I stank. Braedon stank. He wasn't supposed to. He was supposed to smell like shampoo and his yummy cologne.

I lay my head on my bent knees, my face toward him. He had been quiet all day, and the red glow of the sun made his sunburned face seem redder than normal, fatigue making him look older. His eyes met mine.

"How long?" I asked.

"Until what?"

The last bit of sun dropped over the horizon, washing away the light. Until the moon rose, we were almost blind. I could just make out Braedon's form. "How long will they look for us?"

"How would I know?" He didn't even try to sound pleasant. "I wish you wouldn't act like I know everything."

What a jerk. "Aw, poor Braedon. Does that happen to you a lot? Weak women thinking you know everything?"

He stiffened, and I thought I heard him open his mouth and then snap it shut. With a sigh, he rubbed his face and straightened, popping his back. "I don't want to fight with you."

"Then don't throw the first punch."

Braedon laughed. "Is that what you thought it was?"

I gathered my dignity about me like a cloak. "I was asking your opinion, not expecting you to spew wisdom based on your extensive experience of being shipwrecked. I thought having lived near the ocean you might have heard about searches for people lost at sea."

He heaved a sigh. "Point taken, but I don't appreciate the jab about weak women. I've spent my life around strong women, now being no exception." Standing, he touched my shoulder. I hesitated but took the hand he offered, and he pulled me to my feet. He kept my hand in his as we made our way to the center of the small shelter we had made from the sail and a pile of leaves.

The evening breeze increased, bringing with it the smell of flowers and rain. I stared into the darkness. "They're not coming."

He didn't say anything at first. "No," he finally said, his voice tight. It was clear he didn't want to talk about it.

Rolling over so my back was to him, I watched the moon rise over the trees. We had two options. We could stay here, or we could rescue ourselves. A knot formed in my throat. At night, in the dark, with nightmares waiting for me to fall asleep, it was hard to consider going out on the ocean again.

Clouds swallowed the stars and the moon, and finally raindrops smacked against the sail above us. I scooted farther under the sail, away from the rain splatters. I froze when my foot brushed Braedon's.

He touched my shoulder. "Lyn."

When we lay so close under the sail, memories of those last days on the ship would run through my mind. Braedon never mentioned them. It always amazed me that, of all the people on the catamaran excursion, I ended up here with him—a fact I was grateful for. I rolled onto my back, ignoring the desire to keep going until I was cuddled against him. I turned just my head toward him instead.

"I think it's time to make some plans," he said gently.

There was only one thing he could be talking about. "How about the catamaran?"

He shifted an arm under his head as a pillow. "It's too damaged, and the hulls are fiberglass. I have no idea how to fix them with the tools we have."

"Have you ever built a boat?"

"No."

Not only was I going to have to face getting out on the water again, I was also going to have to do it in a homemade boat. A knot in my stomach joined the one in my throat. What a choice. Stay here or go out with the sharks. "How will we get past the waves?"

"Track the tides." Braedon brushed my clenched fist with his fingers.

"It'll take time to prepare." He yawned, the tenseness in his voice lessened, as though having reached a decision lifted his spirits. "We'll be here for a while."

Planning I could handle.

$\mathcal{W}$E SPENT the morning digging a latrine pit. Hot and sticky after our manual labor, we went for an ocean swim to clean off, since Braedon didn't want to risk fouling the lagoon. I hated the sticky residue from swimming in salt water.

"I'd like a shower to be our next project." I shifted the load of wood I was carrying for the bonfire pile on the beach.

Braedon shook his head, concentrating on organizing the wood for the best airflow against the breeze. "A shower's a luxury. We need to put our energy into getting a roof over our heads."

"We have a roof over our heads with the sail. How about we work on a shower and the roof at the same time?"

"No." His house of wood collapsed, and he growled in frustration. "We'll spend our energy on a tree house."

Speechless, I stood watching him as he rebuilt the fire pit, my skin itching from the sea salt. He had never blown me off before, and the longer I thought about it, the angrier I got. I forgot all about my earlier gratitude for his survival knowledge and how glad I had been for his company. And how I had been crushing on him.

I clutched the load of wood tight to my chest. "When were you voted king of the island?"

Braedon twisted to stare at me. "Be reasonable. I have the building experience."

That was his excuse for playing high and mighty? "I should also have a say in which projects we work on."

He tried to hide the flash of impatience that crossed his face before looking at me again. "Do we have to talk about this right now? There's a lot to do."

My nightmares from the night before had already left me

tired and edgy. The skin on my back itched again. I wanted to be clean, and Braedon stood in the way. "I want to talk about it now."

His jaw muscles tightened. "We'll work on the tree house first. End of discussion." He turned back to the woodpile.

"Oh, we will?" I tossed the wood onto his little tower, wrecking it, and stalked away.

He grabbed for my hand, but I danced out of his reach and ran down the beach.

"Lyn! Come back here!"

I ignored him and went back to the lagoon. He didn't follow. Fuming, I made my way to the top of the falls, searching for a good place to divert some of the stream. Scrutinizing the area, I tried to visualize several possibilities. It soon became apparent that redirecting enough water for a decent shower would take time to design and a lot of digging and rock carrying.

I thought about my behavior on the beach. Yeah, I was miserable, but it wasn't like Braedon loved it here. I had overreacted. I consoled myself that it didn't excuse Braedon for playing the boss.

Collapsing to the ground, I gave in to a pity party and considered all the things I missed from home. My thoughts drifted to my family and what they must be thinking. My father had a heart condition, and he wouldn't have taken the news of my disappearance well. It might be easier on him to know I had died than to be left worrying about me. My morbid thoughts moved to Jimmy and Maria, and then to Elle and Jori. I lay in the dirt and cried.

I must have dozed off because when I opened my eyes, Braedon sat beside me, leaning on his elbows, his legs stretched out before him.

Sitting up, I straightened my legs. Even though I hadn't handled myself well, I wasn't going to be the first to speak. I didn't have to wait long.

"I'm sorry I was so rude."

A guy who could admit he was wrong once in a while. How refreshing. But it didn't get him off the hook completely. "And arrogant and offensive."

"Yes," he agreed.

I sighed. My turn. "And right."

His eyes danced. "That too."

"I'm sorry for throwing a tantrum, but please don't blow me off. I don't like being treated like an ignorant child."

Braedon sat silently, and I wondered if he was thinking of telling me I shouldn't act like a child if I didn't want to be treated like one. He chose diplomacy. "I'll try not to do it again." He wiped at the mud on my cheek. "I'm sorry I made you cry."

All my residual anger faded away. "Fine. We'll do the stupid tree house first." I pushed against his shoulder before jumping to my feet and going to wash off my muddy face.

$\mathcal{I}$ TOSSED ON my leafy mattress, sleep eluding me, probably because of my nap. Rolling over to face Braedon's silent form, I watched the movement of his chest's slow, steady breathing. His grooming on the ship had been immaculate, and with a smile I wondered if his short, scruffy beard drove him crazy.

A plop hit the sail, followed by another and another, and then the deluge of the regular evening rain shower started. Braedon stirred but didn't rouse. Listening to the rain, a burst of inspiration came to me.

I slipped out of my bed and stepped into the steady stream—

perfect for a shower. Because of the triangular shape of the sail, it left one corner hanging down and provided some privacy, so I pulled off my cover-up and shimmied out of my swimsuit, careful not to get too close to the edge in the dark.

The water beating against my bare skin relaxed my taut muscles. I promised myself if we ever got back to civilization, I would never take a shower for granted again. Without shampoo, scouring my hair was unlikely to make a difference, but I did it anyway. At least I could braid my long hair and keep it out of the way. The suit came next, but when I squeezed the water from the heavy, knit cover-up, the sound made more noise than I anticipated.

"Lyn?"

I startled like a child caught cheating. "Don't come out!" I shrieked, trying with shaking hands to undo the twisted cover-up.

Braedon must have caught the panic in my voice because I heard him leap from his bed. I barely got the dress unrolled and in front of me.

"What's wrong?" He reached for me, but as soon as he felt my bare back, he let me go like my skin had burned his hands. "Where are your clothes?"

"I told you not to come out!" I accused. "I wanted to take a shower and wash my clothes in fresh water."

The now light sprinkle flattened Braedon's hair as he stood for a second in the dim moonlight breaking through the clouds. I could just make out his shaking head as he turned and went back under the sail. "Unless you plan on coming back to bed naked, you're going to have to sleep in wet clothes."

I hadn't thought about that.

CHAPTER 17

$\mathcal{B}$RAEDON STOOD near the floor's edge and the newly installed railing, the outline of the tree house walls and roof behind him. He squinted at the distant beach. "Do you see something?" I couldn't keep the excitement from my voice.

Braedon shook his head, marking something on a piece of bark with a charred stick. "The moon was full last night. I'm tracking the tides."

We had been there a month. With a sigh, I began to climb down the ladder. Our eyes met and my heart lurched. Just what we needed: me crushing on him. I grabbed the large pot and headed to the falls.

Before filling it, I made sure there was plenty of a plant I had found which grew prolifically around the island. Its stalk, when split open, poofed out with a fluffy, absorbent fiber, and it even had a mild, pleasant fragrance. It was a heaven-sent sanitary supply.

After lunch, we moved to the shady lagoon area and Braedon pulled out some hemp rope he was using to make bowstring. I tried not to watch him too much, but it was hard not to. He glanced up and caught me peeking at him. I flushed, dropping my eyes.

When he went back to work on the rope, I studied his graceful hands. Something about them triggered a memory of my nightmare from the night before ... and that sense of security that let me fall asleep again in peace. My breath caught. How stupid was I not to have put it together sooner?

"It's you, isn't it?" I said. Braedon's head jerked up, and I continued, "You're the one stopping my nightmares."

He nodded. "I tried to wake you the first time but couldn't. I think you could have PTSD."

"Post-Traumatic Stress Disorder?"

"I'm not trying to diagnose you." He set his bow on the ground. "But nightmares can be a symptom of PTSD. Have you had problems with bad dreams before?"

I thought of the months after Jace had died and the nightmares that had driven me to run. When Elle had found out I had been running rather than sleeping, she had suggested the cruise to take my mind off Jace. I nodded.

"You need to talk about it. That's something they recommend for PTSD."

I knew he wanted me to talk about Jace. "I thought you weren't diagnosing me."

He scowled. "I'm not. Don't change the subject."

I could stay on subject. Kind of. "Jimmy's always there. Sometimes Elle and Maria are too, or my family."

Braedon peered at me, his body tense. "Why won't you talk about him?"

I jumped to my feet, but he got in my way. When I tried to go around him, he pinned me to his chest. "Let me go!"

"You always run away. Stay and talk about it."

Weariness swept through me, far beyond the physical stresses of the last few weeks. I stopped fighting and leaned against him, closing my eyes. He circled his arms around me. It made me feel like I did at the end of my nightmares, safe and secure.

"Tell me about him."

I lifted my head. "I won't give him anymore time or energy."

"You really don't see it, do you? He's consuming you, even now."

This time when I pulled away, he let me go—except for one hand.

"Lyn, I can't fight a dead man."

The pain in his voice made me stop. "What do you mean?"

"He has power over you because you won't talk about him." Braedon eased me closer. "He's already come between us once. Tell me it wasn't Ja—"

My fingers flew to his lips, stopping him from saying the name I hadn't spoken aloud since that hospital visit. Elle wouldn't have told Braedon; she had promised. "How do you know his name? Was it Jori?"

He shifted his face away from my hand, his jaw tight. "That's not important."

So it was Jori.

"Say the name, Lyn."

I looked at Braedon and tried to say it. I really did. With my eyes squeezed shut, I concentrated on forcing my lips to form it.

He stepped away, fixating me with hard eyes. "Jace. The bastard's name was Jace."

I tensed reflexively. But instead of pain, Braedon's words brought me incredible satisfaction. I savored the venom and disgust in his tone. "Say it again."

The corners of his mouth twitched, his face softening. "I will … but only after you say it."

Training my eyes firmly on Braedon's, I said, "The bastard's name was Jace."

Braedon cupped my cheek in one hand and said slowly, giving each word special emphasis, "I'm. Not. Jace." He brushed my cheek with his thumb. "I can't change what happened, but I can promise I will never do that to you."

I stared at him and knew he was telling me the truth. I had seen him in the best and the worst of conditions. Of course he wouldn't. I slid my arms around his waist and rested my head on his shoulder. As his arms pulled me close, the familiar feeling brought with it not just a sense of security but of coming home.

He held me in silence for a minute. "You should write Jace a letter."

I looked at him. "Um, he's dead."

"Lucky for him," Braedon growled, and I smiled. "I'm serious about the letter. It's therapeutic to tell the person who's hurt you all the things you want to say."

Braedon had never meant so much to me. He understood me in this, maybe better than I did myself. My heart swelled. I had never thought to meet someone who could make me feel safe on so many levels. I swallowed. "We don't have any paper."

"You can use some of my bark. The sand would also work, but I want you to have something you can throw away." He grinned, a hard gleam in his eyes. "I want you to throw him away."

Sitting, I watched as Braedon retrieved a charred stick from the fire and some of his precious bark pieces. He went back to work on his bow while I wrote. And wrote and wrote. I filled three large sections before I had written it all.

I told Jace I had given him my love and my trust, that I

had thought his words of love and forever had been true. His actions had proved his words to be empty lies that had stolen my self-esteem and made me question if I even deserved to be loved. But he was the liar. He was the cheat. I was done with carrying his betrayal around me like chains. No more.

The setting sun stretched our shadows to the rim of the jungle as we walked together to a large boulder on the beach. Braedon steadied me as I climbed on top of the farthest one out and chucked the bark pieces as far out as I could. As they caught the wind and flew up and then down into the waves, I felt light, like I could fly, no longer burdened by Jace's dishonesty.

Braedon gave me a hand down into the ankle-deep water and put his arm around my shoulders, watching with me as the ocean took the pieces away.

"That felt good." I turned to face him, surprised to see pride in his eyes. I thought about how he had pointed out the elderly couple, of his expression when he concentrated on a piece of music, his courage in stepping forward to check the dead captain. His unquestioning support of my plan to fight the pirates. He had never complained about my nightmares but held me until I slept again. Braedon had freed my heart.

I reached up and cupped his face, his scruffy beard rough in my hands. The words I thought I would never say again flowed easily from my mouth, "I love you, Braedon." I brushed his lips with mine.

The breeze ruffled his hair, and he smiled, his look making me feel warm all over. "I love you too, my Gwendolyn."

I grinned as our lips met again, for once liking the sound of my name.

CHAPTER 18

*M*Y EUPHORIA lasted for days, during which we nearly finished the tree house. Then one afternoon, Braedon, unusually subdued, returned with the fish for dinner.

"I've got the spit ready for you." I bounced over to him, throwing my arms around his neck to kiss him. I couldn't seem to touch him enough, as though I had to reassure myself it wouldn't all disappear.

He returned my embrace, but he didn't laugh as usual at my enthusiasm, instead giving me a preoccupied peck. Rather stiffly, he went to work on the fish. A sense of unease filled me, and I returned to cutting up the fruit. Watching him, I tried to distract myself with the thought that a true sign of love was a man who cleaned and gutted the fish himself.

My old insecurities fought for control, but I could think of no reason why he would be upset. Plus, I had found Braedon to be the kind to get right to the point.

He remained silent about what was bothering him all

throughout our dinner, and it took all my self-control not to quiz him.

When we had finished eating, Braedon exhaled and finally blurted it out. "I was married once. A long time ago." He raised his eyes and met my gaze, his brows squeezed together.

My heart jumped. Did he have kids? No, he would have mentioned children. Why had he been so worried about telling me? I covered his hand with mine. "Do you want to tell me about it?"

His shoulders relaxed. "We were both eighteen and full of ourselves about being old enough to make our own decisions. We eloped." He shook his head. "After six months, my wife got bored playing house with a husband who spent all his time studying. She left me."

I grimaced. "Ouch."

"To be honest, it was a relief. We both knew we'd made a stupid mistake."

"Why did it bother you to tell me?"

Something crossed his face I couldn't read. "I was worried you'd think I'd been hiding something from you."

I slid my arms around his neck, rubbing my cheek against his beard, teasing the real kiss from him that he had deprived me of earlier. A little breathless, I whispered, "Like you said, you're not him."

With a relieved grin, Braedon leaned in for another kiss.

BRAEDON HAMMERED in the last dowel and gave the bamboo a firm push. When it didn't move, he stepped back, scanning our work. "That's it, then."

We stood for a minute with silly grins on our faces, admiring our bamboo tree house. The window openings allowed for plenty of airflow, and the large shutters would keep out most of the rain. Braedon put the hammer down and pulled a small wooden cross from the toolbox, running his fingers over it. I leaned in to read the single word carved into it: Maria.

I took it from him, blinking. "When did you make this? It's beautiful. I can place it while I'm out scavenging." I took his hand. "Do you want to come today?"

He hesitated. "I'd like to, but I've got some … stuff to work on."

Tilting my head, I scrutinized him with narrowed eyes. He was up to something. "Stuff?"

"One project is to work on plans for a raft."

I shuddered. Just thinking about going out on the water almost guaranteed me nightmares.

Braedon put his hands on the back of my neck, his gentle touch sending shivers down my spine. "We won't go out until you're ready."

Meaning it was my job to get myself ready. I sighed and kissed him. "I'm working on it."

$\mathcal{K}$NEELING BY the mound under the shady edge of the jungle, I surveyed my work. I gave the little cross an unnecessary nudge and smoothed out the white sand around the blossoms, breathing in their sweet fragrance.

Would Jimmy and Maria have stayed together once the cruise was over? I sniffed, wiping my nose. I shifted around to face the ocean, staring at the waves crashing against the rocks. If we were going to get off the island, I had to remember my reasons for going on the cruise in the first place. My love of being at sea. My love of water. But all those recent ship memories just made me want to cry.

My mind drifted to daydreams of what it would be like to go home. What would my father say when I introduced him to Braedon? A vision came to me of him sitting comfortably in a lounge chair in my parents' backyard, chatting with my dad while he grilled burgers. Or Braedon shooting some hoops with my brother, Marc.

And my mother—I could see her turning from Braedon to face me and fanning herself, her eyes big and round. The image made me laugh out loud. Yes. These were the things I needed to think about, to plan for, to cling to as I prepared to face the ocean again. We would get home, and all the people I loved would be together again.

A crackling of branches behind me followed immediately by a snuffling noise startled me. I dashed to the water before my brain took control of my instincts, and I stopped. Peering at the heavy foliage, I couldn't make out any animals, but the birds had quieted.

Carefully, I bent over and picked up a decent-sized rock. I cocked my arm back, taking in a deep breath for a kiai, releasing both with as much force as I had. The birds squawked and scattered into the air, and whatever was in the jungle ran away from the noise, its departure marked by the sound of breaking twigs.

Jogging, I headed back up the beach toward our camp. Braedon needed to know there was larger game on this end of the island.

As I reached toward the hanging vegetation to enter our lagoon, it suddenly swished aside. With a yelp, I staggered back, nearly falling to the ground.

Braedon poked his head around the lush foliage, his eyebrows raised. "I apologize for distressing you, my lady. You may enter." He pointed his right arm back toward the lagoon, his left arm holding back the vines.

I stepped past him and paused, my eyes drawn to the four burning bamboo torches. "What's this?"

Our work area, normally scattered with various siesta projects, had been transformed. A small bamboo table sat on a blanket of banana leaves, a coconut bowl filled with flowers set in the center.

I looked at Braedon, who had moved beside me, and I had to cover my mouth. With the vines around him, I hadn't noticed his wardrobe. Along with his ratty T-shirt, he wore a banana leaf bowtie. A bright purple flower peeked out his shirt pocket. His clothing, along with his nappy beard and shaggy hair, was such a contrast to my memory of him in his tuxedo that I giggled.

Braedon raised one eyebrow, his body stiff with mock dignity. Not wanting to spoil whatever he had planned, I smoothed my features. He raised his elbow for me to take and led me to the table, seating me on a banana leaf blanket and placing one of my small woven mats on my lap.

He set before me a clever banana leaf bowl filled with pieces of ripe pineapple. I looked up, expecting him to sit with me, but he continued to stand like a servant waiting to receive a command.

"This is when I would need a clone," he muttered. "I can't be your dinner partner and waiter at the same time."

I reached over and ran my hand up the back of his calf. "I'd rather have you as my dinner partner. I'd rather have you as any kind of partner."

Braedon crossed his legs and sat on the mat to my left.

Since there was only the one bowl, I pushed it between us. I picked up the chop sticks he had carved and chose a large piece of the ripe fruit, one that would come apart easily. Our eyes met as I raised the pineapple to my lips, slowly biting off the end.

I rose on my knees and leaned in to kiss him, enjoying the shared taste of pineapple. He put a stop to it when I smushed his bow tie.

When I finished the last bite, he stood and took the little bowl away, returning with a banana leaf plate of fruit bat meat and a mound of breadfruit. I lifted the meat and something fell on my plate.

Braedon, who had remained standing, went down on one knee beside me. "Go ahead. Pick it up."

With shaking hands, I lifted the dark brown circle, turning it toward the light. At the center of the ring was a small, flattish object. The light from the torches cast it with a soft, warm cream color that changed as I tilted it toward the flame.

He took the ring from me. My heart raced like I had just run a marathon as he lifted my left hand to his lips. "My Gwendolyn."

My eyes filled with tears.

Braedon brushed a loose strand of hair from my face. "Will you marry me?"

I threw my arms around his neck, loving the feeling of him pulling me close.

He tilted his head to look at me. "Is that a yes?"

"Of course it's yes, you silly man."

His rough kiss made my toes tingle. He took my left hand and slid the slender wooden band on my ring finger.

I held it up, tipping it back and forth to catch the light.

Braedon touched it. "I can't guarantee the pearl will stay. You'll want to keep it somewhere safe."

I sighed. "It could be a very long engagement."

"It's a full moon tomorrow night. Let's exchange vows then."

"Isn't that a little fast?"

"Do you want to wait until we get off the island?" He reached over and ran his thumb down my cheek. "It won't change the way I feel."

It wouldn't make any difference to me either. I turned my face and pressed my lips against his.

WE CELEBRATED the completion of the tree house by spending the entire afternoon the next day getting ready for the wedding, including working on vows.

From our little tree house deck, I admired the glitter of the full moon on the water. I leaned on the railing, holding the wedding lei I had made for Braedon. He stepped up behind me, resting a hand on my shoulder, and then sliding it around my waist. I shivered.

"There's a little fruit bat up there to witness our nuptials." He pointed to the top of the Banyan tree.

I leaned my head back against him for a second, completely calm. If anyone had told me at the start of the cruise that I would be getting married in a few months, I would have laughed. So much for all the plans I had made.

Facing him, I put the bright orange and yellow lei over his head and settled it on his shoulders, inhaling the sweet scent. He put a red and pink lei headdress on top of my head. A flower veil.

I pulled one of the three lengths of threaded flowers over my shoulder to admire. "I think you've missed your calling. You should open a flower shop."

Braedon grunted. "If I had my phone, I could take orders."

Laughing, I said, "Okay. Maybe not."

Suddenly serious, he took my hands in his, lifting first one and then the other to his lips. "Gwendolyn Byington North, I, Braedon Fredrick Randolph, take you to be my wife and my friend, to join with you and to share what is to come, to be your faithful husband; a commitment made in love, kept in faith, and eternally made new."

I blinked furiously; I wanted to be able to see him. "I, Gwendolyn Byington North, take you, Braedon Fredrick Randolph, to be my husband, my friend and partner in life, my one true love. I will trust you and love you faithfully through the good times and the bad times, regardless of the obstacles we may face together. I give you my hand, my heart, and my love forever."

Braedon pulled another ring he had carved from his pocket, wider this time and with no gems, and placed it on my left hand. "As I place this ring on your finger, I commit my heart and life to you. I declare to the world that you are mine."

I had woven one for him from my hair. I tugged the hair ring on his finger and met his gaze. "I give you this ring as a symbol of my love and my faith in our strength together."

Braedon took my face in his hands, his thumbs moving down my cheeks, his warm lips soft as they touched mine. He slid one hand to the back of my head while dropping the other to my back, pressing me closer as he deepened the kiss.

I wrapped my arms around his neck, clinging to him as I turned to putty and molded myself against him. The racing of my heart beat a harmony with his where our chests touched. He was mine, and my soul was complete.

Putting his arm behind my knees, he lifted me and carried me through the doorway into our home.

CHAPTER 19

*T*HE FIRST project after our wedding was the construction of a shower. Even though it was not as complicated to build as the house had been, it was still dirty work.

Braedon grinned as he rubbed his skin with the poufy plant to absorb the moisture from our shower. "You were right." His eyes danced. "We should have done this before the tree house. I definitely prefer the view." He picked up a leaf-wrapped parcel and handed it to me.

I unfolded it and stared at the object inside: a carved and surprisingly smooth wooden hair pick. "It's exquisite!" I exclaimed, running my fingers over it.

Braedon held his hand out for me to give it back, taking the end of my mass of hair.

I tried pulling away. "My hair's so nasty and greasy."

He raised one eyebrow and began gently running the pick through the strands. "Aislinn's always had long hair, and my father never had much patience with her about it when we'd go camping. I knew you'd need this."

It took a long time for him to work his way up to my scalp.

"Thank you, my husband." I accepted the comb, running it through my hair before pulling two clumps over my shoulders for a Lady Godiva look.

He strategically adjusted a lock of hair. "Well, my wife, I might even like this look better than that bikini of yours on the ship."

My face flamed at the memory. "You weren't supposed to see me in that."

"That was obvious from the look on your face. That suit haunted my dreams for days." Chuckling, he kissed me and went to work on his bowstring.

I slipped into my damp tankini and sat down to examine Braedon's shirt. I had agreed to mend his clothes when I found I couldn't hit anything with an arrow.

His clothing had gotten so threadbare I spent far too much time sewing up tears. His T-shirt was getting to be mostly stitches.

I sighed in frustration. "If we're here much longer, we're going to end up in grass skirts." We had already discovered the need for some kind of clothing. Partly for protection from the jungle, but mostly because we never got anything done otherwise.

"Not for me, my wife. I'll wear a manly breechcloth." He eyed me knowingly. "We'll have to risk it."

Braedon was referring to his find of a couple of days ago when he had returned from checking out the sounds I had heard by Maria's grave. Wild boars.

"It's too dangerous," I had said when he proposed we hunt them.

"We can use the skin for clothing and I will be glad for the change in diet." He had shot me a sly look. "They have lots of fat on them."

"Fat," I had said with longing, distracted from my fear. "Maybe we can get enough fat to make some soap." He knew my obsession with cleaning my hair. I had once tried using sand to absorb the oils from my scalp, and it had taken him almost half an afternoon to help me get it out of my hair, with him laughing the whole time.

As I sat there by the shower considering Braedon's frayed T-shirt, my fear of a boar hunt returned. I looked at him as he worked on his bow. He seemed so confident and capable that he always managed to convince me.

I stitched a hole in his shirt. Maybe he was right. Maybe we could pull it off. I started a litany of confident statements, but deep down, I was still doubtful.

IT TOOK a couple of days to prepare before we were ready to go hunting. Since we planned to cook the beast in the ground, luau style, we had to dig a big pit. We also built a bamboo corral of sorts in the event we caught one of them alive.

My stomach persisted in churning all day. I didn't mention my worries to Braedon because I wanted to be a team player and was worried I would sound like a whiner. I held up the carrot of homemade soap as a personal incentive.

None of my efforts could control my dreams, however, which changed that night from a watery nightmare to dark fantasies of a fiendish boar with huge tusks ripping Braedon to shreds.

When I woke him for the third time, he asked, "It's different tonight, isn't it?"

I remained silent.

"Lyn. Don't hold back from me."

I told him about the dream.

He pulled me tight, his voice soothing. "You're only scared because you've never hunted before. We'll be fine. Didn't we agree we need this animal?"

I didn't argue, but I wasn't convinced.

$\mathcal{B}$RAEDON PUSHED through the jungle and headed toward me, where I sat next to the fire.

"We're about ready. Come running when I whistle." He paused and eyed me wickedly. "Hmmm ... I like the idea of you coming when I whistle."

"Then you'd better get a dog." I nodded to the jungle. "Where?"

He pointed to a spot on the edge of the foliage.

My stomach knotted. He squeezed my shoulder and left. I closed my eyes with a shiver. We were really going to do it.

A few minutes passed before he whistled. A few minutes where I sat with butterflies fluttering in my gut—that turned into hawks dive-bombing at the lining of my stomach at his signal. I swept up my spear, hands sweaty, and dashed in the direction of the whistle, my heart battering the inside of my chest. Blinded by fear, I didn't see Braedon and was about to plow past him when he grabbed me from behind. He stopped my cry with a swift hand.

"Don't spook them; they're up ahead about thirty yards." He slid his hand from my mouth, turning the gesture into a caress of my cheek. "They're in the closed valley, so they have no place to go but toward us. Their instinct will be to run, but they'll fight if cornered. I've set up several snares along the path, and we only have to drive them in that direction."

I shook my head in denial. No way could it be as easy as he made it out. "What happens if they don't want to go?"

"Use your spear, but remember we're only the sheep dogs driving the cattle," Mr. Calm said.

The knot in my stomach tightened as an image from my dream flashed through my mind.

Braedon gave my neck a peck and stepped around and in front of me, signaling that I should follow as he filed ahead. I stepped behind him along the path for a few yards, and then he stopped and turned.

"I want you to go up there—very quietly." He pointed to a dead end. "Make lots of noise when I raise my third finger. The only place they can go will be toward me. Loudly follow up behind them—but not too close. If we're lucky, one or two will hit my snares."

Gripping my spear, I advanced softly to the spot he had indicated. I took slow, deep breaths. From a distance, I could see the animals rooting in the ground. I glanced back at him; he had raised his right fist.

One finger. I took a cleansing breath.

Two fingers. I relaxed my knees, preparing to run.

Three fingers. I burst from my hiding place, bounding through the jungle. Using one of my best karate kiais, I waved my arms, spear in hand.

The animals bolted just as Braedon had predicted, running straight ahead. When they began to veer off his intended path, he shouted, driving them back against the steep cliff. I took up a rear position, still yelling. It seemed ridiculously easy.

At first.

Then this big, old boar turned back. Toward me.

The beast was fast. I came to my senses and threw my

spear. It hit the boar in the head ... and bounced off. Now he looked ticked!

Spinning, I took off. "Braedon!"

I darted toward a tree with low branches. Twigs and brush ripped at my exposed legs and arms. The thudding sounds of the beast's feet drew closer. The huffing of its breath urged me on.

The tree. I had to get up the tree.

My back prickled as the creature got closer. Then the tree was in reach. I grabbed a lower branch and swung up. But not fast enough. The boar sliced my left calf before running on. An arrow whizzed past me and struck the beast in the rear haunch. It squealed and continued to run with an unbalanced stride. Another arrow struck, bringing it down.

Braedon charged past me with my spear in his hand and slammed it into the animal's ribs. It went still. As he pulled the spear from the boar, he called back to me, "You okay?"

With shaking hands, I dropped from the branch. Pain shot up from my calf. I cried out and staggered, trying to keep all my weight on my right leg. Something warm and moist trickled down my calf.

At my cry, Braedon dashed to me. As soon as he saw the bleeding cut, he swore and picked me up, jogging to our camp on the beach.

"Sit still while I boil some water," he commanded. "Is your tetanus shot current?"

I nodded and clenched my teeth. "Should I put pressure on it?"

"No. It's not bleeding that bad, and the blood will help flush out the wound."

Braedon poked at the embers of the fire. Fortunately, I had already boiled water, even if it had cooled somewhat by now.

He pulled his ragged shirt off to use as a potholder and rinsed out a bottle before filling it with sterilized water. Setting it aside, he poured the rest of our bottles into the pot.

He handed me the bottle with the sterilized water and examined the cut more closely. When he poked around the wound, I moaned as a wave of dizziness and nausea hit me. "None of the muscle tissue appears to have been damaged."

He grabbed his pack and pulled out the catamaran's emergency kit. He lifted my leg and, without looking up, held out his hand. "Bottle."

I passed it to him, wondering if he acted like this during surgery. The image of me as a nurse made me start to laugh, but it turned to a gasp as he poured the still-hot water on my leg. I reflexively tried to jerk away, but his powerful grip held me in place.

Braedon looked at me. "You okay?"

I nodded, clenching my jaw.

He opened up two of the antiseptic wipes, giving his hands a thorough scrub. "Pour the rest of the water over my hands. Slowly." When the water was gone, he had me squeeze some of the antibiotic ointment onto his finger. He spread it into the oozing cut. "Unless it gets infected, you should have a clean scar. You can consider it a war wound."

I stuck my tongue out at him.

"Is that an insult or an invitation?"

Before I could respond, he made it an invitation.

When Braedon had finished with my leg, it looked like it could have been done in an emergency room. Unfortunately, it hurt too much for me to help him haul the beast and two live babies back to camp.

CHAPTER 20

TWENTY MONTHS LATER

*M*Y JAWS clenched tight, I rowed as fast as I could, blinking against the salty spray, frantic to avoid the rocks. Would the softwood hold up if we hit them? Please, please hold up. I had thought going out for a test run would be bad enough. I never imagined coming back might kill us. Another wave smashed over us, driving the softwood outrigger closer to the narrow gap in the boulders.

With aching muscles, I drove my oar into the ocean, swallowing a sob. No sharks. I wouldn't think of sharks.

"Lyn!" Braedon roared, tossing his oar aside and throwing himself at me.

We flew over the side and into a wave, which washed us between the crags. Even as my head went underwater, I could hear the crash of shattering wood. Coughing and gasping, we made it to shore, collapsing on the sand.

My shoulder ached where I had broken my collarbone during our first tropical cyclone. Our injuries had delayed us from working on an escape clear into our second monsoon season. Not again. After giving up on rafts, it had taken us weeks to hollow out a softwood tree. I covered my mouth as tears mixed with the seawater.

The stress had been mounting with every failure. I had often wished our paradisiacal existence lived up to the fantasy, where we only had to walk out the door and pick food off a tree. The reality had us working to near exhaustion.

Slumped over his knees beside me, Braedon suddenly arched his back and let out a roar, the veins in his neck bulging. He raised his clenched fists, slamming them into the sand, the pink scar on his forearm from his cyclone injury turning bright red as the sand flew into the air. It reminded me of him trying to pull me to safety with that mangled mess of an arm. I had vowed then to face my fear of the ocean. Yeah. Look how well that had turned out.

He suddenly twisted to face me, his eyes a little wild, filled with his frustration and fear. I shared his fear … and the desperation. The monsoons would be here again soon. Braedon grabbed me and pressed his salty lips hard against mine, his hands clutching the back of my neck, pulling me down to the sand.

By the time an incoming wave touched our feet, our frantic emotions were spent. We lay in the sand. I didn't think I could get up. Lightning flashed in the distance, and another wave tickled my feet. Instinctively, I untangled myself from Braedon and pulled my knees up.

He watched me, his dark brown eyes drained of hope. The image of the barbeque scene in my father's backyard, the one that had given me the strength to get out on that stupid outrigger in the first place, flashed through my mind. It had to happen.

It had to. I picked up Braedon's ponytail and ran the wet end across his cheek above his beard. "We can't give up."

Brushing a strand of hair behind my ear, Braedon gave me a weak nod. He rose in one fluid movement and pulled me to my feet.

With our arms around each other, we headed toward the lagoon. Braedon pulled aside the curtain of vines, but I turned back toward the water. Against the darkness of the approaching storm, the last of the wreckage of our softwood outrigger—and our dreams—crashed against the rocks.

I rested my head against his shoulder. "Softwood isn't going to work."

He exhaled. "We'll have to use hardwood."

"But the softwood took weeks to hollow out."

He turned to face the jungle. "Does it matter how long it takes? You said it. We can't give up. No matter how long it takes."

We had barely chosen the tree when they came.

𝓘 HAD JUST stepped out of the shower into the late afternoon shadow. I paused, thinking I heard voices, and shook my head at the ridiculous thought.

Then a boy's laugh made me jump. A man called something in a language I couldn't understand. It reminded me of the pirates, and my blood ran cold.

I wiggled into my clothes and stole toward the lower falls. I needed to warn Braedon, yet I couldn't resist taking a peek through the cascading vines. When I couldn't see movement through the filter of leaves, I began to creep out for a better view.

Abruptly a hand grabbed me from the side, and my scream choked off as another hand covered my mouth. I felt a surge of adrenaline until I recognized Braedon. I relaxed and turned to face him.

He had his bow slung over his shoulder along with a quiver of arrows. With a finger held against his lips, he handed me my spear. Nodding in the general direction of the voices, he stole into the jungle. I followed, not sure if I should feel happy or scared. My stomach churned in anticipation.

Peering through the plants, we saw several outrigger canoes on the shore some distance from the opening to the lagoon, perhaps a third of the way to the catamaran. No people. Braedon tapped my arm and indicated we should continue in the direction of the voices.

Still hidden in the jungle foliage, we found them looking at the wreckage of the catamaran. Braedon put a finger to his lips again, and I nodded. We watched.

There were ten Polynesians—six boys, ranging from about fourteen to eighteen years old, and four adult men. They were looking over the catamaran and examining the general area. The boys spoke English.

We stood in the jungle not far from Maria's grave, where I had put fresh flowers just that morning. When a couple of the boys wandered over to it, I held my breath. Braedon tensed beside me, slowly lifting his bow with a nocked arrow. My heart pounded in alarm. Surely he wouldn't have to use it.

One of the boys noticed the little wooden cross on Maria's grave. "Dad! There's a grave here!"

The men closest to them turned and hurried over. Most of the others followed.

"See, Dad?"

The boy's father knelt down at the grave and touched the little marker.

"Who buried her?" his son asked.

The father touched the fresh flowers and stood abruptly, peering into the jungle and up and down the beach. He backed up with his arms outstretched, forcing the others to move away from the jungle.

As if on cue, Braedon stepped out and raised his bow.

The four men seized the boys, pulling them behind them. The father raised his hands and met Braedon's eyes, saying in English, "We don't have weapons."

"What's on your waist, then?" Braedon nodded toward the knife on the man's belt.

An electric thrill crackled through me as I noticed something. I dashed out of the jungle and pushed down Braedon's bow.

"They're Boy Scouts." I pointed at the BSA T-shirt one of the men wore and advanced toward the father with my hand held out. "Are you from American Samoa? I'm Lyn North—"

"Lyn Randolph," Braedon corrected, following closely behind me.

Smiling, I repeated, "Lyn Randolph. This is my husband, Braedon. We've been stranded here for over two years. You're a God send!"

There was no keeping the boys back then, and everyone began to talk at once. Finally, the father put two fingers in his mouth and whistled. Everyone stopped talking. "My name is Moli Tatupu and, yes, we're from American Samoa." He glanced at the catamaran and then back at us. "I think I know who you are. You're those cruise ship people who got taken by pirates a couple years ago."

"What happened to the others?" I clutched Mr. Tatupu's arm. "Did they get away? Was anyone else hurt?"

His face became sympathetic. "Yes, they got away, and no, no one else was hurt too bad. They took the pirates' ship right out from under them in the middle of a storm. The only ones they couldn't find were the four on the catamaran." He looked at the boat again and back at us, his eyebrows raised.

Braedon answered the unasked question. "Jimmy was shot in the escape and died a few hours later. Maria died when the catamaran crashed here."

Anger flashed in Mr. Tatupu's eyes. "I remember the story well because the captain of this boat was my good friend."

Braedon's expression darkened. "I'm sorry for your loss." An awkward moment passed before he pointed back toward the lagoon. "We've got a camp up the beach not far from where you landed. Why don't we all go back there and get something to eat, and we can talk?"

I could have floated in the air as we strolled up the beach. Mr. Tatupu introduced everyone.

"How is it you came to this island, Mr. Tatupu?" Braedon asked.

"Call me Moli. We're here on a summer camping and boating trip. The boys need the experience for merit badges." He chuckled. "Our trip isn't exactly sanctioned by the organization, so it's an unofficial extended father/son overnighter." Moli examined the tall mountain. "My father told me about visiting an island in this area many years ago, so we came looking for it. It's not near any of the regular shipping routes. That's probably why it's been left alone so long."

Braedon met my eyes. "We could have been stuck here for the rest of our lives."

Moli nodded. "I think I'm the only one my father told about it. He said he first heard of it from a European. He wanted to build a vacation resort here but got hurt and gave up."

I grinned at Braedon. "Well, that explains that."

Moli's son, Lua, who had been listening as he walked behind us, asked, "Explains what?"

"You'll see when we get to our camp." Braedon's eyes twinkled.

As we approached the lagoon, Braedon and I took the lead. With a host-like manner, Braedon pulled back the hanging foliage and swung his arm out. I went first, ducking under the greenery and walking ahead to our work area by the falls.

The men gave appropriate *oohs* and *ahhs* as they inspected our workmanship. The boys got excited when I pointed out Braedon's fish trap, which already had two fish in it. Isaac Patu and his son Etano were especially impressed with the shower.

Etano looked around and noted, "You wouldn't have very good protection in here from the weather."

Smirking, Braedon and I said together, "We have a tree house."

"Where?" asked Lua, lifting his head from where he checked the fish trap.

I pointed to the pathway leading to the plateau, and the younger boys darted for it.

Lua, who stayed to hike up the hill with us, said, "This must be the explanation you mentioned. Did you build the tree house?"

"Yes and no." Braedon explained what we had found. "We had to do repairs, but it saved us a lot of work."

"But we did build the tree house," I said, "more than once."

When we reached the top of the plateau, one of the younger boys called back to ask if they could look inside.

Moli looked at me, and I nodded. He yelled to them, "You can go up but don't touch anything." He then turned to us. "You two have done pretty good here. I hope you understand we don't have room to take you back with us. We'll inform the authorities you're here and have someone come and pick you up."

My heart sank, and I clutched Braedon's arm. He remained silent, his face expressionless, but he couldn't hide the disappointment in his eyes.

Lua, the oldest of the boys and nearly eighteen, had stayed with us. "Sure we could, Dad. We've used up half our food. They could use that space."

The fathers shuffled, uncomfortable; it was clear they didn't want to take us. I couldn't blame them.

"I don't know, Lua." Moli didn't look at us.

Lua turned and faced his father. "If I was lost from my family for two years and people came who could take me home right away, I'd want to go with them too."

Hope surged through me, and I blinked back tears as I mouthed a 'thank you' to him. He grinned.

Isaac grunted. "We can talk about it, Moli."

I squeezed Braedon's hand as he led the way to our working area. Giving him a kiss, I held his gaze for an intense moment before we gathered food for dinner. We had to convince them to take us.

As I gathered more fruit, my hands shook and my stomach roiled. I told myself it didn't matter what they decided. We were getting off the island soon, one way or another. But we had to go with them now. I couldn't shake the feeling that if they left without us, no one else would ever come again. They had to take us with them. They just had to.

When everyone returned to the fire, the Scouts added their portion and we shared an excellent meal. In spite of the stress of not knowing what they would decide, it turned into a banquet.

CHAPTER 21

I THOUGHT WE did a good job making our case, but it was the combined efforts of Lua and Etano that convinced Moli and Isaac, the two in charge, to let us come with them. The next day we were packing the four canoes.

I would get to see Elle and my family again.

Lua and Etano sailed with Braedon in their boat, while I went with Moli and his younger son, Kalolo. It was logical to split up the inexperienced passengers.

As we pulled away from the shore, the sky turning pink as the sun peeked over the horizon, a strange feeling swept through me. I couldn't wait to leave the place, yet as I watched the early morning breeze flutter the vines that led to the lagoon, my heart twisted. This had been our first home, the place where Braedon and I had become a family.

I glanced at his boat. He was watching the receding island as well. I wondered what he thought about leaving. He twisted back toward me and met my gaze. Eyes glittering, he smiled at me and then turned to answer a question from one of the boys.

Moli and Kalolo were seasoned sailors, and we pulled away

from the island in no time. The farther we got from land, the more my hands shook.

"You okay, Lyn?" Moli asked after we cleared the hardest part of the current that drove the crashing waves into the beach.

I took a deep, calming breath and forced my hands to unclasp, trying hard not to think of my nightmares. "I'll be fine."

He squinted at me over his shoulder. "Why did you go on a cruise if the water frightens you?"

"It didn't used to scare me." I shifted to drumming my fingers on the supplies stored between my feet, trying not to notice how close the deep water was. "Until the sharks ate Jimmy."

Kalolo choked from behind, and Moli turned around to gape at me, both of them pausing in their strokes.

I continued, my eyes burning, "We had to bury him at sea, and then sharks showed up. I've had nightmares about it ever since." All the talking I had done with Braedon about it hadn't made them go away completely. I scanned the huge expanse of ocean around us, rocking in my seat. "I'm hoping this trip will help me face my fears."

"Those monsters left so many scars," Moli mumbled, his voice gruff.

Grateful for the distraction, I focused my attention on Moli. "Were all the pirates captured? What happened to them?"

Moli gave me a gleeful look. "They caught them all, and everyone got life in prison."

*T*HE WEATHER, which had been decent since the squall that had ruined our outrigger, became stormy on the third day out. As the water got choppier and the clouds darker, images of our last tropical storm on the catamaran flashed through my mind. Had we really begged them to bring us along?

Moli and Kalolo began what became a personal battle with the ocean, fighting against the waves to keep us upright. Between the pelting rain and swells, we lost sight of the other boats, and a sense of dread filled me. I told myself not to make too much of it, that it was my inexperience which frightened me … but then I intercepted a look Moli exchanged with Kalolo.

"Oh, God," I prayed, my hands turning cold.

Moli swiftly reached in front of him—almost without any change in his rhythm—and pulled out something he tossed back at me. I grabbed it just before a wave caught it; it was a small bucket. My heart sank, and I went to work bailing out the water.

The rain, wind, and waves were like a curtain that kept us cocooned alone in our own little world. I'm sure it was only Moli's and Kalolo's superb seamanship that kept us afloat.

Between scoops, I tried to spot the other boats, to spot Braedon. I needed to see him.

My arms and back ached. Dip and scoop. I forced my arms to keep moving. Dip and scoop. My burning muscles made a mockery of my hope for this trip to fix my fear of the water.

I didn't notice when the rain slowed to a drizzle and the waves grew smaller. My hazy mind continued to make my arms follow their painful, mechanical rhythm. I stopped only when Moli's shaking hands reached back and gently pushed my hands down. With bleary eyes, I looked up.

In the dim light of the crescent moon, I couldn't see the other boats. We appeared to be alone. The sound of my heartbeat pulsed in my ears; my eyes stung. Where were the others? I pressed my arms against my stomach. Surely we hadn't managed to survive pirates and a shipwreck only to die while being rescued.

No. The storm had just separated us. They hadn't gone down.

Moli pulled a whistle from under his shirt and blew a loud blast. After the roar of the storm, its shrill sound stabbed my brain. He waited a minute, listening. When he heard nothing, he blew it again and paused to await a response. After the third blow, we heard an answering whistle far away. Hope rushed back into me.

Moli changed his sequence and blew two blasts, repeating this every minute or so.

Kalolo leaned toward me and whispered, "It's our signal. He's giving them directions, and the two blows identify us. They'll come to us."

I sat, exhausted, massaging the aching muscles in my arms and trying to ignore the sick feeling of worry in my gut.

At last, we saw the faint outline of an outrigger in the dim moonlight. Kalolo called out, and someone from the boat shouted back, but they were too far for us to understand. We had to wait for a few more of Moli's whistle blows before we could identify Isaac Patu and two of the boys. It was such a relief to know they were safe, yet my stomach twisted as I scanned the horizon and saw no sign of another boat.

While they made their way to us, the shrill sound of another whistle from the other side reached us. My heart sped up again. Moli continued his regular whistle blows as we waited for the third boat to reach us.

As it approached, we could see something was wrong, which explained its slow progress. When they were close enough for us to understand their shouts, we saw it was two fathers, Eli and Sila, with the youngest boy in the group, Ieti. As Moli continued his now strained whistle blowing, Isaac pulled his boat along Eli's, and they went to work to fix the damage.

Moli persisted with his blowing, and I learned how a whistle could reflect the stress of the blower. The sound grated on my nerves.

They completed the repairs, and our vigil continued. The others sat silently in their boats, keeping alert between Moli's blasts, sometimes searching hopefully. Still Moli blew his whistle.

The rain had stopped and the sky had cleared when Eli brought his outrigger closer to ours.

"What?" Moli growled, refusing to look at the other father. Moli blew the whistle again.

Eli's face was somber. "How long should we wait? If they haven't answered by now, they can't. We need to get help."

Moli paused for a moment and then slumped. I heard a sob from Kalolo. Isaac, whose son Etano was in the missing boat, started to argue with Eli.

A roaring filled my ears, and an odd mixture of numbness and a sick, stabbing pain swirled in my chest. Everything around me took on that horrible nightmare quality I knew too well. It couldn't be real. I had to be in the middle of a nightmare. The boat would come, and we would all laugh at how scared we had been.

I barely noticed when Eli convinced the other two fathers, and they all went to work to persuade Moli. He finally surrendered. "We'll go get help."

"No!" I shouted. "Their boat's a little more damaged, that's all. It's just taking them longer to get here."

Moli turned haunted eyes to me. "If that was the case, they would have returned my whistle calls. The best we can do now is to get others out looking for them." He twisted back to the front, took his oars, and began to pull methodically through the water. Behind me, crying softly, Kalolo did the same, matching the rhythm of his strokes to his father's.

Shaking my head in denial, I wondered again how Braedon and I could have lived through so much only for this to happen. But then I thought of Maria, who had survived only to die on the rocks. The burning in my eyes intensified.

I would wake up at any moment. Braedon would have his arms around me, comforting me as he always did.

But the nightmare didn't end.

THE NEXT day went by in a blur. All I could remember was the quiet and the rowing. Kalolo had stopped crying. I dozed off and on.

I don't know how those men and boys did it. After the dreadful battle with the sea, they rowed through the night and into morning of the next day, fueled by their desire to get help.

They understood what I didn't. We were close enough to the shipping lanes where help could be close. The sun shone near its peak when they spotted a yacht on the horizon. I should have experienced a rush of excitement to see the vessel, but I felt nothing. All my emotions had been encapsulated within the hard knot in my stomach. I didn't dare let them loose until I knew what I was allowed to feel. I refused to accept that it could be grief.

One of the boys pulled out a large piece of bright fabric and waved it while Moli blew his whistle again. It didn't take long for the yacht to notice us.

When we drew abreast of it, Moli called out, "Can we use your radio? We've lost a boat with three men and need to call for help."

An older middle-aged couple stood beside three crewmembers—one of whom pointed a rifle at us. When the wife saw me in the boat, she leaned into her husband and said something we couldn't hear. He nodded and a crewman put a ladder over the side.

Moli boarded first. As I rose to follow him, the woman's eyes widened when she saw my breechcloth and top. I overheard him say something to the woman about me being stranded. She inspected me with sympathy and reached to help me up into the yacht.

"You poor thing." She put an arm around my shoulders. "Come with me, dear. I'll get you something decent to wear."

As I let her pull me into the main cabin, Moli turned to help the others onto the boat.

"I'm Norma." The woman picked up a throw from the sofa and wrapped it around my shoulders as she pushed me into a chair. "What's your name, dear? How long were you lost?"

"Lyn." My eyes followed Moli, who stood using the cockpit radio. "We've been stranded over two years."

The woman made some sympathetic noises as she worked at her bar. I leaned forward, wishing I could hear what Moli was saying. Norma brought over a glass of juice and some crackers, but Moli had finished on the radio and turned to speak to the man I guessed was Norma's husband.

I stood, dropping the throw. "Excuse me." I went to the cockpit.

Moli and the others had decided to go back and search.

"I want to come."

With sad eyes, Moli shook his head. "No offense, but you'd be a liability. The stormy season is starting early. We saw some of it yesterday, and we don't have much time before another big one is due. We've called the Coast Guard for help, but it could take hours for them to get this far out."

"I can't just leave …," I whispered. The knot of emotions in my stomach tightened further.

Moli wouldn't look at me, and Norma took me by the shoulders, trying to direct me to a cabin. Her husband joined her, standing at my other side, as I watched my new friends board their outriggers and row away.

Abandoned, I found I no longer had the will to resist and let them guide me to a small cabin. Norma pointed out the shower, but I crawled onto the narrow bed, turning my back to the door.

Part 3

CHAPTER 22

*D*REAMS HAUNTED by scenes of Jimmy pulling Braedon and the two boys into shark-infested water drove me up on deck. I stood for hours looking for any sign of Moli, the knot in my gut squeezing tighter and tighter.

Norma came searching for me. Kind and patient, she didn't say anything and just stood with me. When the early morning sun began to paint the clouds on the horizon with a vivid array of pinks and reds, she left for a few minutes only to return with a plate of fresh fruit and crackers.

"You really must eat something." She took my arm and pulled me into a chair, handing me the plate before dragging a small table over. When I took a cube of watermelon, she said, "The authorities have contacted your families."

I stared at her, the knot loosening a little. Would my mom and dad come? Would I see Elle? The knot tightened again. What would they tell Aislinn? What *could* they tell her?

My throat contracted, and I couldn't answer. Norma squeezed my shoulder and left me, returning a while later with a handful of clothing for me to try on. Nothing quite fit, the only thing coming close being a single T-shirt. Yet it still felt strange against my skin, and I took it off as soon as Norma left.

For two days, I never managed to sleep more than a few hours at a time. Once a nightmare jerked me awake, I would return to the deck.

Early on the morning of the third day, the sound of knocking on my cabin door woke me. Being the first time I had not been awakened by a nightmare, it left me confused, expecting to see the tree house walls and feel Braedon snuggled beside me.

"My dear," Norma called through the door. "We've docked, and the authorities are here for you."

I bolted upright from my pile of blankets on the floor. "Is there any word from Moli?"

She hesitated. "I'm sorry, but no."

Leaning against the bed's frame for a minute, I rubbed at the ache in my stomach. Why should today be any different? I rose and stepped into the small restroom and cleaned up.

I hadn't done more than sponge myself off since I had come onboard. My ratty braid fell over my shoulder, and I inspected the dark hollows under my eyes, thinking they went well with those in my cheeks.

A sharp knock on the door made me jump. "Lyn! Open up!" a familiar voice shouted.

I dashed to the door and flung it open. Elle launched herself at me, sobbing as she threw her arms around my neck. The knot in my stomach loosened as I hugged her back. I wasn't alone anymore.

After a moment, I pushed her back to look at her. Her long hair had been cut short in a stylish bob that became her, and her face was fuller than I remembered. Then I noticed the small roundness of her stomach. "Are you pregnant?"

She laughed while her makeup ran down her cheeks. "Yes! I'm married now." She threw her arms around me again. "Oh, Lyn, I can't believe you're alive!"

A baby. My chest felt heavy as I patted Elle's back. Braedon and I had talked about having children when we got home but had tried to assure I wouldn't become pregnant while still on the island. How could we have escaped in an outrigger with a child? Still, we had always fantasized about the family we would one day have.

There was a rustling near the door. I glanced over Elle's shoulder and found Aislinn watching us, her eyes glistening. Immediately I let go of Elle and hugged Aislinn tightly.

When she pulled back, I asked, "Is there any word on Braedon?"

Her quivering lips were answer enough.

The lump in my throat threatened to choke me, and I wanted to crawl back under my blankets.

Sniffing, Aislinn pointed to the ring on my left finger. "Did he carve that?"

"My wedding ring? Yes," I croaked, dropping my hand and twisting the ring.

Aislinn blinked. "Wedding? How …?"

"We exchanged vows." Not sure what to make of her expression, I stepped back. Did she think I was lying?

She grabbed my shoulders and hugged me again. The knot in my stomach broke free, letting loose a surge of pain, and for the first time, I cried.

Finally, exhausted, we sat on the bed. I had dreamed of seeing these women so many times, yet now I didn't know what to say.

Elle shifted uncomfortably. "Those government people are

waiting. We need to get going. Do you have anything else to wear?" She picked up the T-shirt I had cast off. "How about this?"

I stood and wiped my eyes, taking the shirt from her. "It feels weird."

"Well, if you walk around Pago Pago in your current get-up, people are going to get an eyeful." Elle crossed her arms, reminding me of my mother.

At the thought, a sudden craving for my mom's comforting arms around me filled me. I peered out the cabin door. "Are my parents coming?"

Elle and Aislinn exchanged a look that turned me cold.

"What happened?" I pressed my fingers against my lips to stop their quivering.

"They were killed in a car crash about eighteen months ago," Elle said quietly, her eyes shining.

I dropped to the bed again and buried my face in my hands. Both my parents were gone. This wasn't what Braedon and I had planned for, dreamed of. What about my barbeque? I looked up. "And my brother?" I prepared myself for another blow.

Elle's face lightened. "Oh, Marc's fine. He joined the Marines and is stationed overseas. We got word to him before we left that you're alive. We're going to set up a video call."

I let my head fall back. I still had Marc. That at least was something to hold on to.

A shout on deck made us all jump, and Aislinn handed me the T-shirt. "They're waiting."

With a grimace, I slipped it over my head. The small thing only came to the top of my breechcloth, still revealing my bony hips.

Aislinn and Elle led the way up on deck where D'Arcy stood beside a younger man. Elle went to the stranger, who I assumed was her husband, and he put his arms around her. The loving gesture sent me into turmoil, jealousy fighting with embarrassment. How could I be so shallow?

D'Arcy came over and hugged me. "Good to see you again." He pointed toward the ramp to shore. "This way."

Elle and her husband stayed behind to speak to the yacht couple, but I couldn't make out what they were saying. I turned and raised my hand to catch Norma's attention, hoping she would understand my thanks.

On the dock, policemen were fighting to hold back a crowd of people. Cameras flashed, and a uniformed man hurried us into a large van. Were these people there to see me?

Once I had ducked inside behind the Armstrongs, I tugged at my short shirt, trying to cover my exposed hips.

Elle and her husband slid in next to me. "Lyn, this is my husband, Malcolm."

"Everyone just calls me Mal." He shook my hand before removing his button-down shirt and handing it to me.

"Thank you." I spread the shirt over my legs and hips.

I had just leaned my head against the window when a flash went off outside. In a deft movement, Elle's husband switched places with me. He held a newspaper against the window, blocking the view.

"What was that about?" I asked as the van pulled away.

"They're just curious about you." He dropped the paper when we had left the group of people behind.

Elle clasped my hand, and everyone sat in silence. At first, I was glad for some peace after the turbulence on the dock, but soon it started to bug me that no one was telling me anything. "Where are we going?"

"To the police station. We have some questions for you, Ms. North," replied one of the uniformed men in the front.

I flinched at the name. Had it only been a few days ago that I had introduced myself to Moli as Lyn North and Braedon had corrected me? Aislinn, who sat behind me, squeezed my shoulder.

They took us to a large building and had us sit in a conference room. It was air-conditioned—and so freezing to me. Trying not to shiver, I answered dozens of questions about everything that had happened.

Jimmy and Maria were easier to talk about, but a hard knot in my throat prevented me from speaking about Braedon. Mal answered for me with the information he had gotten from the yacht couple. I nodded my agreement.

The officials wanted information about the island, but I couldn't tell them its location. They would have to wait and question Moli when he returned.

After what felt like a frozen eternity, they said they were done with me. They requested that I remain in American Samoa for a couple of days in case they had any additional questions, printed my statement, and handed it to me to sign. I picked up the pen and paused, rolling the cheap tube in my fingers, thinking how strange the plastic felt.

Then I realized I didn't know what name to sign. The knot in my throat tightened, and my eyes filled with tears.

Elle moved to my side. "What is it?"

I couldn't speak and shook my head. The man across the table looked alarmed as he handed me a tissue. I almost signed my maiden name rather than deal with an argument but, at the last moment, I thought of Braedon as we exchanged our vows. I was his wife. I signed Randolph.

The policeman took the paper. When he read my signature, he looked about to challenge me, but I clenched my jaw and stared him down. With a shrug, he made a notation on the paper and said we could go.

Relieved to be outside again, I stopped and stretched out my arms to feel the sun's heat. Elle tapped me on the shoulder and pointed at the van. We were driven to a hotel, and Elle and Aislinn led me to my room.

"I'll bring you something of mine to put on, though it might be a little big on you." Aislinn opened my door. "Once you're dressed, we can go down to dinner."

I hesitated, unable to bear the thought of going into a restaurant full of people staring at me. "I'm not particularly hungry."

"You're so thin," Aislinn argued, examining me again. "You need to eat."

I slipped through the door and turned, leaning on the frame, weariness weighing me down. "I'll order in." I paused, realizing I had no money. "Is it okay if I order in?"

Aislinn and Elle exchanged worried glances, and Elle said, "Of course. Just promise you'll eat something."

"I will." I started to close the door.

Aislinn stopped it with her hand. "If you need anything— and I mean *anything*—Elle's room is on that side of yours, and mine is on the other."

"Thanks." I closed the door and immediately went to turn off the air-conditioning and closed the drapes, shutting out the view of civilization. I paused, unsure what to do. I had nothing to hang in the closet, no interest in what might be on the television, no one to write to with the stationary on the desk. Even the bowl of fruit on the small dining table did nothing but make me slightly nauseous.

I finally decided to take a bath in the oversized spa tub. While the tub filled with hot water, I removed my furry top and breechcloth and set my ring by the sink. I examined my gaunt frame in the mirror. I had thought we had eaten pretty well on the island, but I could see the outline of my ribs.

Once in the tub, I slid down so only my face was exposed. I wished I could force my emotions back into a little knot. I told myself Braedon and the boys might still be found, but on the edges of my mind, I only saw the tiny speck of the outrigger almost indiscernible against the wide expanse of the ocean. I lay in the hot water trying to hold the pain at bay.

When the water grew tepid, I got out and wrapped up in a towel. I thought about how hard it would be to untangle my wet hair … and yelped. I had left the bag with my few island possessions on the yacht. It had all the things Braedon had carved for me, including the hair pick. I leaned against the bathroom wall, slid to the floor, and cried.

CHAPTER 23

I WOKE TO the smell of food and the feel of someone rubbing my shoulder. I surged to a sitting position. "Braedon!"

Elle snapped her hand back. "I'm sorry," she whispered. "It's just me."

I clambered to my knees, clutching the towel around me. "Any news?"

"Nothing yet. The Coast Guard has a massive search going, but a tropical storm is headed that way." Elle helped me up. "You've slept a couple of hours. I ordered you some oatmeal. You should eat it before it gets cold."

With hands now almost too heavy to lift, I slipped on a robe and followed her into the bedroom. She stirred the melting brown sugar into the gray mush, added a bit of milk, and passed me the bowl. My stomach grumbled and I took a big bite—and promptly spat it back into the dish.

"What's wrong?" Elle took the bowl from me and peered at the oatmeal.

I swallowed, trying to get the taste out of my mouth. "It's

too sweet." I grabbed the glass of milk from the tray and took a drink. "I'm sorry. Can I get another bowl without any sugar?"

"Sure." Elle set the bowl aside and called room service.

After she hung up, Elle rubbed my back and then scowled, lifting a clump of my hair. "This is a mess. Let me get some things, and I'll help you with it. Oh, and Aislinn gave me these for you." She took a stack of clothes out of a bag and left.

I looked through the clothing and chose the softest items. I didn't like their feel, but I knew I would have to get used to them. If Braedon and I had been going through this transition together, we would have been laughing and rejoicing.

As I was finishing getting dressed, Elle returned, followed by Aislinn.

Elle had me sit down and worked leave-in conditioner into my hair. Aislinn and Elle then each took half my hair and began working out the snarls. I thought of Braedon doing the same thing back on the island, and the now familiar ache in my throat burned again as I tried not to cry. It was a losing battle, and my shoulders shook.

Aislinn knelt beside me with an arm around my shoulders. "We can get you some help, you know. They have counselors."

"I'm okay." I wiped my eyes with the tissue Elle handed me. "It's just that everything reminds me of him." My voice broke. "He carved me a beautiful comb, but I've lost my bag."

Elle slapped her temple. "Mrs. Hathaway gave me a bag for you. I forgot all about it." She moved to the door. "I'll go get it."

I leaned back in the chair. I hadn't lost my treasures. While Aislinn worked on my hair again, I tapped my foot and watched the door.

When Elle finally returned with my woven bag, I bounded out of my chair, leaving a few strands of hair in Aislinn's hands.

"Show us what you have in there," Aislinn suggested, her voice quiet.

As Aislinn and Elle combed the rats and tangles out of my hair, I talked about the items Braedon had carved for me and the stories behind them. It surprised me how good it felt to speak of him.

Elle ran her brush through my hair one last time. "You need to get your hair cut. It's not healthy." She held up the frizzy ends. "I can totally believe you washed it with lye."

The phone rang, and I jumped at the unexpected sound. Aislinn answered, said something I couldn't hear, and hung up. She exchanged glances with Elle and then turned to me. "The Coast Guard found the Scout group." Aislinn's eyes glistened. "But not Braedon or the two boys."

I took her hand. "But they'll keep looking, right?"

"The catamaran was large enough to justify a lengthy search. A homemade outrigger ...."

I pinched the bridge of my nose. "It's my fault," I whispered. "They weren't going to take us. Moli wanted to send someone back for us. It's my fault they were in that storm with an inexperienced passenger."

Elle took both my shoulders and gave me a shake. "Lyn, you're not making sense. *You* were an inexperienced passenger, and you made it. It was just bad luck."

I blinked rapidly to keep from crying again. "Do you have any idea when they'll be here?"

"Tomorrow, we hope." Aislinn indicated the television she had turned on but muted. "I think you should see this."

It was one of the morning news shows ... and I was the

opening story. Aislinn unmuted it. They were reviewing the old kidnapping news. There was even a flash of Elle, Jori, and the others in our group. Then the screen filled with a picture of Braedon and me. It had to be one of Elle's from the cruise.

Aislinn turned off the TV. "You needed to know. The press wants to talk to you."

"No." I slammed my hand on the table. "This is our loss, not theirs. I can't stomach the thought of people watching the story while they eat dinner and then go on with their lives, while we're …." My voice cracked.

Elle squeezed my arm. "We agree."

*D'*ARCY AND Mal arrived a while later and set up a laptop for the video call to Marc. I sat in front of the screen and waited impatiently for the call to connect. Finally, a picture of my little brother came into focus.

"Thank God, Lyn!" Marc shouted, his eyes watering. "I can't believe I'm seeing you. I wish I was there and could give you a huge hug."

Marc looked older than he should have, crow's feet spreading from his eyes. The burden of so many losses had left its mark on him. I blinked rapidly. "Wow, little brother, you're all grown up!"

He rolled his eyes. "To be honest, you look like you could do with a few extra meals." Marc leaned forward, trying to see me better, his voice soft. "Was it very bad?"

I picked at my battered fingernails, trying to decide what to say. I looked up and attempted a smile. "The accommodations stank, but the company was great."

"Is there any news?"

Trying to swallow the lump in my throat, I shook my head. Time for a change of topic. "Tell me what you've been up to."

Marc talked for a while about his decision to join the Marines and the girl he had left in Georgia. There was an awkward pause as we stared at each other. I wanted to ask about our parents, but the words wouldn't come.

My brother's face crumbled. The sob I had been trying to hold back broke loose. A man's hand appeared on-screen, squeezing Marc's shoulder, and Aislinn and Elle each grabbed one of my hands.

Marc wiped his face impatiently. "I'm sorry. This should be a happy time. You're *alive*." He hiccupped and his face went crimson. Marc snorted, and I laughed. It was a little hysterical, but the constricting knot in my throat eased. "We'll talk about them later."

I nodded and raised my hand in the sign language symbol for 'I love you' that our family had always used. He returned it and cut the connection.

ON THE fourth day, Elle arrived early in the morning, tapping on the door before using her key card. I stared at her where I sat frozen in front of the television.

She stopped, grimacing at the screen still showing the Coast Guard spokesman.

I clenched the couch cushion against my chest. "How can they call off the search?"

Elle came over and sat beside me. "Mal's talking to them now."

The pressure on my chest increased. Closing my eyes, I

forced slow breaths. Elle squeezed my hand, and I focused on the movement of my chest, willing it to calm.

There was a tap on the door, and Elle went to open it. Mal came in, and the slight shake of his head told me all I needed to know. I stood on shaky legs and went to the window, opening it a sliver to stare at the reporters huddling against the increasing wind. Last night, the storm that had halted the search had finally broken, bringing a spark of hope.

"I'm sorry, Lyn." Mal's reflection in the glass grew.

The dark, roiling clouds sucked away the light. The first heavy splatters of rain, followed quickly by a tropical deluge, washed away the little flame of hope I had been clinging to. My vision went blurry, and I closed my eyes. "What do we do now?"

Elle's voice came out as a tight whisper. "The police said we can leave whenever we want."

I looked at Elle's image where she had joined her husband behind me, her head resting on his shoulder. "Is this what happened before?"

She nodded, her eyes shining even in the dim reflection.

I turned to face them, my arms folded tightly against my body. "We were still alive. They could be too."

Elle buried her face in Mal's shoulder, and he murmured something softly to her before looking at me. "It's been in the news. Boaters will keep a lookout, and the Coast Guard will notify us if they find anything."

Find any*thing*? My head pounded. "I have to talk to Moli and Isaac."

$\mathcal{I}$ PACED THE hotel room, wishing I could go outside or to the hotel's gym to release some tension. Even after the hotel had banned the press, a few still had found a way inside.

At a knock, I jumped and approached the door with some trepidation, concerned about a repeat of the night before. I had just been about to leave my room with Aislinn and D'Arcy when he had pushed me back inside reporters trying to press in behind him. We had been stuck until the hotel's security had arrived.

"It's Vin." Elle gave the code phrase. In a different time and place, the ridiculousness of it would have made us laugh.

Mal followed her in, carrying a package with a change of clothes. He handed it to me.

As I accepted it, I said to Mal, "Thank you so much for everything you've done for a total stranger."

He flopped on the couch, automatically putting his arm around Elle when she sat next to him. "You're hardly a stranger, Lyn. Elle has told me so much about you in the last two years that I felt like I knew you even before we met."

"How'd you two meet?" I asked.

"During the first search. Aislinn and Elle became close, and I got pulled in." He looked at Elle with soft eyes. "It just kind of happened."

I smiled as she returned his adoring gaze. "How long have you been married?"

"Two years," Elle replied, her eyes on Mal.

"Me too," I whispered. I took the package and went to the bathroom to change.

With the help of some of the hotel staff, we snuck past the press. Mal and D'Arcy, dressed in bright-colored shirts, shorts, and large straw hats, drove to the hotel's loading dock in a rental car with darkened windows to pick us up.

$\mathcal{E}$LLE HAD braided my hair and forced it under a baseball cap. I wore simple jeans and a bright shirt. The uncomfortable clothes and sandals set my mood.

We drove to meet Moli and Isaac in a little hole-in-the-wall diner full of people. I went in alone. Once my eyes adjusted to the darker interior, I saw the two men seated in a booth with tall seat backs near the rear.

Hesitating only a moment, I joined them, sliding onto the cracked vinyl bench across from them. Their eyes were dark with grief, and I recalled the vivid, laughing faces of their sons. I had worked very hard all day not to cry, but I lost it then.

"I'm so sorry," I wept, grabbing a napkin and wiping my nose. In my selfishness, I had stolen Lua and Etano from their families.

Moli frowned, leaning forward as if to hear better. "Mrs. Armstrong told me you feel responsible for what happened. You're wrong." His voice was stern. "Don't take credit for other people's choices. Our sons wanted to do this. It was their choice."

Isaac asked, his bereaved face kind, "Do you think you brought on the storm? Are you so powerful as that?"

I shook my head, but I wasn't convinced.

Moli watched me with discerning eyes. "I'm a spiritual man. I've lost my eldest son, but I believe he's joined our ancestors. I'll see him again. Your husband was a strong man, and even though I didn't know him long, I liked him and thought I understood him. He'd want you to be strong too."

I stared down at my hands, but Moli reached across the table and forced me to look at him. "You have many people who love you, Lyn, including your husband's family. You're their only connection to him now. They thought you were dead, and now they have the joy of your return."

Moli and Isaac rose from the booth, each shaking my hand. They left without another word.

I sat in the booth, thinking about what they had said. The logical part of me knew they were right, but the emotional part of me continued to feel guilty. Of course I had wanted the boys on our side, but I hadn't had to convince them. Was Moli right? Was I doing them an injustice by taking credit for their choice?

I rubbed my temples, trying to clear my mind. Why was I doing and thinking things that only made me hurt more? I didn't just feel accountable for having wanted to leave right away; I felt guilty because I was alive and Braedon and the boys probably were not.

Elle slid into the seat opposite me.

I watched her for a moment. "Do you think I'll ever feel good about being alive again?"

Elle considered me. "Believe it or not, I understand how you feel."

I shook my head, but she grasped my hand and squeezed it hard.

"Did it ever occur to you how I might have felt when they couldn't find the catamaran?" She swallowed, and her eyes misted.

A lump grew in my throat, and I squeezed her hand back. I had known her for a very long time, and if I had thought of anyone but myself, I would have realized how she had felt. "You're beating yourself up right now, aren't you? Because you'd accepted we were dead and moved on."

She crumbled then, and I moved over to her side of the

table and held her while she cried. It was strange, but with the reversal of our roles, I felt strong again—well, stronger. I cried with her. Cried for the lost lives, the lost futures, the years that could not be recovered, and the goodbyes that would never be said.

When we had cried ourselves out, I asked, "What happened on the boat with the pirates?"

Elle sniffed, grabbing some more napkins and wiping her face. "When Jori tried to give me his shirt, it started an argument with the pirates. Then there was a shout down on the catamaran, and the pirates looked away from us. Jori and the other two guys you practiced self-defense with took advantage of the moment and jumped the pirates. It was scary for a while. Jori got hit in the face with a rifle butt." Her lips trembled. "It was crazy. He was bleeding, and the storm hit, and people were shooting guns."

I smiled for the first time in days.

"What's funny?"

"We were part of the plan. I'm glad it worked and you guys got away. Is Jori okay?"

"Broke his cheekbone and had to have a bunch of plastic surgery. I called him when we got back to the States, to see how he was doing. He said there'd be no more modeling for him … but he sounded happy about it."

"I'm not surprised. He hated it."

"Doesn't matter anyway." Her voice became bubbly. "He's made a big hit in the art world."

"Good for him. Do you ever hear from him?"

Elle got a tender look on her face. "We kind of adopted him, but that's a story for another time. He's in Finland now for a series of shows. Do you think you'd like to talk to him?"

Jori was so tied in my memory to Braedon that the familiar knot formed in my throat. "I … I can't. Not yet. He'll want to know about Jimmy and Braedon." I briefly closed my eyes and squeezed the bridge of my nose. "Maybe I'll be ready when he comes back to the States."

"All right."

I leaned back in my seat and felt some of the stress from the last few days leave my shoulders. "I guess Jimmy, Maria, and … Braedon were the only casualties."

"They confirmed some of those pirates trafficked in women," Elle said, a sick expression on her face. "That's what they had planned for us."

We sat in silence for a moment. "I'm ready."

Elle's eyebrows furrowed. "Ready for what?"

"To go home."

CHAPTER 24

ON THE flight to Hawaii from American Samoa, I had time to observe Elle and Aislinn together. They were more than sisters-in-law; they were very close friends. I was glad they'd had each other. They were a lot alike too, and probably better suited than Elle and I had been. The last two years had changed us, and I didn't know what that meant for our friendship.

As I stared out the window, I wondered about my future. It was like my past had been wiped away. I would never go shopping with my mom again. No more stargazing with my dad. My brother serving overseas. What was I going to do?

Brought by neighbors, Kate waited at the airport in New York to greet us. The tiny girl had grown a lot but still remembered me. The feel of her gloved hand as she held mine made me feel better.

I knew Elle expected me to stay with her, but Aislinn surprised me when she said, "You're welcome to stay at our house for a while, Lyn. I have a lot of Braedon's things. I'm not pushing them at you, but I thought you might like to see them when you're ready."

As we made our way to collect our luggage, I considered her offer. By the time we got outside, I had made up my mind. After my realization about Elle, I sensed Aislinn needed a chance to grieve. She had just lost her brother for the second time. Maybe I could help.

I looked at Elle, hoping she understood. She nodded, so I said, "I'd love to go with you, Aislinn."

She blinked tears away, confirming my suspicions.

Elle took Kate's hand. "Mal and I can take this little minx in our car."

"Good thinking." Mal tugged on the braid that hung from under Kate's knit cap and grabbed some luggage.

Elle hugged me while Kate watched me with doleful eyes.

"I'll see you in a little while," I assured her.

New York in January can be bitter cold, and we arrived during a bad spell. A gust of frigid wind sent snow scurrying around us as we left the airport, ripping the breath from my lungs. For the first time, I was glad for all the clothes they had made me put on.

D'Arcy played chauffeur, leaving Aislinn and me to sit in the back. Not sure what she needed, I hoped she would say something. When she remained silent, I asked, "How long before you all gave up on us?"

She closed her eyes and leaned her head against the seat. "A year."

A year of searching. A year of waiting, ever hopeful that news would come that we had been found alive. A year of continual disappointments. "That's a long time. I'm sure everyone told you to let it go long before that."

Aislinn smiled bitterly. "Yet you were both alive when we gave up." Her voice broke. "I feel like I betrayed him."

I put my arm around her, and she laid her head on my shoulder and cried. What a mess we all were. Talking about Braedon seemed to have helped before, so I decided to tell her about our time on the catamaran. Once I got to Jimmy's burial, I couldn't continue.

Aislinn lifted her head, wiping her eyes. "Thank you."

We sat in silence the rest of the way and finally entered a gated community.

It had just begun to snow, and I shivered. We pulled up to a large house and D'Arcy activated the garage door opener and drove in. My teeth were still chattering by the time we got in the house.

"I've got the luggage," D'Arcy called as he went back into the garage.

I followed Aislinn into the kitchen where we were met by Kate, who had just arrived together with Elle and Mal.

"Mommy, can I make Aunt Lyn a cocoa?"

"If she wants one."

"That would be nice. Can you put extra water in it?" I asked.

Aislinn pointed to a knife. "Would you like to help cut up the vegetables for the salad while you wait for your drink?"

"Sure." After washing my hands, I inspected the workmanship of the knife. "What we could have done with a knife like this." I winked at Kate. "We didn't get a lot of vegetables on the island. Mostly only during the monsoons when the bamboo sprouted."

With care, Kate set the cup of hot chocolate she had heated in the microwave by my hand. I put down the knife and picked up the cup, warming my hands on the sides.

"Aren't monsoons really bad storms?" Kate asked.

I nodded. "We'd stay in a cave then and could only check on our tree house when the weather let up." I almost rolled my shoulder at the memory.

Kate's eyes grew large. "You built a tree house?"

"In a Banyan tree."

"Oh, we saw those in Hawaii." Kate turned to her mother. "Where's Uncle Mal and Aunt Elle?"

"Went to get pizza, you little munchkin." D'Arcy stomped his feet at the door. With a leap, he swept Kate in his arms and tickled her. She giggled, and he headed toward the dining room. "Why don't we go set the table?"

It was easy to imagine Braedon here, joking with D'Arcy, teasing Kate and Aislinn while he helped prepare the table. The lump in my throat choked me and made my eyes water. I glanced at Aislinn.

She had been watching me, her own eyes misty. We must have been thinking the same thing.

"What about your father?"

Looking uncomfortable, she shook her head. "He was going to come, but when he found out ...." She dropped her eyes to the celery on the counter. "Well ... when he found out about you, he stayed in Montana."

My stomach twisted. "Me?"

"Don't worry about him." Aislinn met my eyes. "He's dealing with grief in his own way."

I went back to chopping, unsettled. "Braedon talked about him a lot, and I'd hoped to meet him."

"Maybe. Someday." Aislinn sounded doubtful. "When he's ready."

By the time the pizza arrived, I had little appetite and only ate some salad. While the others chatted, I wondered what issue Braedon's father had with me. I didn't realize I had dozed off until my head dropped, and I jerked awake.

Elle laughed. "You need to go take a nap. The jetlag's hitting you hard."

"I think I will, if that's okay." I rose.

"Can I come with you?" Kate asked.

"Kate …," Aislinn warned.

"No, it's okay. I don't mind."

Kate skipped to join me, clasping my hand. She led me to the bedroom. "This is Uncle Bray's room when he stays here. Mama thought you'd like to be in here."

"She's right." I scanned the room with interest, my weariness forgotten. I ran my hand over the old-fashioned quilt on the bed.

"Want me to show you something of Uncle Bray's?"

She went straight to a bookcase, grabbed a photo album, and climbed onto the bed. We propped up the pillows, and she opened the book.

The album held pictures from Braedon's summers in Montana. I could see why he had loved the ranch. The rough land in the west is so different to the soft hills of the east. It takes a special kind of person to live there and love it.

Braedon looked about twelve in one of the first pictures. I touched his face. He seemed very happy.

"That's Grampa." Kate pointed at a man standing by as Braedon mounted a horse in another snapshot.

It was easy to tell they were father and son, and I could see how Braedon might have looked if he had … I shut down that thought and turned the page where a younger Aislinn grinned for the camera.

"You look a lot like your mother." I glanced at the little girl. "Does your mom like to visit Montana?"

"She does, but she likes it better here," Kate paused as her face became contemplative. "She doesn't love Montana like Uncle Bray does."

"Do you like it in Montana?"

"Yes, but I think I'm like Mama. I like it better here."

As we made our way through the album, Kate told me who the people were and talked about the places. When we were finished, she paused in thought. "Aunt Lyn, can I ask you a question?"

"Sure." I hoped I could answer whatever that grave little face portended.

"I always thought I was going to be the flower girl at Uncle Bray's wedding." She sounded distressed. "When did you and him get married?"

"I was wondering the same thing," came a voice from the doorway.

Both Kate and I started, and Kate cried, "Daddy! You scared us!"

D'Arcy grinned. "Bath time for you, little lady. You have school tomorrow."

She groaned but didn't argue, giving me a quick hug and scooting off the bed. She embraced her father as she went by. D'Arcy remained leaning against the doorframe, watching me, and I knew he was waiting for me to answer his question.

I twisted my wooden ring. "Braedon and I exchanged vows about two years ago."

D'Arcy remained silent for a minute. "Before Hawaii, Aislinn wondered if you two might make a match ...."

"Before I behaved like an idiot." I leaned my head against the headboard.

The corner of his mouth twitched. "Sounds like you came around." He looked over his shoulder in the direction Kate had gone before turning back to me. "I hope it's okay that Kate calls you Aunt Lyn. It was Aislinn's idea."

I smiled, my heart heavy. "I like it. It makes me feel like I might have had a place here."

Straightening and striding to the bed, D'Arcy snapped, "You do have a place here, Lyn. I don't care what Jack says."

"Jack?" I stared up at him, surprised at his vehemence.

D'Arcy swore. "I wasn't supposed to say anything. Don't tell Aislinn."

"Tell Aislinn what? I have no idea what you're talking about."

"Let's leave it at that, then. I just came up to make sure you know you're welcome to stay with us as long as you like, and staying at Elle's is a given." He patted my shoulder and left.

I sat there for a few minutes, thinking about D'Arcy's kind offer. They had already done so much, and they had no obligation to me. I wondered how long I could stay here or even with Elle. But what was I doing here exactly?

Even more than on the plane, the reality of my parents' loss struck me. Knowing they wouldn't be there, ready to welcome me home, to help me build a new life, made me feel adrift. I had been dead to everyone I knew for over two years. What should I do? Where could I go? Parents gone, Marc abroad, and Elle married and living on the East Coast. All my plans with Braedon destroyed.

Alone, I opened the photo album and examined the pictures again. They filled me with an even stronger desire to visit his father's ranch. I wanted to see the places Braedon had talked about so fondly and meet the people he had loved.

The sense of needing to do *something* began that night, though it was some time before I knew what it was.

Exhausted, I returned the photo album to the bookcase and put on my new pajamas. Pulling the heavy quilt and a pillow off the bed, I lay on the floor. I had thought we had made our bed pretty soft on the island, but I found my back ached when I slept in a bed now. Like my taste buds, my back would need to adjust to being home again.

$\mathcal{I}$ woke only a couple of hours later feeling hungry, so I tiptoed down the stairs to get a piece of fruit. As I slipped past the door to the family room, I heard my name and stopped. I had never been an eavesdropper before, but curiosity made me pause.

"… I understand, Elle," Mal was saying, "but since she doesn't have anyone else, we need to understand how she grieves. Was this how she reacted when her fiancé died?"

Elle let out a heavy sigh as though in surrender. "No. When Jace died, she cried that night, but once we visited that girl in the hospital, she never cried over him again."

I leaned against the wall and closed my eyes.

"At first I thought it was a good sign she didn't waste any time grieving the scumbag. I admired her strength until I realized she'd refused every invitation for a date. She'd come with me to group activities, but any suggestion that we go on a double date and she had other plans. And God help any guy who asked her out, because she'd turned into an ice queen."

"So she cut herself off?" Mal asked. "Do we need to

schedule some therapy for her? Should we talk about Braedon or should we avoid discussing him?"

Aislinn said, "I think she needs to talk about him … and she needs to know we're grieving too. Don't you think she did well talking to me in the car today, honey?"

"Yeah, she did," D'Arcy replied. "Mal, unless she's covering things up, I think she's done pretty well considering everything. We have to remember she's not just worrying that Braedon will never be found; she's lost her parents too. I wonder if I'd do as well if I'd been through two years in survival mode only to come back here to find—" his voice cracked, and he paused before continuing, "to find Aislinn and Kate dead, you gone off to Timbuktu, and my home sold … hey, lovey, don't. I'm sorry."

Aislinn had begun to cry, so I crept away, went back upstairs, and crawled under my covers. It bothered me at first because I didn't like people talking about me, but then I felt ashamed. They hadn't been malicious. They were concerned about me. These wonderful people had stopped their lives and come halfway across the world to help me. I could pretend they only did it for Elle, but I knew they weren't being fake.

An almost overwhelming desire to tell Braedon how much I loved his family filled me. Nighttime was hardest for me anyway. I ached to feel his body close to mine, and his arm around my waist as I drifted to sleep.

For a fleeting moment, as sorrow gripped me, I wished I had never met him. Then I shuddered as an even greater pain caused me to gasp. No Braedon? That was the stupidest thought I had ever had.

$\mathcal{E}$LLE AND Mal came over the next morning while we were still eating breakfast. Eggs were what I craved the most. I had missed them on the island, and they were easy to cook in a variety of ways—without salt.

Pulling up the chair beside me, Mal flipped it so he could sit on it backward. "Lyn, we keep getting calls from the press. Everyone wants to interview you—and I mean *everyone*. I even got a call from a big daytime talk show. You know, that classy Native American, Olivia Howard. She wants to do an entire show about you."

Aislinn bristled. "Lyn's not interested, Mal, and we support her."

"I'm good with that," he said easily. "But as the family spokesman, I need to provide some kind of statement."

I stared at him. "Family spokesman?"

D'Arcy put his arm around his wife. "During the search for the catamaran, we were being pestered by the press, so we designated Mal as the family spokesman. He specializes in communications, so he's comfortable in front of a camera, and he was more emotionally removed from what happened."

I regarded Mal and Elle. They probably would have never met if not for the pirate attack. I raised my orange juice in a toast. "To unexpected blessings."

Everyone raised their glasses and murmured agreement.

CHAPTER 25

OVER THE next few weeks, I finally stopped jumping at the sound of any phone call, thinking the Coast Guard might be calling to tell us they had found Braedon and the boys. I stayed a couple of weeks at Aislinn's house and a couple with Elle. I got used to wearing clothing again and forced myself to sleep in a bed. I could even drink a cup of hot chocolate at three-quarter strength.

I spent a lot of time on the Internet reading about world events and catching up on what I had missed. Having such a huge gap left me feeling even more disconnected. We had a new president, and I knew nothing about the campaign issues.

Aislinn had a piano, and I spent a lot of time playing. It was in a room far from the bedrooms, so I could use it when I had trouble sleeping without bothering anyone. I lost myself in the music and found it therapeutic.

I continued to dislike being in public, but Elle and Aislinn lured me out one morning with the temptation of looking for sheet music. When we arrived at a small shopping complex,

I started toward the music store, but Elle snagged my elbow. "We're going to hit the music store *after* the spa."

Aislinn took my other arm. "We're going to get manicures and pedicures, and you're going to have your hair done."

I pulled back. "Not my hair."

"Yes, your hair," Elle insisted. "It's not healthy, Lyn. We brought a bag so you can keep what they cut off."

Aislinn held up a gallon-sized plastic bag.

They shepherded me into a high-class spa. I had always frequented the dollar cut type places. Wary, I checked for other customers, but we were the only ones there except for the receptionist.

After she confirmed our appointment, she led us through an elegant door and down a hallway with a plush carpet, expensive artwork, and velvet-covered chairs. As she separated me from the others, I glared at Elle.

The receptionist left me with a hairstylist, who complained about my hair and asked what I had been doing to let it get so damaged. All I could think of was everything Braedon and I had gone through to make our rudimentary soap. The memory made the scar on my leg itch. I was done.

I stood up just as the owner approached from behind me. "My name is Patricia," she introduced herself and turned to the hairstylist. "I'll be doing Mrs. Randolph's hair." When the other woman left, looking abashed, Patricia gently pushed me back in the chair. She picked up one of my hands, rubbed the skin, and examined my nails.

"I assume they have you on a good vitamin regime now." She then pulled at a few strands of my hair. "I'm sure your limited diet contributed to the poor condition of your hair and skin." She dropped the strand and smiled. "Under the circumstances, I would have expected your skin to look much worse."

The fact that she knew who I was and was so matter-of-fact about it put me at ease. I rubbed my hand, which looked much better than it had on the island. "I made a sort of lotion from coconut milk."

"I can't even imagine how much work that would take. Well, we'll provide everything you need today, and I'll give Mrs. Armstrong a list of products to help." Patricia's eyes twinkled. "And you won't have to make any of it yourself."

I spent the rest of the morning being soaked, deep conditioned, buffed, and painted. I tried to argue that my hair looked so much better after being conditioned and didn't need to be cut anymore, but Patricia was resolute. I finally gave in. She kept it long but had to layer it to cut off the damaged ends.

I had only one more unpleasant experience. During the full-body massage, I got to thinking about the island. When the therapist saw the tears running down the sides of my cheeks, she asked if she had gone too deep.

Patricia, who was sitting to the side, came to me and asked, "Are you all right?" She seemed to understand it was more than physical pain.

I shook my head and whispered, "No, but I will be."

She watched me, sympathetic. "Tell me if I can do anything."

I looked away to the wall. "You can't bring him back."

Patricia touched my hand. "No, I'm sorry to say I can't." She nodded to the therapist.

When everything was done, including the application of a little makeup, Patricia stood behind me before a full-length mirror. She fluffed and patted my hair as I examined my reflection.

"Mrs. Randolph, I think you'll be able to move around in public a little easier now. You don't look so much like the wild woman dressed in animal skins from the news."

I smiled.

After we purchased some music, we had lunch at a nice restaurant. No one gave me a second glance. I began to believe I might yet fit back in the real world.

$\mathcal{D}$URING THOSE weeks, in the back of my mind, I waited. It was more than the limbo of waiting for the slim chance that Braedon and the boys might be found. I needed to do something, but I didn't know what. The last two years of my life had been focused on surviving, and before that, my job had given me purpose. While I began to feel like a civilized woman again, I still felt lost. I needed to move ahead, but I had no idea what direction to take.

I decided to ask Marc if anything was left from our parents' estate during a chat the following week.

"I'm sorry," he said, dismayed. "You were declared dead, and I inherited everything. I sold the house, but once I paid off the mortgage and the funerals, there was barely enough to settle my school loans." Marc perked up. "Hey, my car's paid off. I can get a loan against it and send it to you."

"No, that's not necessary. I just need to do some traveling, and I don't have any money." I leaned back in my chair. "I'll see about getting a job. You did what you should have, so don't worry."

His face became somber. "It must be strange for you, not having a home to go to."

"Yeah, it is."

Aislinn entered the den. "She does too have a home, Marc—here. You of all people know that."

He put on a brooding expression that shifted to a mock seductive leer. "Hey, Ash! You're lookin' *good* ... as always."

Aislinn looked at me. "Your brother is such a flirt."

I eyed him. "Into older women now, huh, little brother? What would your Georgia peach think of this?"

Marc waved a hand at me. "She knows about Ash." He turned puppy dog eyes to Aislinn and exhaled. "The one who could have been the love of my life ... if I'd been born *twenty* years earlier."

"Ouch!" Aislinn cringed, laughing.

Marc twisted in his seat when someone called his name. He turned back. "Hey, I gotta run." He gave me the sign language symbol.

"Love you, too," I said, and Marc logged off.

I grinned at Aislinn. "I can't tell you how weird it still is that you even know him."

She came to sit beside me. "You do have money. Or you will when we work through the legal issues."

"What do you mean?"

"Braedon's estate."

I held up my hand. "That's yours."

"It is not!" She sat up. "It belongs to his wife. We could've had him declared dead a long time ago, but we decided to wait the seven years. D'Arcy, Mal, and I have been talking. We think we should appeal to the court for a death declaration now. If there's any legal concern about your claim to his estate, I'll just gift it to you. There's close to a million dollars in the account."

I gaped at her. "I can't take that." I felt dizzy. "Why would you even consider this? I have no legal claim."

Aislinn slid her chair until we were facing each other. "I wish you could have seen Braedon before he met you. He dated plenty, but it was like he was just going through the motions. Even that first day when the ship was departing and we met you on the deck, I saw how he looked at you." Her smile became sad. "He was so devastated when you wouldn't see him. This is his money, and he would have wanted you to have it."

She took my hands in hers. "I've already been in touch with our attorney, and he's working on it. In the meantime, we've opened an account in your name. You said last night you have some business to take care of before you decide what to do long term. Well, you've got the money to do it."

I didn't know what to say.

CHAPTER 26

I BEGAN TO make plans, and it felt good to have purpose again. Even though Elle and Aislinn repeated several times that they wanted me to stay, they also encouraged me to do what I felt was necessary.

Aislinn and I spent the day before I left together, just the two of us. We went to Long Island, where she gave me a tour of Winterwood, her and Braedon's childhood home. The name seemed appropriate, dressed as it was in winter snow. Though it was too cold to stay outside long, I had her show me her secret garden and the ghost path that had frightened Braedon as a boy.

We went to lunch, and I told her everything I could think of that I hadn't mentioned about the island. I tried to give her the two years with Braedon she had missed.

"You'll come back here, won't you?" she asked as we drove back.

"Everything's so different from what Braedon and I planned." I looked out my window, sliding my hand along the door. "Who knows? When I go back to the Springs I may decide I want to stay there after all … but I doubt it."

She glanced over her shoulder and changed lanes. "You can live here. We'd love to have you close."

"I don't know." I rubbed my temple. "Let me do these visits before I decide anything."

Resigned, she asked, "Where are you going first?

"Colorado Springs. And then Texas."

"Jimmy's and Maria's families?"

I nodded.

"Anywhere else?"

I hesitated for a long moment. "Montana."

"To see my father?" Her eyes opened wide.

"I want to meet him. I want to see the ranch Braedon loved so much." I leaned the back of my head against the window and looked at her. "Did you know Braedon planned to move out west?"

"Kate said something about that, but I thought she'd misunderstood him. They loved Braedon at Cornell, and I thought he enjoyed working there."

"He did love it, but he told me Cornell was never more than a place to get experience." I shifted my gaze to the passing landscape. "He'd been considering the move even before your mother died, so he could be closer to your father. And then when we met …." I squeezed my eyes shut.

Aislinn put her hand over mine. "Just stay in touch, okay?"

"I will."

THE NEXT morning, as we loaded my luggage into Aislinn's car,

Mal said from the doorway, "We're going to have to come up with another plan."

I frowned. "Why?"

"The press." He grimaced.

"But we went out yesterday with no problem."

Mal leaned against Aislinn's car and folded his arms. "It's funny how that works," he reflected. "The more mysterious someone is, the more intrigued the press gets. It was a slow news day yesterday, and your story got attention again. They want to hear from you. Have I mentioned we got a call from a TV producer who wants to do a movie?"

"What is wrong with these people?" I shouted, heat flushing through my body. "They just want to be entertained by our pain. It makes me sick!"

Startled by my outburst, Mal straightened. He put a hand on my arm. "There's some truth to that, but telling your story is also a way to let the public know about people you loved. You haven't said a lot about Jimmy and Maria, but until you were found no one knew what happened to them either."

He hesitated and then spoke slowly, his voice firm. "You can't talk to everyone who cared about them. Hearing about their last days might be part of the healing process for the friends you don't visit. I know it's all still too raw for you right now, but give it some time and think about it."

He twisted to regard D'Arcy, who had entered the garage. "I've talked to Mr. Statler down the street. He said he'd be glad to drive her to the airport."

That's how I ended up riding to the airport wearing old Mr. Statler's wife's knitted cap, scarf, and coat. He had no idea who I was and talked all the way to the airport, which suited me just fine.

$\mathcal{I}$T WAS surreal to fly into Colorado Springs after so long, a very different return from the one Elle and I had planned three years earlier. Luckily, no one paid any attention to me. My story didn't seem to be making headlines here, which was a pleasant surprise.

Everything had a dreamlike quality as I drove through areas I should have recognized but didn't. It reminded me of a mixed-up collage with pieces from my memories pasted on places I had never seen.

I drove to the cemetery first. The plain headstone Marc had chosen fit the simple couple our parents had been. I knelt on the grave, despite the snow, and arranged the silk flowers I had brought with me.

By the time I finished, my body shook with the cold, my toes numb. Stiff, I rose to my feet and stared at the grave. They were gone. Really gone.

In the morning, I made a trip to the high school where I had taught. I didn't go in but parked outside and watched the comings and goings. Life had moved on, and I wasn't a part of the place anymore.

Sitting in my motel room the second night, I tried to think who else I should visit in Colorado. I couldn't think of anyone. It wasn't my home anymore.

I booked a flight to Houston, Texas for the next morning. Jimmy's ranch was northwest of Sealy, and Maria's home was in a small farming community close to Houston. I decided to hit Jimmy's first.

While I had the agent on the phone, I considered getting tickets to Montana, but memories of what Aislinn had said about her father held me back. The last thing I wanted to do was to cause him further grief. She and I had agreed if I decided to go, I would call her so she could let him know of my imminent arrival—imminent being the key word.

CHAPTER 27

So at the end of February, I flew into Houston. With the city close to the Gulf Coast, the milder weather was a relief after New York and Colorado. It seemed like Jimmy's entire family waited for me as I pulled up the long drive to the white clapboard farmhouse.

They prepared a huge meal for me, and we exchanged stories about him. When I reached the part where he was shot while fighting the pirates, I worried it would distress them. They thought it was heroic, however, and just the kind of thing Jimmy would have and should have done.

When I pulled out my keys, Mrs. Hewitt jumped to her feet, replacing a flash of disappointment with a big grin. She followed me outside once I had hugged the others goodbye.

Mrs. Hewitt embraced me, her eyes glistening. "Thank you so much for coming. The people from the cruise line could never tell us enough." She breathed out a sigh. "With the four of you disappearing, well ... it's just good to know. If a mother has to lose a son, it's nice to know he went down fighting."

I drove away, surprised at how good I felt, and that night in the motel was free of dreams.

The next day, I met with Maria's grandmother, and that meeting was nothing like the one with Jimmy's family. Maria's parents hadn't been a part of her life for several years, and her younger siblings had been divided up and sent to live with other family members. The grandmother I met had one grandchild with her, a sullen youth of about fifteen. When I introduced myself, he barely nodded and quickly left the room. The old woman spoke poor English, and I think she feared I wanted something from her.

I was impressed that Maria had done so well coming from this home. It was a shame that of the three who had died, the only one I could report a burial place for didn't have anyone who cared.

Indecision still plagued me. While my need to do something had diminished, it was still there. I didn't know where to go next, but I knew I wasn't ready to return to New York. After a drive to Galveston and some time spent watching the open water of the Gulf of Mexico, I returned to the airport and got a flight to Montana.

Landing in the cold weather of Great Falls, I shivered all the way to my motel room and cranked up the heater as soon as I arrived. After a shower, I crawled into bed, wishing I knew what to do. Knowing that Braedon's favorite childhood home was so close felt like an itch I couldn't scratch.

It took me forever to fall asleep, and I dreamed I went to the ranch. In the dream, I drove up to the house, and Braedon stepped out of the front door to welcome me. The constant ache, the one that sometimes threatened to overwhelm me, disappeared, replaced by a sense of peace.

When I awoke to reality, a crushing weight bore down on me, twisting my stomach in knots and sending a vicious wave of nausea. I wanted to go to Lewistown, even knowing Braedon wouldn't be there, but I was afraid. I took a trip to the mall and wandered around the stores, thinking about what had brought me on this journey in the first place.

After sitting through a movie I didn't watch, I got up, went to my rental car, and headed down the highway. It had started snowing during the movie, but Lewistown was only a couple of hours away. The Randolph Ranch lay northwest of the town. Even if I never got up the courage to knock on the door, I could at least drive past.

I didn't feel very well when I started out, sluggish from the restless night. Maria's grandmother had also insisted on feeding me an iffy-looking dish while at her house. Things there had been so dismal I hadn't been able to refuse her offer.

The more I drove, the more I regretted eating it. I had almost decided to find a motel when the worst of the nausea passed. By then the weather had gotten interesting to drive in, and I worried the storm would worsen.

I needed a break anyway, so I decided to go into Lewistown first. While there, I got directions to the ranch. The attendant eyed me curiously, making me wonder if the Randolphs didn't get many visitors.

I didn't phone Aislinn until I left town. It would have served me right if Braedon's father had been away when I showed up.

My nervousness increased as I drove away from the lights of town, and not just because I wasn't wanted or expected. Darkness came early in February. I had waited too long to start out, and the bad weather had lengthened the drive. I cursed myself for not getting a room in town and waiting until tomorrow. Yet if I waited, I might not have the courage again to visit.

I had only gone a couple of miles when the visibility got so bad I had to slow to a crawl. I hadn't done a lot of driving since I had returned to civilization. As I crept along inside my little dome of light, huge flakes fell like a curtain, hiding everything behind it.

There were no lights I could see. Even at my reduced speed, I should have already reached the turnoff to the ranch. I would have to turn around, but the road didn't look very wide. If I tried turning around, I might end up in a ditch. My stomach churned. What if I got lost out here? How ironic to have survived all that time on a tropical island only to freeze to death in Montana.

I had just decided to stop when a huge red truck burst out of a side road I hadn't noticed and skidded to a stop in front of me. Already jumpy, I braked, sliding a little and just missing the truck. White knuckles clenching the steering wheel, my heart thumped and my knees trembled.

The driver flashed the truck's headlights at me, but I wasn't sure what that meant. Through the oscillating window wipers, I could make out the driver-side window roll down and a gloved hand jab violently toward the direction from which the truck had just come.

As I decided to take the driver's help, I wondered where else in the world I would even consider following instructions given like that by a stranger.

The driver honked, flashed the truck's lights, and waved again. Seemed like someone wasn't happy. My hands shook, and my stomach lurched.

Swallowing to keep from retching, I flashed my lights back. The truck turned in the drive, and I followed its disappearing trail. I tried to stay close to the rear lights as it made its way up a long lane, the driving snow obscuring almost everything else. I coughed, telling myself I would *not* throw up.

Finally, in the distance, I could make out some dim lights I hoped were from a house. The truck drove up close to them, and I pulled next to it. The driver, head covered by a hat, got out, his entire body pulsing with anger.

I opened my door, hoping the fresh air would clear my head and help my stomach, but the driver ripped the door from my hand and shouted, "What the hell do you think you're doing coming out here in weather like this?"

I promptly threw up on his boots.

CHAPTER 28

A ROAR OF laughter came from the porch as the man jumped back, cursing. He glared at me as he wiped his shoes off in the snow. I covered my mouth in dismay but felt another heave coming.

"Watch out!" shouted the voice from the porch. "She's going to do it again!"

I did, and then a wave of dizziness struck me, and I swayed. Swearing, the man grabbed me before I could do a face plant in the snow. He put his arm under my knees and picked me up, muttering under his breath as he slid up the snowy steps.

The young man on the porch opened the door and followed us into the house.

"Is he back?" a woman's voice called from another room.

"Better get out here quick! She's sick," called the young man.

A plump, motherly looking woman in jeans and an apron came through a door, took one look at the man standing with me in his arms, and seized control.

"Well, don't just stand there, you old fool! She can't drive back to town in this weather. Take her upstairs to the bedroom."

Grumbling, the man carried me up the stairs and dumped me on my feet by a four-poster bed. I clutched one of the posts.

The woman nudged the man out of her way. He glowered at me for a second and then stomped out. The woman shut the door behind him and came to me, examining my face.

I clutched my arms to my chest. "I'm so sorry. I think I ate something yesterday that gave me food poisoning."

"Don't you worry about it." She pulled a pair of flannel pajamas from a dresser drawer. "I'm Emily Walters. Get out of those soiled clothes, so I can get them washed, and you can get into that tub." She pointed to a bathroom and handed me an empty trash can. "In case you feel like you're going to throw up again."

She went into the bathroom, and I followed, watching as she turned on the water. Self-conscious, I took off my clothes as fast as I could, ordering myself to ignore the painful abdominal gurgling.

"You're sure a thin thing," she commented.

My face flamed. "I didn't used to be," I said a little harsher than necessary. Then I had to grab the trash can as my stomach heaved, too sick to consider my humiliating state of undress.

When I stopped vomiting, Mrs. Walters helped me into the steaming water. She rinsed the trash can before handing it back to me. "I'll get these clothes into the wash and bring you up something to help your stomach." She left.

I leaned back in the old-fashioned tub, not knowing if I was even in the right place. The heat from the water felt good, and my stomach settled down. When Mrs. Walters returned with a cup of herbal tea, I was able to sip some of it.

"Don't drink it too fast, hon." She sat next to me. "Don't want it coming right back up."

I took a taste. "Is this the Randolph Ranch?"

"Yes, it is." She chuckled, "And you puked on the boots of His Highness John Randolph himself."

"Oh, Lord," I breathed, closing my eyes.

"You're Lyn North." A statement.

"Did Aislinn call to say I was coming?"

"Yes again, and Sir John was madder than I've seen him since—"

"Should I leave?" I interrupted.

Mrs. Walters appraised me. "Aislinn said Braedon wanted to marry you."

I almost dropped the cup. "He *did* marry me."

"On that ship?"

"No. On the island."

"Oh, really? And who performed the ceremony?"

I hesitated. "A fruit bat."

She cocked her head and then burst out laughing. "Okay. I get what you're saying. What'd you two do, exchange vows or something? Sounds kind of romantic and like something Braedon would do." She put her fingers into the cooling water.

"Time for you to get out." She took the cup from me and set it on the counter before holding up a large, fluffy towel. "You bring any clothes with you?"

Shivering, I stepped out of the tub and draped the towel over my shoulders. "Yes, but they're in my car."

"Well, you'll just have to wait for your other clothes to dry to have fresh undies." She handed over a pair of pajamas and turned to leave.

"Thank you, Mrs. Walters."

Glancing back at me, she grinned and then left the room.

Once dressed, I went back into the bedroom, where Mrs.

Walters had turned back the bedding. There were electric blanket controls on the nightstand, and they were on high. *Bless you, Mrs. Walters.* I climbed into the bed and fell asleep immediately.

❧

I STARTED AWAKE. The soft light from the nightstand lamp showed a figure standing just outside the open door. I sat up, pulling the blankets up around my neck.

The driver from earlier strode into the room and sat in the chair by the bed, glowering at me again. Here, out of his hat and coat, was the older version of the man from the photos. Jack Randolph would never have been called handsome, but there was a rugged sort of beauty in his silver hair and chiseled face. I recalled Braedon talking about how his mother, the debutant, had fallen for this cowboy. I could see why—his strong character showed through.

"Why are you here?" he demanded.

I slid my feet from under the covers. I felt at a disadvantage to be lying in bed when facing this man. "I wanted to meet you."

Jack Randolph stood up. "Why?"

I stood up too. Was he playing some kind of power game with me, trying to keep my head below his? He wasn't as tall as Braedon, but he was still taller than me. "Because you were special to him."

He scowled, his entire body tight with dislike. "Don't you mean because you wanted to con me like you've conned Aislinn? Prance over here from that island claiming he'd *married* you. Figured as a widow you could get your hands on his estate—"

My veins strained against my skin, and I slapped him. "How dare you?"

"You're nothing but a gold-digging tramp!" He grabbed my arm.

My training kicked in, and I pinned his hand to my arm, turned my own so I had him in a wristlock, and he dropped to his knees, grimacing in pain.

Mrs. Walters and two young men rushed through the bedroom door. I let Jack go and stepped out of his reach, stunned at what I had done. My anger was gone as quickly as it had come, leaving me in a terrible position.

Mrs. Walters and the two guys stood for a second in shock and then began laughing. Jack rose, looking daggers at all of us, and rubbed his hand and arm.

I swallowed. "I'll leave in the morning if the roads are open."

The others went silent. Jack gave a curt nod and turned to leave.

"But I *will* tell you what I came here to say." I stepped forward.

"And what is that?" He spun back to me, spitting out the words.

"Thank you," I said softly, my eyes burning.

He gaped at me. "What …why?"

Now I did cry. "Because you taught him things that saved our lives. Because you taught him how to be strong and brave … and gave him a high code of ethics to live up to." I sniffed, swallowing to get rid of the painful lump in my throat. "And you gave him his happiest childhood memories."

Jack stood frozen in place. Just as I saw the hint of a shine in his eyes, he turned and left. Mrs. Walters quietly pushed the two young men from the room and shut the door behind her, leaving me alone again.

Numb, I stood for a moment and then pulled out my cell

phone. It would be late in New York, but I dialed the number anyway. When Aislinn's sleepy voice answered, I demanded, "Why didn't you tell me your father is a petty tyrant?"

"What happened?" she asked, very awake now.

I explained.

"He called you *what*?"

My shoulders sagged. "A gold-digging tramp."

"What did you say?" she whispered.

I closed my eyes. "I slapped him."

She groaned.

It embarrassed me that I had struck Braedon's father. It wasn't something I would normally have done. "Then he grabbed my arm, so I took him down."

Aislinn was quiet for a moment. "Took him down? Like a karate take down, the kind Braedon told me about?"

"Yes," I breathed.

"He's not a violent man, not with women. He wouldn't have done anything to you," Aislinn said weakly.

"Well, I'm just batting a thousand tonight." I sighed, sitting on the edge of the bed. "I also vomited on his shoes when I first got here."

There was dead silence on the other end.

I looked at my phone to make sure we hadn't been disconnected. "Aislinn?"

Before she answered, someone rapped on the door, and I tossed the phone behind me and stood up. "Come in."

Jack Randolph opened the door and scrutinized me.

"Can I help you with anything, Mr. Randolph?" I kept my tone as frigid as the air outside.

He rubbed the back of his neck. "I'm sorry." He shoved his hands in his pockets.

I stared at him, unsure what to say. Was this some kind of trick?

"Please don't leave in the morning ... unless you want to, that is." Jack's shoes suddenly fascinated him. "I wouldn't blame you if you did want to." He began to leave, and to my dismay, I could see the red imprint of my hand on his cheek.

"I owe you an apology too," I reached toward him but dropped my hand. "About the take down ...."

I could see the corner of his mouth quirk up ... it was *so* like Braedon's. "I've never had anyone get me on the ground like that before."

My knees went wobbly for a moment. "It's a technique the police sometimes use to subdue criminals."

He frowned. "You're a cop?"

I shook my head. "I'm a high school music teacher."

Now he did grin. "I hope you'll stay."

I smiled back at him. "I will."

Jack left, shutting the door behind him. I sat on the bed, feeling a little dazed.

"Lyn!" Aislinn's voiced shouted. I had forgotten all about her.

I snatched up the phone "Aislinn—did you hear that?"

"Most of it. Good for you! I can't *ever* remember my father apologizing to *anyone*!"

"Why the quick turnaround?" I asked, confused.

She laughed. "My father's always been one to blow up fast, but once he gets something off his chest, he's over it. You must have said the right thing. It makes me think he wanted to believe you all along."

CHAPTER 29

I HAD A hard time sleeping again after all the fuss and was surprised when I woke up alert, but the clock on the nightstand said it was only 5:30 a.m. I lay in the bed trying to decide what to do. Mrs. Walters had taken my clothing. I wondered if there might be something in the room I could put on.

The closet had some men's clothing in it, all much too large for me. I moved to the dresser and opened a couple of drawers. They were full of personal items, so I didn't look any further. It seemed this room belonged to someone, and I hoped I hadn't put anyone out for the night.

I finally discovered a robe hanging on a hook behind the bathroom door. I wrapped it around me and slipped into some large slippers I found in the closet. Opening the door, I tiptoed to the top of the stairs. I heard voices coming from below, so I headed for them, trying not to trip on my oversized footwear.

Jack was pouring a cup of coffee while Mrs. Walters opened a package of bacon. They looked up when I entered. She gave me an encouraging smile, and he raised his cup in salute. "Want some coffee?" He acted like nothing had happened the night before.

"I don't drink it. Do you have any hot chocolate?"

He pointed to a cupboard, and I found several cans of gourmet hot chocolate inside. A kitchen after my own heart.

As I stirred my cocoa, the first smell of cooking bacon hit. A sharp pain stabbed my stomach, and I knew I wasn't in the clear yet. I set the cup down abruptly, spilling some of it, and jumped out of the oversized slippers. I raced from the kitchen back to the bathroom, where I threw up again.

I cursed that food in Texas. At this rate, I would lose all the weight I had gained since my return to civilization. I heard the door open and groaned. I hated being sick where anyone could see me.

"I'm sorry, Mrs. Walters," I gasped between dry heaves. "I think it's food poisoning from an enchilada I ate."

A deep voice said, "Don't worry about it. If need be, we can take you to the doctor."

Braedon's father put his hand on the top of my head and held my hair back. It reminded me of when his son had done the same for me on the catamaran. I started to cry. He murmured soothing words.

Once the heaves finally stopped, he helped me to my feet before retreating from the bathroom. I rinsed my mouth and splashed water over my face. When I came out, Jack was leaning against the dresser, his arms crossed. He glanced around the room. "This was Braedon's room when he stayed here."

My heart raced. "Those are his clothes in the closet and the dresser?"

"Yep."

Scanning the room, I asked, "Why did you never get rid of them?"

Jack shook his head, his throat working in a way I knew all too well.

I went over and touched his arm. "I'm sorry. Stupid question."

He coughed and cleared his throat. It amazed me that he could keep the tears back with the intensity of emotion I felt coming from him. He reached behind him and handed me my cocoa. The abandoned slippers rested on the floor by the dresser.

"How about you try sipping this and come downstairs when the meat smell's cleared out in a bit?" He gave me a stern look. "You aren't one of those vegetarians or vegans are you?"

In response, I reached down, lifted the leg of my pajama pants, and showed him my six-inch scar. "I got it when Braedon and I went boar hunting. We needed the skins because our clothes were falling apart ... and I wanted soap."

Jack considered me for a moment, as though the last bit of his preconceived ideas about me didn't fit anymore. "How'd you get the cut?"

"I didn't run fast enough. I was supposed to be directing the herd to Braedon's snares, but a big old boar decided he didn't want to be herded. I threw my spear at him but it glanced off— and don't you even be thinking it was just because I'm a girl!" I glared at him, and he chuckled. He sounded like Braedon, and my heart twisted.

I rubbed the clean, straight scar. "Braedon took that beast down with two arrows. He was so fast."

"Yeah, he loved hunting with a bow. He didn't need to kill like some people do. What he loved was the hunt, pitting himself against nature. *Knowing* he could take an animal down with his brains and skill was enough for him."

We stood in silence for a moment. "Is there any chance someone could get my clothes from the car?"

Jack nodded and strode from the room. I sat on the bed with my lukewarm chocolate and stroked the bedspread. Braedon had slept in this bed. I sniffed the cocoa. When my stomach didn't seem to mind, I took a sip.

After a few minutes, one of the young men from last night tapped on the door and slid my suitcase in. His close-cut, sandy-colored hair was covered with melting snow.

"Is it still snowing?" I went to the window and pulled aside the curtain. Against the reflected light of the window, larges flakes fell.

"Yes, ma'am. The forecast is calling for snow all day," he replied, still holding the doorknob in his hand.

"I'm sorry I made you go out." When he began to shut the door, I asked, "What's your name?"

He dipped his head and touched a knuckle to his forehead. "Ethan, ma'am."

"Thank you, Ethan."

He paused. "Uh, ma'am …?"

"Yes?"

"Is there any chance you could show me … us, I mean, what you did to Mr. Randolph? That was wicked!"

I laughed. "If there's time. I'm not sure how long I'll be here."

Nodding, he closed the door.

I locked the door, got dressed, and headed back downstairs. The faint scent of bacon coming from the kitchen sent my stomach roiling, so I followed the sound of voices coming from another direction.

Mrs. Walters sat at a desk doing paperwork, Jack cleaned a rifle, and Ethan worked on something made of leather in a large room that seemed to serve as both a living and a dining room. Classical music played in the background.

A set of huge windows, the centerpiece of the room, highlighted the blowing snow. The house seemed more modern than I had expected. The living room combined logs and stone with rustic decorations and a large fireplace. I was struck by the sense of *home* the scene gave me.

Everyone looked up when I entered, and I held up my empty cup. "I didn't dare put it in the kitchen. I'm sorry to be so much trouble."

Mrs. Walters came and took the cup from me. "Don't you worry about it. Can I get you some toast?"

My stomach rumbled. "I'd like to give some a try." She nodded and left for the kitchen.

I went over to where Jack and Ethan worked. "Is there anything I can do?"

"Sure." Jack plunged the rod back and forth in the barrel. "Tell me about those pirates and that island."

I spent the morning curled up in a chair by the fire, covered with a quilt, answering their questions. Surprisingly, I found it easy to talk about Braedon around them.

A little while into my story, the other young man, introduced as Owen, came in. He looked like a younger version of Ethan but with longer, darker hair. Owen came over and warmed his hands by the fire, listening to me with rapt attention.

When Mrs. Walters rose from the desk to fix lunch, I got up to help, but she insisted I rest. We had a hearty soup and homemade bread at a dining table at the end of the large room. I managed to keep down some food and felt much better.

After lunch, Jack and the boys had work to do out in the barn. I overheard them say something as they left about how bad the storm was. They worried about not being able to get out to feed the herd. Some of the horses and cattle could die.

Mrs. Walters said she had things to do upstairs, and I found myself alone. A baby grand piano sat in a corner, and I went over to examine it. It was in tune, and I sat down and began to play. The piano was a beautiful instrument with magnificent sound. It had to have been Braedon's.

When I finished playing the songs I knew by heart, I searched for some music. A bookcase full of sheet music and music books stood behind the piano. I flipped through them until I found one of the pieces I had heard Braedon play on the ship. As I held the music, I imagined him with that very paper in his hands. I brushed it against my cheek, musing about the injustice that these sheets were here when he was not.

I worked my way through the number, repeating difficult passages until I was comfortable with them.

From behind me, Ethan said. "That was one of Braedon's favorite songs."

Spinning, I saw the others had returned and had been listening. My face warmed. "I know. He used to play it for me on the ship." Self-conscious, I stood and moved to close the fallboard.

"Don't stop playing just because of us." Jack sat in a recliner and opened a newspaper.

Mrs. Walters had already taken her seat at the desk and began shuffling through her papers. "No one's played the piano in a long time. I'd like to hear some more."

Ethan and Owen nodded in agreement and took out their leather projects.

Braedon was a talented pianist, and I worried I would disappoint them. "I can't play like Braedon."

Jack snorted. "None of us can play at all. Go ahead. I've been having that thing tuned every six months. It'll be nice to get something out of the investment."

I hesitated but sat on the bench, opening the fallboard again. I pulled out a New Age piece from Braedon's collection. As I lost myself in the music, I was able to ignore the others. Because they didn't say anything when I finished the song, I picked out another, continuing until my back started to ache.

I closed the fallboard and returned the music to the bookshelf. I wasn't sure what to do next.

Emily and the boys had drifted off, but Jack sat watching me. "Do you play chess?"

"I know how to play, but I'm not very good."

He gave me a dubious look. "Like you can't play the piano?"

I tilted my head. "I never said I couldn't play. I said I couldn't play like Braedon."

"All right. All right." From behind his chair, Jack pulled out a small table with a beautiful carved chess set. "Bring a chair over," he commanded, using a tone that echoed faintly of the one Braedon had used sometimes when we argued.

This time, I did as told and put my seat across from him. While I didn't play very often, I could usually give even good players a run for their money.

"Tell me about Braedon as a boy," I said a few minutes into our first game.

Jack considered the board. "Well, he was a clever little kid, always keeping himself entertained. Pretty quiet but determined not to let anything keep him down. The only one who could bully him was Aislinn, and she played on his feelings. He put up a tough exterior to hide a soft heart."

I grinned. "I wonder where he got that from." Jack scowled, so I said softly, "Braedon didn't want to appear weak."

"No." He stretched out the word. "He didn't. I'm not sure if it was his mother's fault or mine. He'd study things out, decide what he wanted, and then you better get out of his way. If he wanted it, he'd get it."

I remembered the plan to win me over that Braedon had told me about, starting with the music he had written and his nearby but unintimidating presence during the fun part of the snorkeling trip. That made me smile.

Noticing my expression, Jack asked, "What are you thinking?"

I told him.

Jack moved his knight. "That sounds like him. Did he tell you he was married once?"

I shifted my bishop. "Yes."

"Fool kids." Jack curled his lip. "It must have been the only thing he did without thinking it to death first."

An image of Braedon's face as he made his vow to me brought a lump to my throat. How different things might have been if my trip had gone according to plan.

I whispered, "You know what's the hardest thing for me? I have *nothing* of his—not even the right to his name." I jumped up.

Like his son, Jack was faster. He pushed the little chess table over as he pulled me into his arms and held me while I wept. He cried a little too. We broke apart when we heard

Mrs. Walters enter. Jack handed me a clean handkerchief and, coughing, left the room.

She watched him go before looking at me. "I'm glad to see that. He's been grieving alone too long. He can be a cross old coot on the best of days, but he's been unbearable since he heard the news."

"He's lucky to have you here," I said after blowing my nose. "Where's Mr. Walters?"

"Died fifteen years ago."

"I'm sorry."

She shrugged, pulling out some dishes from the hutch. "I'm used to it now."

I joined her. "Did you have any children?"

With a big grin, she said, "Ethan and Owen are mine."

"They're nice boys."

"Well, I like them." She passed me some dishes. "How about you help me set the table?"

I took them and went to work.

*A*FTER DINNER, Ethan asked, "Do you think you could show us what you did to Mr. Randolph?"

Jack glowered at the reference and continued marking a crossword puzzle.

"Okay. You two come stand by me, facing each other. I'll show you how joint locks work." I sneakily watched Jack as I went through the demonstration. He feigned a lack of interest, but I could tell he took in everything I said to the boys.

"How do you know this stuff?" Owen asked after he tapped out for the third time.

I shifted his fingers in the hold he was attempting on Ethan. "I have a black belt in karate."

Jack leapt from his chair. "Well, that explains it, then!"

We stared at him.

"There's no shame in being taken down by a black belt." Jack marched over to where the boys and I stood. He held his hand out to me. "Here. Show me what you're teaching them. I won't have them thinking they can pull any of this on me."

The boys kept silent but smirked when Jack wasn't looking.

$\mathcal{E}$VERYONE PREPARED to go to bed early. The forecast called for the storm to stop in the middle of the night, and the guys wanted to be out first thing in the morning to check on the animals. As I folded up the blanket I had used, Jack hung back, waiting for the others to leave us.

Once we were alone, he said, "The roads should be cleared later tomorrow."

I nodded and put the blanket on the end of the sofa. "Thank you for today. I'm glad I got to see this place and meet you all. Braedon talked so much about it." I hesitated. "I think I needed something to help me say ... goodbye." I sniffed.

Jack clenched and unclenched his fists at his side, seeming to struggle with something. "I know I sort of apologized—in general. But ... I'm sorry about what I called you."

I touched his arm. "It's all good. You—"

"No," he interrupted, shaking off my hand. "It's not all good. I guess I ...."

"Needed to blame me for being alive when Braedon wasn't?" I asked softly.

Jack nodded, staring at his shoes. "Yes." He met my eyes. "I never thought maybe you'd be hurting too."

I couldn't think of what to say.

"Do you think you might consider staying a little longer?"

Surprised, I opened my mouth to answer, but Jack interrupted me. "I know it's a lot to ask, but it would mean a lot to me. I … I need …," he choked on the word and coughed to cover it up.

This self-reliant man was asking me for help. I reached out and touched his arm again. "I would love to stay for a while, Mr. Randolph."

His face lit up. "Call me Jack."

I considered him for a long moment.

"What?" He shifted under my scrutiny. I almost smiled, thinking he wasn't used to being uncomfortable.

"Why did you never remarry?"

Jack shrugged. "I made such a mess of the first one I guess I didn't trust my judgment."

I thought about the comfortable home he had here with a nice woman taking care of him and even boys to help raise. "Not even Mrs. Walters? Is she seeing someone?"

He frowned.

I grinned. "Sorry. None of my business." I kissed him on the cheek. "Good night, Jack."

When I got up to my room, I called Aislinn to let her know Jack had invited me to stay in Montana for a while, and I had agreed. I looked at the room with different eyes now. All this stuff had been Braedon's. I had even worn his pajamas to bed last night.

I went to the closet and searched through the clothes inside. I wasn't sure I would be able to smell anything after this long, but I lucked out and found a sweater that smelled faintly of Braedon's aftershave. It took me back to the first time we had danced. I slipped into his pajamas again and crawled into the bed, pulling the sweater up against my cheek.

I had the best night's sleep since leaving the island.

CHAPTER 30

I OVERSLEPT THE next morning and missed breakfast, which was fortunate because the food poisoning reared its nasty head again. Once I cleared my stomach, I felt much better.

Bacon seemed to be a staple breakfast food, the lingering smell hitting me when I came down the stairs. I stayed clear of the kitchen and went searching for the others, but it seemed no one was in the house.

Grabbing my purse and coat, I went out into the clear, frigid morning. I raised my hand to block the brilliant morning light reflecting off the snow. White-coated mountains shone in the distance.

Footprints in the otherwise pristine snow pointed me in the direction I needed to go, and I followed them to a large barn. As I approached the building, music blared from a partially open door. I called out and knocked. Ethan poked his head out, drying his hands on a towel.

I looked around. "Is everyone still out feeding the herds?"

"Yeah. And checking to see if we lost any." He grabbed his

coat and closed the door. "Mr. Randolph told me to follow you into town, so you could turn in your rental car. You ready?"

"Yes, but I think I should follow you."

We headed toward the cars.

"Did they go out on horseback?" I scanned the field beyond the barn.

He laughed and opened my door. "No, ma'am. We use a special kind of tractor."

By the time we got to town, I regretted not having my sunglasses against the blinding glare. Ethan walked into the business with me and handed my keys to the clerk.

She kept looking at me from the corners of her eyes. Ethan seemed to know her but didn't introduce me to the girl or acknowledge me in any way. He simply explained the car needed to be returned to Great Falls.

I completed the paperwork, and Ethan held the door open for me. Just after I had crossed the threshold, he leaned back into the office. "Oh, yeah, April. This is Mr. Randolph's daughter-in-law, Lyn. She was married to Braedon. Lyn, this is April Watts." He waved at the gaping girl, gave my back a gentle nudge as I stared at him, and followed me out of the building.

"What was that about?" I exclaimed when we were inside the truck.

He chuckled. "Mr. Randolph said we might as well get the word out about you. One little comment here and by tonight the whole town will know."

So much for my privacy. "No. No. No," I moaned, punctuating each word with a bang of my head against the window.

Ethan put the keys in the ignition. "Mr. Randolph just wants people to make you feel welcome. He's pretty particular about folks, but when he decides he likes someone, he really likes them. And he likes you."

"And he thinks I will feel welcome by having strangers talk about me behind my back?" It miffed me that Jack was doing all this without telling me, but it also warmed me that I had won his approval.

Ethan shrugged. "You'll see."

"The press better not find me because I'm suddenly the talk of the town." I hated being the center of attention. That was something for Elle, not me. With that thought, I remembered I needed to call her and pulled out my phone.

"I hear you've won over Mr. Grumpy Smurf," Elle launched right in.

I burst out laughing. "What did you call him?"

"You heard me. I met him when he came to New York two years ago. Egad, what a grouch!"

"Elle, I doubt you saw him at his best."

Her voice got gleeful. "Did you really throw up on him?"

"I'm going to kill Aislinn!" I explained about the blizzard and my food poisoning.

"Sorry you're sick, especially after Aislinn and I worked so hard to get some weight back on you. Oh, I almost forgot. Mal says there are still people trying to find out where you are. And those people from Olivia Howard's show called again."

I closed my eyes and took a deep breath. "Elle, please don't tell anyone where I'm at. Just say I want to be left alone."

"Don't worry. We won't, but I agree with Mal. You ought to consider Olivia's offer. She's a class act and would do your story right. I think people should know how wonderful Braedon was."

I rubbed my temple. "The people who matter already know

how wonderful Braedon was. I don't have to go on national television to tell them that."

"Just think about it, okay? I have to run. Love you!"

"Love you too." I hung up and stared at the passing white landscape.

"Mrs. Randolph …."

I spun to look at Ethan. "What did you call me?" Even though he had told the girl I was Braedon's wife, I had gotten used to being called Ms. North again.

Ethan stared at me, confused. "Uh … Mrs. Randolph?"

"You do know the government probably won't recognize our marriage?"

He watched me from the corner of his eye. "That's not what Mr. Randolph says."

I clenched my jaw. "What *does* Mr. Randolph say?"

"That you and Braedon exchanged vows before God, and that's married to him." He laughed. "Mr. Randolph says there are ways to get around a technicality."

"Jack's been doing a lot of talking about me when I'm not there."

Ethan took a deep breath. "He's been like my father since my own dad died, Mrs. Randolph. And since he found out about Braedon this time … well, he's started talking to me some."

I was right. These boys were like sons to Jack. The thought made me happy. "Why do you keep calling him Mr. Randolph? And for heaven's sake don't call me Mrs. Randolph again. How old are you? I doubt I'm more than ten years older than you."

"I'm eighteen … and I have to call him that."

"Why?"

He hesitated. "Because that's what I've always called him."

I rolled my eyes. "Try calling him Jack sometime and

see what happens. It was appropriate for you to call him Mr. Randolph when you were little and he was your mother's employer. You're like a son to him now."

Ethan's faced brightened. I wondered how long these people had just plugged along doing what they had always done and never considered doing something different.

After we parked in front of the house, Ethan switched off the ignition and turned to me, his left arm flung over the steering wheel. "Are people really wanting you to tell your story on TV?"

I picked up my purse from the floor. "Yes."

"Holy sh ... cow! Like who?"

"Olivia Howard."

"Holy cow!" he repeated, his eyes sparkling.

I grabbed his arm. "Ethan, I don't want the press to know I'm here."

His face fell, and he muttered something about wanting to know someone on TV. I continued to hold him with my gaze, and he finally sighed, nodded, and stepped out to get my door.

*T*HAT NIGHT, Jack sought me out again after the others had left for bed. He handed me a manila envelope. It contained the photo of Braedon and me on the formal night before Hawaii.

I dropped to the couch, drinking in Braedon's smiling image and tracing his face with my finger. I had forgotten how hot he had looked in his tuxedo ....

"Aislinn sent it to me after they returned." Jack sat beside me.

I handed him the photo. "Thank you for showing it to me. I

never did see it. That's the night he scared me off." I laughed, but it turned into a sniff. "I wish I could have that week back."

Jack put his arm around my shoulders and pushed the picture back in my hands. "I think this belongs to you, but maybe you'll let me look at it sometimes." He handed me a clean handkerchief, and I blew my nose.

*T*HE VERY evening after our discussion in the truck, Ethan, ever so casually, called Jack by his first name when asking for something at dinner. Jack didn't say anything, but he couldn't hide the hint of a smile.

I soon got into a routine. I began calling Mrs. Walters by her first name, Emily. I started helping out with chores, such as cleaning the house. I didn't know how Emily had managed the eight bedrooms alone before.

Ethan had been right that people would be curious about me after his little introduction. Folks from town began dropping by the ranch under the guise of borrowing this or returning that. Jack always introduced me as his daughter-in-law, and the visitors offered me their condolences. I relaxed when no one from the press showed up.

When we went to church on Sunday, the minister asked Jack if he planned to have a memorial service for Braedon. Jack told him to mind his own business.

I wasn't ready to give up on Braedon either, but I wondered if a service might be nice. I tried to broach the topic, but the expression on Jack's face made me decide it was best to take our time. Still, I felt like we were making progress. I think we were good for each other in that.

When I told Emily I wanted to do more, she insisted I

needed to rest up and get my strength back first. Though she never came right out and said it, I knew she wanted to fatten me up, and it was working. I slowly gained weight again, though I had a hard time throwing off the residual food poisoning. A college roommate of mine once had battled food poising for three weeks, so I wasn't worried about it too much. I wasn't violently ill after all.

Jack had a gym in the basement, put in by Braedon. I took advantage of it to slowly start working my forms again. It was bittersweet to go through the katas, since the last time I had done them had been on the island with Braedon. He would have been ready to test for his brown belt by now.

One night, as I cuddled against Braedon's old sweater, it struck me how much this place had come to feel like home, like I belonged here. Could these people fill the hole created by the loss of Braedon and my family?

$\mathcal{W}$HEN I had been there about two weeks, Jack invited me to go with them to feed the cattle and horses. He said it was a good time for me to go because things were going to get a little crazy in a few weeks when the calving started.

Jack and I sat on the slow-moving tractor, dispensing hay to the animals, while Ethan and Owen followed us on snowmobiles checking if the fence needed repairs. When they found a section, I went over to ask if I could help. Ethan laughed at me.

With tight lips, I swept him. Ethan went over on his back, his eyes widening as he hit the packed snow. Owen stared at us, his jaw hanging loose.

Ethan leapt to his feet, his eyes blazing. "Why'd you do that?"

I advanced on him, and he stepped back like a well-mannered cowboy would. "Don't act like I'm helpless." I tried to glare at him but spoiled it by giggling.

Even though I had insulted his dignity, his good nature won out. He laughed.

I slapped him on the arm. "Give me a chance. Heck, I've hunted boar."

He gave me a light shove before showing me how to work the wire to reinforce the fence.

As we walked back from the barn, I scooped up a huge handful of snow and chucked it at Ethan. I'm a terrible shot and hit Jack instead. With a shriek, I backed away. "It was an accident! I meant to hit Ethan!"

That guaranteed Jack and Ethan would team up against me. They each grabbed a handful of snow. I dashed behind Owen, who threw one snowball that caught Ethan in the face, seized my arm, and pulled me with him behind Jack's truck.

"Owen, I'll make them, and you throw."

With a wicked grin, he started launching lethal ice missiles at the others, who had taken cover behind a corner of the house. The game ended when I hit the front window and brought Emily out.

Covered in snow, we laughed as we entered the house under Emily's watchful gaze. While we went to our rooms to change, she set food and hot drinks on the table. I had my first hearty appetite in months.

After dinner, while I carried in the ice cream that went with her chocolate cake, Emily said, "Don't forget the Chamber dance is next Saturday."

Jack tipped his chair back, chewing on a toothpick. He eyed me. "You interested in going to the dance with us?"

I hesitated. I had just had my most normal day yet, and I didn't want to stir up memories.

Emily gave me a sympathetic nod. "You and Braedon used to go dancing on the ship, didn't you?"

I sighed. "Yes."

She looked to Jack and the boys for support and said, "They have a disco theme this year. I don't think there'll be much about one of the Chamber shindigs that'll remind you of dancing with Braedon. You'll be too busy keeping your feet out from under cowboy boots."

That might be okay. I agreed to go.

CHAPTER 31

*T*HE NIGHT of the dance, everyone quit work a little early and Jack took us to a fun little place called Bon Tons Soda Fountain. Familiar faces greeted us in the small, narrow restaurant with its old-fashioned black and white checkerboard floor tiles and red vinyl covered seats.

When we finished eating, I wanted to look at the displays at the Lewistown Art Center. I had noticed it when I first arrived but hadn't had an opportunity yet to go inside.

Jack and Emily needed something at the Paint and Glass store down the street, and Ethan wanted to check out a rifle at the Sport Center, but Owen came with me.

The Art Center wasn't a large building, but there were several artists featured. I was drawn to a large section dedicated to someone named Virtanen. Owen said he was a local artist and even taught a few special classes at the high school when he was in the area. As I stood trying to decide which piece to buy, Jack stuck his head in the door and told us to hurry. I promised myself to come back when I had more time.

The large Trade Center building by the fairgrounds was

already full of people when we arrived. While a number of people had honored the disco theme and had dressed in leisure suits, bell-bottom pants, and platform shoes, many, like us, were dressed in nice but normal clothing.

I spotted the reporter for the local paper wandering around taking pictures of the event. Alarmed, I ducked behind Ethan when he headed in our direction. Ethan whispered over his shoulder, "I think it's safe to have your picture taken here. He's just got a small photography business on the side." Ethan pulled me out front, and we all leaned in for a group picture.

A while later, Ethan and I finished a dance and stopped to get some punch. Jack and Emily were dancing together again, and Ethan watched them. I thought they made a nice couple. "Do they dance together a lot?"

"No," he replied in wonder.

I followed their movement with interest. If Jack looked my way, I snapped my gaze to a couple next to them. I glanced up at Ethan, eyes dancing.

*O*N MONDAY morning, the guys had already gone when I came downstairs. Emily handed me a bowl of hot oatmeal. "Have you seen this?" She pointed to the local paper on the counter. The front page had an article and pictures from the dance, including a good one of us standing by the refreshment table.

The hair stood up on the back of my neck, and I coughed on a mouthful of oatmeal. My face plastered all over the Lewistown paper was like a target pointed right here. What should I do? I soon realized there was nothing I *could* do. It was too late. I looked at Emily, who watched me in concern. There was no point in alarming her. I cleared my throat. "Where is everyone?"

"A couple of the cattle calved last night." She wrote something on her notepad. "It's starting a little early this year. The next couple of months are going to be busy."

I perked up. "Can I help?"

Emily tilted her head, considering me over her reading glasses. "Jack wants you to get stronger first ... now don't look at me like that. You're just now getting rid of that hollow look in your face. And I know you're still throwing up; I heard you this morning. You can help next year." She turned back to her list. "If you want to help, I've got a whole list of things for you to do."

"All right." I mulled over what she had just said. I could help next year? Were they thinking I might make this my permanent home?

"The first thing you can do is take Owen to school and then pick him up in the afternoon. We need the truck for errands. While you're in town, I need you to stop at the grocery store." Emily handed me a piece of paper. "Here's the list." She held the corner of the list when I tried to take it. "Are you all right with this?"

"Sure," I replied just as Owen came dashing in.

"Sorry I'm late," he said as his mother handed him his backpack. "Jack says both the calves should make it."

"Good. Lyn's taking you today." Emily tossed him the truck keys.

"Okay." Owen caught them. "You ready, Lyn?"

I snagged my coat, picked up my purse, and followed him out to the small truck. While he drove to the school, I asked him, "Are you and Ethan planning to become ranchers?"

"Not Ethan. He wants to become a doctor, like Braedon. He starts college in the fall."

"And you?"

Owen huffed as he pulled into the school. "Yeah, I want to be a rancher. I wish Jack would let me do more now." He put the truck in park, opened the door, and got out. I handed him his backpack and slid into the driver's seat.

"I'll be back at three."

He grinned. "I'll be here."

As I entered the grocery store, the smell from the bakery told me they had been busy, and I wondered if I should get a treat to go with dinner. I recognized one of the clerks and waved to her.

I got a cart and started working through Emily's list. Judging by its length, she must have wanted to stock up for the busy days ahead. If she planned on me taking over some of the cooking responsibilities, I hoped she had the recipes set aside. I was a solid cook if not a particularly creative one.

As I knelt on the floor to compare flour brands, I noticed what could only be described as tittering from the front of the store. One of the clerks said, "I think she's over there."

I turned my attention back to the list and realized I hadn't paid any attention to the brands Emily preferred and decided I had better call her. As I reached into my pocket for my phone, I heard the clicking of shoes on the tile floor. They turned up my aisle.

I was about to press the call button when a voice behind me said, "Lyn. It *is* you."

Frozen in place, I stared at the numbers on my display. I knew that voice. Standing slowly, I turned to face him. It all came back then—the smell of salt, the feel of the humid air, even the movement of the ship. Elle marching past the leering pirates. I hadn't cried in almost a week, but suddenly I was bawling.

Jori strode over and put his arms around me, and I sobbed into his shirt. Behind him, I could hear concerned voices, but no one approached us. After a minute, he said over his shoulder, "Miss, could you get her some water?"

"No." I lifted my head. "It's okay. I've been doing so well. I don't know where that came from." I put away my phone and wiped at my eyes. "My makeup must be a mess … oh, no. Look what I've done to your shirt!"

"Don't worry about my shirt." Jori produced a clean handkerchief that smelled of his distinctive cologne, one that brought back more memories. I unsuccessfully tried to wipe my face. He took the handkerchief from me and removed the smudges to my makeup. "There you are. Almost as good as new."

I gazed at his face and reached up to touch the scar on his left cheek. While I could see why he couldn't model anymore, I thought the imperfection actually added to his beauty. Perhaps because I knew how he had earned it. I tugged at a strand of his long, silky hair. "You've let your hair grow long too. I like it."

"They're calling you Mrs. Randolph."

"Braedon and I exchanged vows on the island." I was pleased my voice didn't crack.

Jori touched my cheek. "See, I was right about you two, wasn't I?"

I blinked against the tears. "You were especially right to call me an idiot."

"Do you need anything else, Mr. Virtanen?" interrupted a clerk.

"Virtanen!" I grabbed his arm. "Those are your paintings at the Art Center."

Jori smiled his beautiful smile. "Do you like them?"

"I almost bought a piece the other day. But what's a Seattleite doing here? Owen called you a local artist."

The clerk frowned and interrupted again. "I thought you were from Finland, Mr. Virtanen."

He flashed her a look of irritation. "I am, but I was living in Seattle when I met Lyn." Jori turned a sad smile to me. "I live part of the year in Finland now. My agent has a gallery in Helsinki."

"What brought you to Montana?"

"Braedon. He told me so much about this place, I had to see it. I've come here the last two springs. There's quite a market in Europe for art inspired by the American West. I was surprised when the school asked me to do some teaching here last year, but I've enjoyed it." He put his hands in his pockets. "I also went to Colorado Springs. I wanted to meet your parents, but I waited too long. I went to their funeral."

A sharp stinging hit my eyes, and I jerked his handkerchief up again.

Jori touched my shoulder. "I'm sorry ...."

I sniffed and changed the subject. "Elle told me your work's all the rage."

He got that surprisingly humble expression I loved. "I was fortunate. One of my drawings caught the eye of someone influential, who in turn had connections to other influential people."

I couldn't remember anyone at the ranch mentioning him. "Does Jack, uh, Mr. Randolph, know about you?"

"No. I'd hoped to introduce myself last year, but when I

talked with some people around town, they warned me against bringing Braedon up. So I spent my time painting and meeting the people here." Jori picked up a can from my basket and rolled it in his hand, staring at it. "When the work I did here sold so well in Europe, it made sense to come back and give it another try." He looked up, tossing the can back. "Especially once I heard you'd been found."

"You have to come for dinner and meet Jack. Let me give you my number."

"I already have it." He chuckled. "Elle called me last night and said she thought you might be ready to see me."

"She knew you were here and didn't tell me?" I reached for my cell phone.

Laughing, Jori pushed my hand away from my purse. "We're talking about Elle here. She always has the answer for what's best for everyone." He glanced at my cart. "I don't have class today. Can I help you with your shopping?"

"Sure, but I'm almost done." I picked up the list. "You have to tell me everything you've been up to and about your latest flirts."

Jori drove the cart while I got the last items on the list and helped me load the groceries into the truck.

"Do you want to come out to the ranch? I'm cooking lunch today." He hesitated, and I reached for the truck door. "That's okay. I'm sure you have things to do."

He covered my hand on the handle. "I only hesitate because of your father-in-law."

I turned to face him. "You've waited a long time to meet him. Just do it."

Jori thought for a moment and exhaled, his breath fogging in the cold air. "I'll follow you in my car."

CHAPTER 32

*T*HE WEATHER had been warming over the past few days and most of the snow from the recent storms had melted, leaving muddy roads.

I parked by the door, and Jori pulled his little sports car up next to it, his sketchbook and a pencil in his pocket. "This is even better than I imagined!" His face glowed as he stared at the house. He took two bags from the truck and followed me up the stairs.

"You've never even driven by before?" I asked as we put the groceries inside the door and began taking off our shoes and jackets.

Jori ducked his head, looking sheepish as he picked up the grocery bags again.

"Silly man," I said as we walked through the large living room into the kitchen. "Do you mind getting the rest, while I start putting these away? Then you can look around the main floor."

With a happy grin, he bowed and hurried from the room. Alone, I leaned against the counter and watched him slide his feet into his stylish loafers. Jori in Lewistown. Who would have thought?

Which made me remember that stinker Elle. I called her while I started emptying the bags. No one answered, so I left a scathing message for her to call me.

Jori didn't say anything as he brought in the last of the bags and then left to explore. Once I finished, I found him in the large living room, furiously sketching as though he would never have another chance. I came over and sat down on the arm of the chair he was in, so I could see what he was drawing.

He had already completed several pictures and was working on the beautiful view through the window. I reached forward and picked up the other sketches. As always, his drawings touched me.

"I really like these, though to be honest I haven't seen any of your works I haven't liked." I stood up and stretched. "I'm going to start cooking. You can keep going if you want or come in and help me."

"I'll help." He set the sketchpad on the table and rose from the chair. "What are you making?"

"Soup and bread … well, Emily got the bread started in the machine this morning."

I gave him an apron to tie over his designer slacks. After washing our hands, I cut the meat and got it browning, and he chopped the vegetables. "So, tell me what you've been up to," I said as we worked.

He made light of the estrangement with his family, spoke in amazement about his rise to fame, and talked happily about his move back to Finland. I could tell he was avoiding some issues by the way he glossed over them, but I didn't press him. He would share them when and if he wanted to.

Once we had the soup simmering, we returned to the living room, and I showed him pictures of Braedon from several photo albums.

"Considering how you cried as soon as you saw me, it may be too soon, but ... are you up to talking about it?"

I squeezed the bridge of my nose. I wasn't going to cry again.

Jori pulled my hand from my face. "You're not ready. It's okay." He gestured toward the piano. "Do you still play?"

"Yes." I appreciated his sensitivity. "I play a lot. It's been very healing."

He moved to the piano and picked up the sheets off the bookshelf. "Play for me. I used to love listening to you on the ship." He set the music near the keyboard.

I played the piece, and as I neared the end, he said, "Another." I gave myself to the music and jumped when the front door opened and Ethan, followed by Emily and then Jack, entered.

Ethan stared as Jori rose from the couch. "Mr. Virtanen? What are you doing here?"

I quickly closed the fallboard. Remembering Ethan's comment about having taken a class from Jori last year, I said, "Ethan, Jori's an old friend of mine. Can you introduce him to Jack and your mother while I set the table?" I dashed into the kitchen where the alarm for the bread had just gone off.

When I returned to the dining area with the dishes, I watched to see how Jack was reacting to Jori. It wasn't encouraging if Jack's expression was any indication.

"Come help with the table while they finish getting cleaned up, Jori," I called. "Lunch will be ready in five minutes, you guys."

Jori hurried to help me. "I should have left sooner."

I giggled and told him about my introduction to Jack. Jori's expression became grim. "What's wrong?" I murmured.

"He shouldn't have called you a tramp."

"Shh ... here they come."

Jack's glower as he sat at the table shut down all conversation. He didn't ask Jori any questions or ask about my morning like he normally did.

The longer the uncomfortable silence went on the angrier I got. Clenching my fork, I finally asked, "So, do you always treat guests at your table like this, Jack?"

From the corner of my eye, I saw Jori's ears go red. Emily and Ethan froze.

When Jack started to sputter, I said, "Jori is a dear friend to both Braedon and me from the ship. He came to Montana two years ago because he wanted to meet *you*."

"I apologize, Mr. Randolph. I shouldn't have come." Jori started to rise.

"Sit down there, young man," Jack barked.

"Now, Jack," chided Emily as I pulled at Jori's sleeve. He sat, his body rigid, his face flushed. I knew from experience how unpredictable his temper could be and hoped he wouldn't lose it.

Jack appeared to like the flash of anger, however, and smiled for the first time. "So tell me why you've wanted to meet me."

I glared at Jack, wondering if he took this approach with every new person.

Jori looked at me before taking a calming breath. Stiff at first, he began to share some of his shipboard experiences with Braedon, most of which I had been a part of. Jori turned on his charm, and everyone relaxed.

With some reluctance, Jack checked the clock. "Well, it's time we got back to work."

Jori stood and offered his hand to Jack. "I'm glad I got to meet you, Sir. If it's all right with you, I'll help Lyn clean up, and then I must get to an appointment."

"Sure thing." Jack took his hand and squeezed it.

I groaned at the masculine grip contest that resulted. Jack strode from the table, and I had to choke back a laugh when Jori turned to me, eyes wide and right hand clutched to his chest, and mouthed 'ow.'

At the door, Jack called back to Jori. "Call me Jack. And you're welcome to come back anytime you want."

Jori turned and dropped his customary bow.

When Jack returned from his chores, I was waiting for him with my arms across my chest. He eyed me as he took off his hat and coat. Without saying anything, I followed his progress to his recliner with my eyes. He picked up the newspaper and pretended I wasn't there. I tapped my foot.

He grunted and dropped his hands to his lap, the paper crumpling. "Out with it, girl."

"What was that all about with Jori during lunch?"

Jack's cheeks went red, and he looked like he wanted to be anywhere else.

"Out with it, Jack."

"I don't have any use for prissy, pretty boys."

"That doesn't justify you being rude to my friend."

"I said he could come back, didn't I? But he better not start courting you." Jack picked up the paper again, watching me over the top. "Now let me read in peace."

I couldn't believe Jori had made both Jack and Braedon feel threatened.

*T*HE CALVING season was indeed upon us, and I didn't see much of the others over the next few days. I focused on working around the house and keeping everyone fed and in clean clothes. Jori came by a couple of times.

After dinner one night, I walked him to his car. He opened the door and hesitated. "You need to get out. Everyone's so busy with the calves, you spend too much time here alone. Let me take you to a movie."

Once he mentioned it, I realized he was right. I was starting to feel a little stir-crazy. "I would love to."

"I'll pick you up on Friday at seven." He kissed my cheek before getting into his car.

I stood on the porch and watched the little red car speed away, grateful to have such a good friend.

Owen came to stand beside me. He stared at the disappearing taillights. "I ... I'm flabbergasted."

The teacher in me grinned at his word choice. "About what?"

"About Mr. Virtanen taking you out. We all thought he was gay."

"Jori gay?" I burst out laughing. "Why would anyone ever think that?"

"Because women have been throwing themselves at him since he first came here." Owen smirked. "At school we love watching how he fends them off. And some of them ... well, we couldn't figure out why he turned them away ... unless he was gay."

"He used to be quite the ladies' man. He's definitely not gay." The idea made me giggle again.

*J*ORI TOOK me to dinner at the Bistro before the movie. Because of Owen's admission, I paid more attention to the people around us. There were many hopeful glances from women when he held my chair for me to sit.

I giggled at one particularly shocked woman's expression and buried my face in my menu.

"What are you laughing at?"

"Do you know what your reputation is here?"

He arched a brow. "I shouldn't have any reputation here."

I fought to control the twitching at the corners of my mouth and failed. When I leaned in conspiratorially, he moved forward until our heads were nearly touching. I whispered, "Owen told me everyone thinks you're gay."

Jori sat upright. "Why would they think that?"

I told him what Owen had said, and Jori muttered something that might have been a Finnish curse. "I date. Just not here." His eyes narrowed. "What did you tell him?"

I smoothed the soft paper napkin in my lap. "That you're not gay."

"That's all you said?"

"Well, I said on the ship you had a reputation as a ladies' man."

Jori exhaled a deep breath. "So I'm either a player or I'm gay?"

"I'm just the messenger." I caught a glare directed at me from a table of women and coughed to cover a laugh.

He started to look over his shoulder, but I grabbed his sleeve and he turned back.

"Let's just say that being seen with a girl tonight could

change your reputation here, but you'll need to be prepared to fight off more fans." I indicated the table of women and giggled again.

"Let's order," he growled, signaling the server.

Later, when the waiter removed our dishes, Jori leaned back in his chair. "Can you tell me how Jimmy died?"

Like he had turned on a faucet, the tears flowed as I talked about the young Texan. It naturally led to Maria's death, and the island. And Braedon.

Jori had to request more napkins even after he let me borrow another one of his monogrammed handkerchiefs.

"I'm sorry," I sniffed.

"No." He reached across the table and pressed my hand for a moment, the skin of his fingers rough with calluses. "I'm sorry. I shouldn't have brought it up. I—"

I interrupted him. "They were your friends too. You have the right to know." I paused. "I'm starting to sound like Elle's husband."

Jori perked up. "What's Mal say?"

I told him about the Olivia Howard interview, expecting him to agree with me.

A funny look crossed his face. "I think he's right. You should do it."

I threw his handkerchief at him, but it fell short. "Why do you care?"

He shrugged, snatching the fabric square before I could take it back. "It would be good for you."

"Right." He was such a liar. There was something else going on, but I decided to let it go. "Now give that back. I need to wash that first."

"I can wash it." He checked his watch. "We need to leave

if we're going to make the show." He stood and pulled out my chair for me.

"You've been such a supportive friend." I gave him a quick hug and whispered, "Now, put your arm around my shoulders when we go out. My contribution to redeeming your reputation."

He did as requested. "Did you see their faces?" I said with a laugh when we were back in the car.

"I'm not sure I'm going to like your kind of help," he replied, watching the women stare out the restaurant window at us.

𝓘 OVERSLEPT THE next morning. The others had already gone out, so I went about my usual routine. After lunch, I returned to the previous day's project of working my way through the unused rooms—cleaning, airing, changing sheets on the beds, and so on.

While vacuuming, I thought I heard something and shut off the machine. Someone downstairs was shouting. I wondered if it was Jack. He would erupt once in a while. He had a temper like a volcano, building up pressure and then releasing. Once he blew, it was over.

I listened for a minute, but this shouting didn't sound like one of those episodes. I ran down the stairs to see what was wrong.

Owen stood in the open doorway, cool air blowing in. I could just barely see Ethan and Jack and a couple of men by a car with an out-of-state license plate. Jack yelled at them while Ethan tried to calm him down. I wondered where Emily might be. She could usually get him to settle down. Then I remembered she had gone into town.

"Owen, what's going on?" I asked as I walked up next to him.

At the sound of my voice, all the men turned toward us, and one of the visitors lifted a camera and took a picture, the flash blinding me. Owen shoved me back into the house, crowding in behind me, and slammed the door shut. I hit the step wrong, twisted my ankle … and went down as excruciating pain consumed me.

I cried out and pulled in my leg, trying not to move my ankle. Owen dashed to my side. "I'm sorry. I'm so sorry." He tried to help me up.

"No," I moaned, pushing him away. "Give me a minute." I clenched my fists, my eyes watering. Once the initial agony had passed and I could breathe again, I said, "Okay. Help me stand."

He put my arm over his shoulder and supported my hops to the couch. I couldn't find any position that didn't hurt. Owen stood staring at me, his face an image of misery.

"I need some ice!" I groaned.

He fled to the kitchen and returned with ice wrapped in a towel. He put it gently on my ankle, but I still yelped at the contact. When he jerked the icepack back, I hissed, "Put it back! I have to stop the swelling." I bit back a cry as he pressed the pack against the quickly bruising flesh. The numbing cold eased the pain to a manageable level.

Outside, the shouting continued. "Owen, can you see what's happening?"

He ran to the door, and I shouted, "No! Look through the window."

"Sorry." He peered through the curtain. "I think they're leaving now." He looked at me over his shoulder. "I sure hope Jack didn't hit one of them. We don't need the police coming around. That would draw even more reporters."

Reporters. My stomach sank. So much for the local photographer being safe.

When Owen returned and reached to check the ice pack, I held up my hands. "Don't touch it! Go get Jack and tell him I need to see a doctor."

Owen bolted to the window again and, seeing it was safe, yanked the door open and yelled, "Jack! We need to get Lyn to the hospital."

Jack and Ethan raced into the house and to the couch. I flinched as Jack moved the ice. He swore and told Ethan to get the truck.

If I hadn't been in so much pain, it would have been funny the way they danced around and argued with each other about how best to get me into the truck without jarring my ankle. Finally, with Jack in the driver's seat, me in the middle leaning against him—which made shifting a little complicated—and Ethan in the front holding up my leg, we made the bumpy ride.

Fortunately, the emergency room wasn't very busy, and they got me in to see the doctor right away.

"You're lucky, Mrs. Randolph." The doctor wrote something in my chart. "It's just a sprain." He looked up. "I know—is there ever *just* a sprain? But take it easy for a couple of days, and you should be fine. How are you feeling otherwise?"

I shrugged, but Jack said, "She's had a touch of food poisoning she can't seem to shake off."

The doctor examined me further. "Now, didn't you just come back after being in the tropics for a couple of years?"

That was a diplomatic way of putting it. "There are some pretty nasty diseases out there, so let's test some blood just to be sure."

Once a nurse had drawn a sample, the doctor returned with an air cast for my ankle and instructions to stay off it for a day or two. He handed me a prescription for pain medication and said we could go.

The men insisted on carrying me into the house. Emily had returned, and Owen had let her know what had happened. She immediately ushered me to Jack's recliner and propped up my foot. Jack brought me some Tylenol and then sat on the coffee table in front of me.

"Who were those men?" I asked after swallowing the pills.

Jack growled, "Paparazzi."

I laid my head back and closed my eyes. "So they've found out where I am."

He studied me. "People are just curious, I figure. We don't watch a lot of television around here, but we do watch some. To tell you the truth, we've kept it off, so you wouldn't see how much you showed up."

I sat up. "I should be old news by now."

Jack shrugged. "I've been talking to Mal about it …."

I clenched the pillow. "Not that again!"

Jack leaned closer. "You're doing a lot better now. Maybe if you just agree to give an exclusive interview, everyone else will leave you alone." He patted my hand. "Give it some thought. Do the interview and put it behind you."

I threw a pillow at him, missing. "Easy for you to say!"

Grinning, he picked up the pillow and tossed it back at me. He didn't miss.

$\mathscr{J}$ORI CAME by that evening after hearing in town about my accident. He brought flowers and stayed for dinner.

"Hey, Mr. Virtanen," Owen said, as they cleared the dinner table. "I hear you're leaving early this year."

Jack was helping me into my chair, and I jerked my head around to stare at Jori.

His eyes met mine. "I've got a big show in New York in April. They've been working on it for a year."

"Will you be back?" I asked, settling the pillow behind my head.

He shook his head. "I've got two shows scheduled in Europe right after New York."

Until I knew he would be leaving, I hadn't realized how important his friendship had become to me. "Fine. Go gallivanting all over Europe and leave us with the cows."

"Hey!" Jack closed a button on his jacket, preparing to check on his stock one more time before bed. "Don't go badmouthing my cattle until you've spent more time with them."

When Jori and I were alone, I asked, "Will you write?"

He sat on the coffee table in front of my chair. "Of course. And call." He leaned forward and tugged at a strand of my hair, reminding me once again of my brother. "You can visit me, if you'd like. It would be fun to show you Finland."

The idea appealed to me, but I wasn't sure if I was up yet to traveling outside of the States.

Jori stood. "If not this year, then next. And I'll be back here next spring." He put on his jacket and leaned over to kiss the top of my head before leaving. "Don't go tripping over anything else."

CHAPTER 33

I TRIED WALKING with the air cast the next day. Being careful, I could hobble around enough to help with simple chores. As I worked, I considered my situation and Emily's comment that I could help out with the next calving season.

This family felt like a part of me, and I had grown to love them. I could imagine making my home here. We thought alike and connected on an emotional level. But a lot of it was because of Braedon. My dream in Great Falls hadn't been that far off. He *was* everywhere on the ranch.

It wasn't just the photos of him and Aislinn that covered the walls, but the memories the others had of him. He had worked on or designed so many things. Or certain spots had been his favorite places to ride or his preferred trail to hike.

But should I make my permanent home here? It made me happy to putter around the house and help out where I could, but I didn't fool myself that I was doing anything other than healing, which I couldn't do for the rest of my life.

The phone rang as I helped Emily sort through some fabric scraps for a quilt. She got up to answer it.

"Lyn, it's for you." She carried in the cordless receiver.

"Did Jack forget something?" I took the phone she offered. "Hello?"

"Mrs. Randolph?"

"Yes."

The woman identified herself as the nurse for some doctor I had never heard of.

"I'm sorry. I have no idea what you're talking about. What test?"

She paused and I heard paper shuffling. "From your emergency room visit. Your blood test was positive."

I remembered the doctor saying something about tropical diseases and swallowed a sudden lump in my throat. "For ... for what?"

"Your pregnancy test, Mrs. Randolph. You'll want to schedule an appointment soon. And don't take any medication without your doctor's approval. Congratulations." She hung up.

At the beep-beep sound from the phone, Emily rushed to my side and took it from me. "What is it?"

Why would someone do that to me? My heart felt like it had been ripped from my chest. "That was a sick joke."

Emily pushed some buttons on the phone. "That's the hospital's number. You said something about a test."

My knees went wobbly, and I had to sit down. "A pregnancy test."

"When did you have your last period?" Emily asked, her voice calm.

My mouth opened and then snapped shut. I hadn't paid attention. "I haven't had it since we left the island."

My heart raced. Could it be true? "Maybe it wasn't food poisoning after all," I breathed, touching my abdomen tenuously.

Her eyes danced. "No, honey. It wasn't food poisoning."

A baby. Braedon's baby. My entire body flooded with joy; I felt giddy and euphoric. I clutched Emily's hands. "This can't be true. I've wanted it too much!"

The roar of Jack's truck as he pulled up outside brought us to our feet. I continued to grip Emily's hand as we faced the door, not knowing if I could say the words, as if speaking them aloud would make it a mistake.

Jack hesitated at the open door, watching us, seeming to know something was up. He shut the door against the cold, never taking his eyes off us. "Out with it."

Emily beat me to it, releasing my hand and clapping hers together. "The rabbit died, Jack!"

He stared at me for a second before raising a finger. "That blood test!" He ran over, a huge grin on his face as he swept me off my feet and twirled me in a circle. When he set me down, he put his face inches from mine. "Are you happy?"

My answer was to burst into tears.

THAT NIGHT we had a party of sorts. I had called Elle earlier and told her to go over to Aislinn's house that evening so we could talk to everyone at once. I think they were as stunned as I was at the news.

Jack hung back as everyone else went up the stairs to bed, leaning against the fireplace. I joined him there.

"You'll stay here now, won't you? Make your home with us?" His intense blue eyes begged me to make it so.

I let out a deep breath. I meant to repay Braedon's estate for my expenses, but now I had an ER visit and a baby coming. "You sure you're okay with that? I'm turning out to be kind of expensive."

"Don't be stupid." Jack said, suddenly cross. "You're my daughter now, and I take care of my family. Money's no problem. My great-grandfather may have started *this* ranch, but my grandfather started a couple more in Texas, and one of them had oil on it. By the time he sold it, he'd made millions."

He chuckled at my expression.

"You didn't really think I could be a prosperous rancher without either a wife who had a job in town or an independent income, did you? And I'll bet you thought my lack of money came between Braedon's mother and me. No, they just didn't approve of my social standing."

Jack glanced around the large room with fondness. "Here, we've got everything we need and a little of what we want. That's all that's necessary to be happy. This house may seem large, but I came from a big family. We needed the space." He winked at me. "Besides, you can only be in one room at a time."

"Braedon was definitely his father's son. He wasn't materialistic either."

That seemed to please Jack a lot.

ONE LITTLE incident showed how fast things were moving between Jack and Emily. It happened the first day I was fully up and about again. I had already gone to bed but had forgotten my book in the living room. When I got to the stairs, Ethan and Owen stood at the bottom, peering stealthily into the kitchen.

I could tell they were trying to be quiet, so I tiptoed down to join them. Music came faintly from the kitchen, where Jack and Emily slow danced. Jack stopped and bent to kiss her—and it got hot pretty fast.

I grabbed the boys' shirts and dragged them back up the stairs. They both had grins as wide as Jack Skellington's.

"Don't you dare say anything about this to either one of them!" I told the boys firmly when we reached the top of the stairs.

Owen shook his head. "Oh, we can have fun with this one!"

Ethan, however, turned serious. "No, Lyn's right. That could ruin this. You know how Jack is. Let's not mess this up for them."

Owen paused, considering it, and then grunted. "You're probably right. But all I can say is, it's about time."

J ORI DROPPED by in the early afternoon the next day when everyone else was gone.

"I'm in the kitchen," I shouted as I hobbled to the oven to put in a cake.

He peeked around the doorway, his face alight. He held his arms behind him as though keeping something hidden from me.

Wary, I waited to see what he was up to.

Jori stepped into the room, swinging his arm around and presenting me with a beautiful bouquet of balloons. One of them had the image of a baby on it.

I hugged him.

He slid into one of the breakfast bar chairs. "So a part of Braedon will live on after all. I'm happy for you."

"I still can't believe it."

He tilted his head. "You look different already. You have a glow about you."

"It's the hormones."

"No. This comes from knowing, I think." He checked his watch and rose. "I've got a class. I need to go."

"Thank you for bringing these." He hugged me goodbye, and I asked, "Would you like to come for dinner?"

"I would, but I have a date." He shook a finger at me. "Since you helped me put a new spin on my reputation, I decided I'd better keep it going."

"Don't go breaking any hearts," I warned.

He winked as he turned to leave. "No promises."

$\mathcal{J}$ACK ACCOMPANIED me to my first doctor's appointment. He must have driven the receptionist crazy with his pacing around before the nurse called me into the consultation room. The doctor put to rest my biggest concern about my malnourished state at conception. Everything looked fine.

When the doctor was about to listen to my baby's heartbeat, I said, "Jack will never forgive you if he's not here for this."

"Good idea." The doctor poked his head out the door and asked his nurse to bring him in.

In a minute, my father-in-law burst into the examination room, brimming with excitement. When the doctor rolled the device over my belly, I reached out and took Jack's hand. He covered it with his other hand, and we listened to the sound of the galloping heartbeat coming out of the speaker. We looked at each other, our eyes misting.

If only Braedon could have been there.

*W*E HAD a few more altercations with the press. Mal continued to push me about doing an interview because Olivia Howard's show persisted in calling him. The pressure from her people had ratcheted up again now they knew I was staying with Braedon's family. Mal could tell they were starting to wear me down.

What helped me decide was the news coverage of a ceremony honoring Moli and the Scouts for their part in the rescue. While I watched, I realized how much I did want people to know about Jimmy, Maria, and Braedon. I also wanted them to know about those wonderful boys who had been lost.

I talked it over with Jack, and we called Mal to discuss conditions.

"I have to be able to control how this interview goes," I told him, "including approving the final piece. Or it doesn't happen."

"That should be no problem," he replied, his excitement coming through the phone. "They really want this. I think they'll agree to just about anything you request. I'll negotiate a healthy fee."

"They pay fees for interviews?" An idea began to form in my mind.

"Sometimes they do."

After thinking about it for a couple of days and discussing it with Jori, I called Mal again. "I want you to negotiate the largest sum you can get."

"Okay." His voice became soft. "Can you tell me why you need so much?"

"I want the money to go to the families of the two boys who were lost. I want the contract to guarantee it."

"Great idea! I don't think I'll have a problem selling that at all."

CHAPTER 34

*J*ACK KEPT a small jet at the Lewistown Airport and flew me to New York in mid-April to film the show.

Aislinn, D'Arcy, Elle, Mal, and Jori—who had already gone to New York for his show—met us at the airport. *The Olivia Howard Show* sent a limo to pick us up, and we were put in a suite in a fancy hotel.

I couldn't believe how huge Elle had gotten. Her delivery date was close.

With a free evening, we went out to dinner and then to Jori's art show. When we arrived at the gallery, there was the usual twittering as people recognized him. He played the host, taking us around and showing his pieces. The art on display put his pictures in Montana to shame; these were his best works.

Jori and I got a little ahead of the others and, as we came around a corner, I found myself on board the ship again. The pictures in the alcove were all from Elle's little group: in the gym during a self-defense class, during a dinner gathering on the sky deck, dancing in the Crow's Nest. And a beautiful oil painting of Jimmy and Maria.

Jori put his arm around me. "Why are you crying? Didn't I capture them right?"

"Of course you captured them right." I leaned against him and stared at the pictures. "Jori, this is incredible. Can I get a copy to give to Jimmy's family?"

"I've been thinking about giving them the original since you told me about your visit," he said quietly.

"How hard is it to have prints made? You know," I continued without letting him answer, "I wish I could take these to the interview tomorrow."

"That would be an excellent idea," D'Arcy commented as he and the others joined us, "if the gallery owners will release them."

Mal examined the pictures. "They will. Why miss out on an opportunity to have their gallery showcased on *The Olivia Howard Show*?"

I winked at Jori who wore an almost fatalistic expression I didn't understand. "Wouldn't hurt our resident artist either. Right?"

He grinned. "Right."

$\mathcal{E}$LLE AND Aislinn helped me with my hair the next morning, rolling and twisting it into a very feminine braid.

Olivia greeted us when we arrived, which I understood was not common. Even more beautiful in person, she was younger than I had thought, perhaps only a couple of years older than me.

I introduced her to everyone, and her eyes danced when I presented her to Jori. He took the hand Olivia extended to him, and she said, "So, we meet at last." He bowed, seeming to hold on a little longer than necessary.

Shooting Jori a quick glance, I explained about his painting to Olivia. "I would love to show them if you think there'd be time."

Her eyes never left Jori as she said, "I have seen some of Mr. Virtanen's work at the Schulze Gallery. I would love to include a piece in today's taping."

One of Olivia's staff members then asked me to follow him to the other side of the stage. Taking a deep breath, I squeezed Elle's hand and followed the man to a room where a woman touched up my hair and makeup. From there, they sent me to the Green Room, where another staff member kitted me out with a microphone and explained what would happen.

I watched Olivia's introduction on a monitor in the room, so I wasn't surprised when another staffer came to lead me down a long hall to a door that opened onto the stage. They had allowed the others to wait there to watch and listen rather than sending them with me to the Green Room. Aislinn and Elle hugged me. Jack kissed my forehead, and Jori rubbed my shoulder.

Walking on stage, I swore everyone could hear my knees knocking because they shook so hard. I had never had such a bad case of stage fright before. My years as a choir director were supposed to help me. Epic fail.

Olivia Howard played upon her Native American beauty in the way she styled her glossy black hair, her makeup accenting her high cheekbones. She was a brilliant, talented, confident woman, and an accomplished interviewer.

Quickly putting me at ease, she made it feel like we were having a casual conversation. It just happened to be taking place in front of an audience of several hundred and cameras that would take it to millions.

She invited me to talk first about my life before the cruise. The topic moved on to the ship and finally the excursion. All my experience in talking about what had happened, especially about Jimmy and Maria, didn't help. I took more tissues from the box Olivia handed to me and wiped my eyes. Maybe it was pregnancy hormones kicking in. Maybe it was the people in the audience who cried with me.

It was a relief when she had her staff bring out Jori's painting and invited him, Elle, Aislinn, and D'Arcy to join us on stage. I was glad not to be the focus of attention for a few minutes.

Olivia had each of them share a memory of Jimmy and Maria. With their unique experiences, they helped me see new facets of the pair. I realized, for the first time, the sense in doing this. Our combined experiences might help their friends find some peace when they had a chance to view it.

After a break, Olivia moved on to questions about how we survived on the island and how our romance had blossomed. The audience loved the marriage ceremony.

She had me explain about the hunt, my injury, preparing the meat for eating, and the hide for clothing. At her request, I had brought along my furry top and breechcloth. Probing questions followed about the work involved in making everything we owned, the intense storms, and the growing need to get back to civilization.

Olivia, very gently, mentioned my pregnancy. I knew she had planned to bring it up, but I flushed anyway. She asked if Braedon had known about the baby. I could only shake my head as the audience and I cried.

By the next break, I felt drained and exhausted. Standing, I wiped my eyes and stretched my legs while Olivia talked with one of her staff members. I couldn't wait for this to end.

One of her crew called over, "Hey, Olivia. I think you'll want to see this."

The man projected a live news broadcast on the screen behind where I sat. It showed the lights of what must be a Coast Guard cutter approaching a dock.

My stomach lurched, and I clutched the arms of my chair. I recognized that dock, even in the dark. I spun to look for Elle and Aislinn. They stood near the entrance to the stage, staring at the screen. Elle's wide eyes met mine for a moment, and she clutched Aislinn's hand. I saw recognition in D'Arcy eyes as he gripped his wife's arm on one side and Jack's on the other.

The reporter on the screen said, "For those of you just joining this special report, a Coast Guard cutter found a damaged homemade outrigger limping its way to Pago Pago a couple of hours ago."

Dizziness overwhelmed me, and my knees went weak. Jack's strong hands grabbed my shoulders. Elle and the others, including Olivia and her camera crew, hurried to join us.

I gripped Jack's cold hand, suddenly afraid. What if it wasn't them? Had anyone else gone missing we didn't know about? Were my hopes being raised only to be dashed? I didn't know if I could take it. I couldn't breathe and began to gasp for air.

"You're okay. You're going to be fine," Jori whispered to me. "Take a slow, deep breath. Come on."

I gripped his hand with my free one and did as he said, forcing in the air.

"That's it." He held my hand.

I jerked my head back to the screen when the reporter said,

"I'm seeing more movement on deck. Yes, some figures are coming to the gangway. They have blankets around them, so it must be the rescued men. We should be able to speak to them soon."

In the dark shadows, I couldn't make out any details. Why didn't the idiot reporter just announce their names? My throat tightened. Were Moli and Isaac in the crowd? Or were they home asleep in their beds?

The first of the three shrouded figures reached the pier. A very tall shrouded figure. The reporter approached, the light from his camera glaring. The man raised his hand against the brilliance.

"Braedon!" I cried out, jumping to my feet and reaching for the screen, my hand shaking. The shadows under his eyes made his face appear gaunt, almost ghost-like. I'd had so many dreams like this. While I had never dreamed *this* scenario, it would fit the theme. Was I imagining everything?

"I need to get word to my wife and family." Braedon pleaded. "Can you get hold of Lyn? Tell her we're alive."

"This way, Mr. Randolph." Two men came between him and the reporter. The camera turned to Lua and Etano. They were alive too.

My heart thrashed inside my chest. I wanted to believe what I saw so badly but couldn't trust the image or the words. Then the people in the audience, who had been quiet as their eyes had darted between me and the screen, cheered, jumping up and hugging each other.

Only when I glanced at the others—Jack with tears running down his face, Aislinn and D'Arcy, Elle and Mal, all crying and clutching each other—did I finally believe it. Jack hugged me and hurried off to grab Aislinn.

"He's alive!" Jori grabbed my shoulders, his face bright with happiness. "You need to go to him."

Yes. I had to get to American Samoa. Dazed, I turned to Olivia, who was approaching us, her eyes glittering. "I'm so sorry, Olivia." I edged toward the exit. "I have to leave."

Jack seized my arm. "Wait a minute. Where are you going?"

What an idiot. "American Samoa."

I could almost see the wheels turning in Olivia's mind. "How are you going to get there?"

Another idiot. What was wrong with these people? "Fly." I took a step toward the exit.

"I have a private plane," she offered.

I edged a little farther. "So do we."

Disconcerted, she glanced at Jack for confirmation. He nodded but added, "I wouldn't take it on that long a flight, though, Lyn."

Irritation flashed through me. Were they trying to keep me from Braedon? "Then I'll go commercial."

"I have a plane that can be in the air in less than two hours," Olivia offered again. "Plus, I can smooth the way for you to get to him quicker. All you have to do is allow me to come with you and film your reunion."

"Let's go." I turned toward the door.

"Wait!" she laughed. "Is there anyone else who should come with you?"

"Everyone here with me now." I looked at Jack, feeling bad Emily and the boys would have to stay behind because of the calving.

Jori shook his head. "This is your time. I'll be here when you bring him home."

"Right." I hugged him and turned back to Olivia. "Six of us then, unless Aislinn and D'Arcy want to bring Kate."

"I can't go." Elle touched her big belly, her disappointment apparent. "I'm too close to my due date. Mal and I will watch Kate; the four of you go."

"Four then," I confirmed to Olivia, hugged Elle, and almost ran out of the studio.

$\mathcal{F}$OR MONTHS, I had felt like I was living in a nightmare. Now I found myself in a dream I desperately wanted to be real.

The next two chaotic hours flew past as we quickly packed our things.

On the plane, Olivia took advantage of the euphoria to grill me about my time on the island, this time focusing on Braedon. Where before she had gone easy with her questions for fear of bringing up difficult memories, she now sought the deep emotions of what I had been through.

Afterward, I managed to doze despite my agitated mind. When I woke, all the others in the cabin slept except Aislinn. "How much longer?" I asked.

She checked her watch. "Maybe an hour."

A thrill raced up my spine. An hour. Sixty minutes and I would see Braedon. I tapped my fingernails on my armrest and forced myself to breathe normally.

The others slowly woke up as well, and Olivia went to the back of the plane to freshen up.

I did the same once she had finished, changing into a summer shift. Aislinn came in and helped me straighten my hair. She pulled out a few strands to hang loose around my face, which gave it a softer look. I even had some curves again, not to mention the little roundness of my normally flat stomach.

The captain called over the speaker that it was time to take our seats and put on our seatbelts. As we descended, Aislinn clasped my hand. Jack reached over and placed his hand over ours.

Olivia began to interview me again. Her questions were all about how I had felt when I thought Braedon was dead, how I had managed to get on without him, and what I thought as we approached the airport.

*H*ER STAFF had arranged a private room at the airport for our meeting. We had seen the news before we left New York and knew reporters were already following Braedon. I didn't want to see him again in front of a huge audience. My wish for privacy worked in Olivia's favor as well.

It felt like an eternity for the plane to taxi to the terminal. When it finally came to a stop, I ripped off my seatbelt and dashed to the door, Aislinn and Jack not far behind me.

I wanted to scream at the steward to hurry as I waited for him to open the door. If I had known how, I would have done it myself. As soon as there was enough room, I squeezed through the opening and tore down the ramp.

I stumbled and clutched my stomach, forcing myself to slow down, fearing a tumble. In the distance, through a small window, I could see the fuzzy outline of people moving on the other side. My eyes burned. Braedon was on the other side of that door. I reached my hand to the knob, but my fingers shook so badly I couldn't get it to turn.

CHAPTER 35

A SHRIEK OF frustration swelled in my chest. A hand reached from behind me and pulled my fingers away. "Let me do it," Jack said. "At this rate you'll never get to him."

I let Jack open the door for me. My perception of time slowed as Braedon turned toward the sound of the opening door. For a second I stood frozen in place, examining him head-to-toe. He had trimmed his hair and shaved, the hollows in his cheeks more pronounced without his beard.

Our eyes met, and his face lit up. In two long strides, he swept me into his arms and pulled me close, kissing my forehead, my wet cheeks, and, finally, my mouth.

I clung to him, remembering the feel of his arms around me, the way I fit against him, the sound of his breath as he buried his face in the hair at my neck. I listened to the beating of his heart. He was alive. Really alive.

After what seemed like an eternity, he pulled back and searched my face, looking me up and down. I placed his hand on the small bulge of my stomach. "You're going to be a daddy."

His eyes widened as his palm cupped the tiny mound. A little fiercely, he kissed me again, and we clung to each other.

Finally, we saw teary-eyed Aislinn, who waited to be noticed. I motioned her to join us, and Braedon pulled her into our hug. After a long embrace, she stepped back so he could put both arms around me again, but she kept her hand on his shoulder as though she too feared he would disappear again.

Jack stood just out of reach, so I leaned over and grabbed his sleeve. He hesitated a moment, but Braedon threw his arms around him, and Jack gripped him back, tears running down his face. With my arm around Aislinn, I sobbed.

Olivia and her staff stayed in the background and filmed. When I spotted Lua and Etano, I dragged Braedon over to them and threw my arms around the grinning boys and their parents.

"Olivia! You've got to meet everyone." I waved her over.

Once they were talking, Braedon and I slipped over to a couch where he pulled me on his lap. He embraced me, one hand resting on my belly. I laid my head on his shoulder, savoring the moment. "What happened?" I finally asked.

"We took a big wave and it did a lot of damage—and Lua was injured. You should have seen him and Etano. They were incredible, even with Lua's broken arm. We ended up on a slip of an island with a few trees and no fresh water. If not for the monsoons, we'd have died." Braedon shook his head. "A tiny cave gave us a little shelter from the worst of the storms, but we couldn't keep a fire going."

Braedon nuzzled my neck. "Our island seems like a five-star hotel by comparison. We couldn't do much more than repair the outrigger until Lua's arm healed, and by then the worst of the monsoons were on us. We had to sit there and wait until we thought we had a chance to make it back home." Braedon looked up at me, his hand caressing my cheek. "We thought we were the only survivors until the Coast Guard found us."

"I know the feeling," I said softly.

Olivia allowed us a few minutes alone before it was time to depart. She had made arrangements with a friend for us to use a secure vacation home on the island.

Once inside a car, Braedon pulled me close. I couldn't keep from touching his cheeks. It had been so long since I had seen him without a beard.

"I've got a surprise planned for you when we get there," he whispered.

"How did you have time to plan a surprise?"

"I have connections." He glanced at Olivia, who smirked, trying unsuccessfully to look innocent.

I wanted to press him about it but decided to let him have his little secret.

"How did you end up at my dad's house?" Braedon asked. "I thought you'd go home to Colorado."

I explained about my parents and brother. "They had me declared dead. I didn't have anywhere to go."

Aislinn, who sat on Braedon's other side, leaned forward to glare at me.

Hastily, I added, "I didn't have anywhere in *Colorado* to go. Aislinn and Elle both offered to let me stay with them, and I did for the first few weeks I was back. But I had things to do."

Braedon raised his eyebrows. "Like what?"

I stroked his smooth cheek, going over the hollow indentation. "Like visit Colorado and then Texas, just like we always planned."

"How did that go?"

I told him about my visits. "But I ate something at Maria's

grandmother's that I thought gave me food poisoning." I giggled. "I went to Montana after Texas."

Braedon chuckled. "Is that when you threw up on my father?"

I choked. "How did you know that?"

"Elle."

Olivia twisted around from the front seat and touched my knee. "I'd like to hear about that, but another time. We're here."

We drove through a security gate and up to a lovely house with wide porches and large windows. Giving Braedon all my attention, I barely noticed the servants who carried our luggage inside.

A young woman escorted us to our room. I stepped in, but Braedon stayed at the door. "I'll see you downstairs."

"What?" I whirled around.

"My surprise." He grinned, kissing me lightly, and left.

How could he leave me again? I was about to follow him when Aislinn appeared in the doorway. Pushing me back into the room, she shut the door. "We've got to get you ready." She went to the closet and pulled out a garment bag.

"Ready for what?"

Aislinn's eyes twinkled. "For your wedding."

My heart melted. "You guys arranged a wedding?"

"Olivia's people did it. Mal used some of his connections to get a hold of Braedon to let him know we'd be coming. Braedon was adamant he wanted this done first thing."

"But what about Elle and Emily and the boys?" I asked as Aislinn unzipped the bag.

"Olivia's staff has arranged a satellite feed, and everyone will be able to watch it, even Marc." Aislinn handed me a robe and a towel. "There will be two-way video, so you can see them too." She pulled my hair up into a shower cap and turned me toward the bathroom. "Go take a quick shower. We don't have much time."

When I stepped out of the shower, I called, "Don't we need a license?"

"Braedon wasn't kidding when he said he had connections. One of his college roommates is the nephew of a local judge. A call to him and we didn't have to worry about a thing. The uncle arranged for a special license you'll sign tonight before the ceremony—he'll be here as a witness."

I put the underwear on Aislinn had left on the counter for me. "But what am I going to wear?"

From behind me, Aislinn commanded, "Close your eyes and don't turn around. Just raise your arms."

She slid something soft and silky over my head and turned me toward the full-length mirror.

"Elle helped Braedon pick it out. Luckily, a local shop had what he wanted."

I stared at the white creation. It reminded me a lot of the gray dress I had worn the night before Hawaii. My heart fluttered at the thought of Braedon somewhere in the house getting ready too.

After a single sharp knock on the door, one of Olivia's staff came in with a case of makeup. She worked on my face for a few minutes and then stepped back for me to see the result. My face looked natural but somehow softer.

The woman left, and Aislinn followed her out, pausing at the door. She eyed me sternly. "Wait here for five minutes. Don't you dare come out a moment sooner."

Five minutes. I paced, and my imagination went into overdrive. What if it had been just a dream? What if I woke up when I went out the door? No, that couldn't happen. Even my darkest side couldn't be that cruel. I rubbed my shaking hands over my stomach, trying to console myself with the thought of the baby. I checked the clock.

Three minutes.

What was Elle thinking, stuck back in New York? And poor Kate. She would be so disappointed to once again miss out on being the flower girl. I would find a way to make it up to her. I peeked at the clock.

Two minutes.

I couldn't take this. Had they made arrangements for Emily and the boys? I imagined them gathered in the big living room, watching us on the television. I wished they could be here with us. Would Jori be linked in? I looked at the clock again.

One minute!

The blood pulsed at my temples, and my hands were wet with perspiration. I wiped them off on a small hand towel and did a final check of my hair and dress. Glancing at the clock, I waited anxiously for the last seconds to pass. I took a deep breath and opened the door.

Braedon stood before me in a white tuxedo jacket and black slacks, leaning against the opposite wall, messing with his cufflinks … just as he had that night before Hawaii. He looked up and one of his slow, appreciative smiles grew across his face, the kind that made me feel warm all over.

"The first time I waited outside your door dressed in a tux, I frightened you away," he said, his voice soft. "It didn't even occur to me until just now that perhaps I should have asked you to marry me again. I've been presumptuous. Have I scared you away again?"

The pain in my heart was exquisite; I almost couldn't

breathe. I drank in the look of him and then launched myself into his arms. "Not likely." I didn't care the least if I ruffled my dress, hair, or lipstick.

Breathless, he pushed me from him, keeping his hands on my shoulders. "So will you marry me, again, my Gwendolyn?"

I stroked his face, running my hands down his smooth cheeks. "Oh, yes."

Braedon kissed me one more time and then touched my mouth, tidying my lipstick. I wiped the color from his lips. He linked my arm with his, and we descended the stairs.

When we came into view, everyone turned toward us and became quiet. Emotion swelled within me as I looked at the people we loved gathered before us.

Braedon whispered, "Lua and Etano are my groomsmen."

"Good choice." I squeezed his arm.

A Samoan in a minister's garb stood smiling before a fountain. Olivia waited off to the side, her eyes gleaming and a satisfied smile on her face.

Before the minister began the ceremony, Olivia's staff turned on the connections with the families in New York, Montana, and the Middle East. Including Jori, dressed in a black tuxedo.

Braedon said softly, "Jori's my best man."

"Perfect." I sniffed and blinked my eyes. I needed to get control of my emotions or I would end up a blubbering mess.

The connection to Montana went live. Their eyes latched onto Braedon first, and Owen cried, "Dude, you're really alive! Awesome!"

Ethan, standing beside his brother, did a mock double take of me, whistled, and exclaimed, "Woo hoo, Lyn. You lookin' fine!" He then eyed Braedon and shouted, "You better make it official quick, Bray! I'm thinking I could get interested in older women!"

I laughed. His behavior reminded me so much of the way my brother teased Aislinn. Braedon shook his head and leaned toward me. "I can't tell you how weird it is that you two know each other."

Tightening my hold on his arm, I replied, "Another feeling I completely understand."

I exclaimed when I saw little Kate on the monitor, wearing a beautiful dress and holding a basket. She waved at us and gleefully tossed a fistful of rose petals in the air. I blew her a kiss, and she grinned. Elle and Mal stood behind her, Elle already in tears. I had to look away to keep my own at bay.

From the final monitor, Marc saluted me. Arrayed behind him was a room full of uniformed men and women. His entire section must have been there. I tugged at Braedon's sleeve and pointed. "My brother."

As Braedon lifted his hand in greeting, the minister coughed to get our attention. We faced him.

And so I married Braedon for the second time, not in a tree house, but by a fountain. No fruit bat, but we had plenty of company this time.

"No more getting away from me now," Braedon whispered before he kissed me.

Everyone came forward to congratulate us. Aislinn cried, and I could hear cheers over the speakers from family and friends far away.

Jack embraced Braedon. "You've got a good one."

My father-in-law then hugged me. I whispered, "Your wedding should be the next one on the schedule." He gave me a sharp look, but I pretended not to see and turned to Lua and Etano. "You two look wonderful in tuxedos!"

"And you clean up real pretty," Lua teased.

I pointed at them. "We have things to talk about, but it'll wait until tomorrow." The boys looked concerned, and I knew I had to handle this right or risk offending them.

It was late, so Olivia's team had scheduled the reception for the next day. She had waited to congratulate us last. "I heard what you said to Etano and Lua, Lyn." She handed me an envelope.

Braedon stretched and feigned a yawn. "We'll see you all in the morning." He took my hand and led me back up the stairs to our room.

CHAPTER 36

*A*FTER A very late and active night, we slept in. When I first woke up, I didn't remember where I was. The feel of my husband's arm over my waist and his body pressed against my back brought it all back. I began to cry.

Braedon rolled me over to face him. "It can't be a good sign when a bride wakes up after her wedding night and cries. What's wrong?"

He wasn't a dream; he had really come back to me. Throwing my arms around his neck, I kissed him. My response distracted us for a while.

Later, as we snuggled together, he asked again, "Why were you crying?"

I cuddled my head into the curve of his shoulder. "Because I'm happy."

"A happy cry, then?"

I ran my hand over his shoulder and down his bicep, relishing the feel of his warm skin against mine. So much better than my dreams. "I *am* pregnant, you know. I'm allowed to cry." I sighed and admitted, "I expected to be back in my bed in Montana … alone."

He kissed my forehead. "No more of that." Braedon chuckled. "You took the perfect approach with my father, you know. He's got a big heart, but he has no patience with weak people. If you'd let him, he'd have run all over you." He played with a strand of my hair.

"What happens now, Braedon?" I whispered.

He ran the strand of hair over my face, giving me shivers. "Do you want to live in Colorado?"

"No, there's nothing for me there anymore." I ran my finger along the line of his eyebrow, the curve of his cheekbone, and finally the circle of his lips. "I'd like our baby to be born in Montana."

He leaned forward and kissed me. "I'd like that too." He rolled over to his back and pulled me close. "For the first time in my life, I'm having a hard time getting my mind around something."

"What?"

"For as long as I can remember, I've been either in school or working. Then those years on the island followed by months thinking you were dead. Now you're here, alive, and …." He swallowed. "I don't want to go back to work right away."

I snorted and covered my mouth at the noise. "Well, it's not like you have to."

Braedon shook his head. "I know it's not a money issue, but it doesn't feel right not to be planning to go to work."

I searched his face. "Do you have anything in mind?"

He stared at the ceiling for a moment before turning to me. "You know, I think I want to be a rancher for a little while."

"I'd love for you to be a rancher for a while. I'm not ready to leave my new family." I leaned over and kissed him. It was time to get distracted again.

*L*ATER, WE showered, dressed, and went in search of food. The sun shone near its peak when we came down the stairs. Everyone, including the Scouts and their families, sat by the pool or was eating from a spread in the dining room.

Olivia hadn't wasted the morning, having spent the time interviewing each of the Scouts about their experiences. Once she finished, she would have enough material for a two-hour TV special.

Jack, Aislinn, and D'Arcy joined us as soon as we came outside. I sat quietly and ate while Braedon's family finally had a chance to talk to him about what had happened.

When he left for a minute to refill his plate, Jack reached over and clasped my hand. "Kid, you look happier than I've ever seen you."

"I can't even put it in words."

When Braedon returned, I rose from the table and kissed him on the cheek. "You talk with your family. I have some business to take care of."

He looked at me quizzically, but I shook my head. I would tell him about it once I found out if I would be successful. I found Lua and Etano lounging by the pool.

"*Talofa*, Lyn!" Lua called when he saw me approaching. He and Etano scooted over to make room on their towels so I could sit with them.

"How's your arm?" I asked Lua.

In answer, he lifted his wrist and bent his elbow. He grimaced only once. "Almost as good as new. The doctor said it's taken so long to heal because of our poor nutrition. Plus, I pulled a muscle rowing. Now I'm eating good again, I should do great."

"Excellent." I paused, wondering how to bring up my gift.

Etano had been watching me. "What's wrong?"

I decided to just come right out with it. "I have a gift for the two of you."

They exchanged uneasy glances and Lua looked around for his father, who stood talking with Olivia. Lua beckoned him to join us. We rose as Moli approached.

Rubbing his chin, Lua announced, "Lyn says she has a gift for us."

Moli pursed his lips, his eyes narrowing.

I held up my hands. "It's a gift to help with college."

Their faces relaxed.

"I didn't want to do the interview with Olivia, but I agreed to it on one condition—that the fee be paid to Lua's and Etano's families."

"Now, Lyn—" Moli began, alarmed.

I interrupted, "It's enough for college—anywhere they want to go." That was not completely true, but I felt sure Braedon would agree to make up any difference.

Frowning, Moli demanded, "How much is it?"

I passed him the check Olivia had given me earlier.

The boys leaned over to examine it and gasped. Moli tried to hand it back to me, but I stepped away and put my hands behind my back.

"I'm here because of you, Moli. Lua and Etano brought Braedon back. Are you going to make me feel obligated to you forever?" I tapped the check in Moli's hand. "This isn't enough, but it's the best I can give."

His mouth pinched, Moli glanced at the boys and then back at me. "All right."

I threw my arms around him and then each of the boys. "Thank you! And I mean what I said about any college. If you want to go to the mainland, you can. Braedon went to Harvard, and he's got connections there."

From their expressions, I knew I had gone too far. "It all depends on what you want to study. It's up to you." I hurried away before they could argue and went in search of Braedon.

I didn't see him and wondered if he had gone back inside for more food. I stopped by Olivia, who sat holding a book and observing everyone.

She waved me over to sit by her, so I took the lounge chair at her side and laid back, enjoying the sun. I wished Braedon would come back. I had been away from him for a whole ten minutes, and I was already getting edgy. When Olivia didn't say anything, I turned my head toward her and found her watching me.

"What?"

She smiled and looked down at her book. "Thank you for letting me be a part of this."

"You made it all happen. I swear you're like my fairy godmother ... well, maybe Braedon qualifies as that since he got the dress." We laughed. "But seriously, Olivia, you've been incredible."

"Oh, don't make me out to be too altruistic, Lyn. This was very much a business decision ...." She paused, and I raised my eyebrows at her. "At least in the beginning. But I admit I've gotten emotionally involved in your story. You're a fortunate woman."

I sighed, nodding. "You know, three months ago I'd have

disagreed with you. But now ...." Braedon entered the pool area from the grounds with his father, and I smiled. "Did I tell you that when things were getting too serious too fast between us on the ship I avoided him for four days and then tried to ignore him for another three?"

Her eyes opened wide. "Tell me!"

Embarrassed, I shared all the gruesome details.

Olivia frowned, confused. "The obvious question is why."

"I couldn't trust myself to fall in love with a fairy tale." I tilted my head and watched Braedon. "I mean, look at him."

She peered at my husband, who now stood talking with Moli. "Well, he's not exactly my type ...."

I gave her a 'be serious' look. "I knew I was falling hard."

Olivia considered me. "You ought to write this all down."

I laughed. "Me? Who'd want to read about me?"

She smirked. "Well, don't tell that to my advertisers, because we're counting on lots of people being interested in your story." She patted my hand. "I'm truly happy for you, Lyn. You got your fairy tale after all, didn't you?"

Braedon, who had been working his way toward me, stepped to my side and touched my hair.

I reached up to take his hand and grinned at Olivia. "Yes, I did, didn't I?"

$\mathcal{D}$ONNA K. Weaver has always loved reading and creating stories, thus she's been ever entertained. A Navy brat and US Army veteran, she's lived in many US states as well as South Korea, the Philippines, and Germany. An avid cruiser, she's sailed the Pacific four times. When she retired from Shorei Kempo Karate with a black belt, she decided it was time to put her imaginary friends and places on paper. She lives in Utah with her husband. They have six children and eight grandchildren.

ACKNOWLEDGEMENTS

$\mathcal{F}$IRST AND foremost, I need to thank my husband, Edward, who helpfully sought comfort from *StarCraft2* and *MineCraft* while I was writing. My beta readers Rachelle (the first person to ever read anything I wrote—and yeah, she's still talking to me), Carole, Mellie, Kelsey, Bobbie, and Sarah all provided valuable insight that helped to make a better story. My Pied Piper critique partners Robin, Meredith, Donea, and Shanna, plus critiquers Melanie, Laura, Natalie, Heidi, and Jennifer all succeeded in messing with my head and forcing me to view the story differently, and I so appreciated the brainstorming sessions with fellow members of the iWriteNetwork.

I'd like to thank my son David who was so kind to point out that I'd emasculated the love interest; my nurse son-in-law, Spencer, who provided valuable input on many of the medical issues; and my brother David for his help with the geology of the island. I send many thanks to Captain Matt Faria from Captain Andy's Sailing Adventures on Kauai who put up with my sailing questions during a catamaran trip to the Na Pali Coast. I would also like to express my gratitude to KellyAnne Terry, the library director for the Lewistown Library, who took time out of her busy schedule to meet with me and talk ranching.

I appreciate the wonderful input and expertise of Rhemalda editors Kat and Diane for polishing the book, but I owe so much to Emmaline Hoffmeister, Rhemalda vice president. It was her encouragement, support, and enthusiasm for the story that let it see the light of day. Thank you!

SNEAK PEEK
Torn Canvas
Book 2 in the *Safe Harbors* series

OLIVIA LEANED against the corner of the office wall, her forehead pressed on the window. She had to get a grip. The view of the Manhattan buildings from her office, so different from anything she had experienced as a child, usually soothed her. Far below, the light changed, and the crowd that had gathered at the corner crossed the street. People scurrying along in their busy lives. Real people with real problems.

Closing her eyes, Olivia relaxed her fingers and took a deep breath. She straightened, smoothed her skirt, and returned to the desk. Spread out were the photos of six up-and-coming models. Three men and three women. Frivolous lightweights, if her staff's research was to be believed.

Olivia took another calming breath and picked up one of the photos. Was she being unfair, judgmental? The young man was definitely hot with his blond, almost white hair and light gray eyes. Add his nicely sculpted body and he was the most physically attractive of the group of beautiful models. His reputation was also the worst of them all. Nothing short of a 'man ho' who got paid to have his picture taken. Beauty with no substance. How cliché. And they wanted her to interview the lot. Gag.

Then why did she keep coming back to his picture? Olivia tilted the photo for better light and leaned in for a closer look. There was something more behind his smiling face. Something in his eyes. It teased her. Made her think there was some more to him than the stories of his escapades. That something was the story Olivia wanted to do; she was sure of it.

The general manager kept insisting on more trending stories, more sensational topics. Why? He had known the kinds of stories Olivia did when he had offered her the contract last year. Surrendering now to his brain fluff would lead to trash like Jerry Springer did. Shows that catered to some of the worst aspects of human nature. Olivia shuddered. She would walk away from her contract first.

A groan rose from her chest. "Give me something, please!" Rather than crush the picture, she released it.

An older woman popped her head in the door. "Did you call, Ms. Howard?"

"No." Olivia dropped into her chair. How had her entire career come to rest on this pathetic group?

"Ms. Howard, José's here. I know you've got a meeting in fifteen minutes—"

"Send him in." His job title might be "fact checker", but his experience as a private investigator had made him much more. This might be just what she needed.

The wiry Hispanic man tipped his head, brushing aside a strand of graying hair. At his grin, her pulse quickened. He had something for her. Please let it be about one of the models. Olivia's eyes flicked to the blond man's picture. Let her instincts about him be right.

"What have you got?" she asked.

"I think you're going to like this."

"Just tell me."

José set a neat folder in front of her and took a seat in the chair on the other side of the desk. Olivia opened the file and hesitated at the newspaper headline. A car/train accident? She glanced up.

"Just read it, Ms. Howard. I've got something else for you when you're done."

Olivia checked her watch. Ten minutes. She began skimming the page. Driver fell asleep—crashed her car into train barriers—car stuck on tracks—driver crawled out broken window. Olivia straightened. A set of twins had been trapped in the car seats in the back.

"Look at these before you read any further." José placed a stack of printed papers on her desk, keeping one back.

"José, I'm running out of time." He pointed at the pictures. If he wasn't so good at what he did ….

Olivia quickly shifted to the grainy photos that showed a man trying to open the car's doors. She vaguely remembered the story from late last summer. In spite of the approaching train, the stranger had crawled inside the car and pulled out the children, one at a time. The mother had reported that he and the last child pulled from the vehicle had almost been struck by flying debris as the train hit the car. The man had checked the child in his arms, made sure the mother and other child were fine, and jogged away.

"This is my kind of story." Olivia shook her head, her frustration increasing. "But there's no one to interview. I'd also like to know what that idiot with the camera was doing taking pictures instead of helping." She stood, her heart sick. "I have to go."

"Maybe you do have an interview." Grinning, José handed her the last picture.

Her hands shook a little as she stared at the photo of a man with pale blond hair holding a child and looking over his shoulder. She picked up the model shot. It was him.

"Why didn't this come out before?"

José shrugged. "Other people asked the same thing you did. I already called this Jori Virtanen's agency."

"Yo-ree?" She checked the name at the bottom of the picture again.

"He's Finnish, so it's a soft 'j'. Not a cool Spanish 'h' like mine. Virtanen's on a long cruise. Won't be back for a few weeks."

"Perfect." Olivia straightened her suit and, with the hint of a smile, headed to her meeting.

Proof

Made in the USA
Charleston, SC
07 October 2013